BOOKS BY SUSANNE DUNLAP

IN THE *Shadow*
OF THE *Lamp*

SUSANNE DUNLAP

BLOOMSBURY

NEW YORK BERLIN LONDON SYDNEY

First published in the United States of America in April 2011
by Bloomsbury Books for Young Readers
Paperback edition published in March 2012
www.bloomsburyteens.com

For information about permission to reproduce selections from this book, write to
Permissions, Bloomsbury BFYR, 175 Fifth Avenue, New York, New York 10010

The Library of Congress has cataloged the hardcover edition as follows:
Dunlap, Susanne Emily.
In the shadow of the lamp / by Susanne Dunlap. — 1st U.S. ed.
        p.   cm.
Summary: Sixteen-year-old Molly Fraser works as a nurse with Florence Nightingale during
the Crimean War to earn a salary to help her family survive in nineteenth-century England.
ISBN 978-1-59990-565-5 (hardcover)
1. Nightingale, Florence, 1820–1910—Juvenile fiction. 2. Crimean War, 1853–1856—
Juvenile fiction. 3. England—Social conditions—19th century—Juvenile fiction.
[1. Nightingale, Florence, 1820–1910—Fiction. 2. Crimean War, 1853–1856—Fiction.
3. England—Social conditions—19th century—Fiction. 4. Nurses—Fiction.] I. Title.
PZ7.D92123In 2011   [Fic]—dc22   2010021158

ISBN 978-1-59990-753-6 (paperback)

Book design by Donna Mark
Typeset by Westchester Book Composition
Printed in the U.S.A. by Quad/Graphics, Fairfield, Pennsylvania
2 4 6 8 10 9 7 5 3 1

To my beloved brothers:
Keith, who builds worlds out of words,
and Duff, who builds worlds

IN THE *Shadow*

OF THE *Lamp*

Chapter 1

I was only fifteen when I went into service. Scullery maid first, but the master thought me too pretty to hide away in the kitchen. Anyway, that's what Will, the valet and my friend, told me later. So when I turned sixteen they made me an under parlormaid. Instead of washing dishes, I cleaned grates, mended linens, and swept the stair carpets.

I got higher wages—four shillings and eight pence a week—and could take more home to my mum in the East End so she could get shoes for the little ones. That made her proud. And the work wasn't nearly so hard as scullery maid.

At first it was me and Janet. But then Janet got diphtheria.

Poor Janet. She was the same age as I was and she died. Cook blamed it on her coming from the country estate where the air was fresh, and said the London fog didn't suit her. No one would go in and see her while she was so sick. Except me. I couldn't bear to think of her suffering all alone. She could hardly draw breath her throat was so swelled up, and the room smelled horrible.

They said to stay away, but something about Janet pulled at me. I didn't know what it was then. I went up to her room, just as bare when she was sick as it was before, only with some sweet-smelling oil in the lamp so the stink wouldn't be too awful for the doctor.

"You awake, Janet?" I asked from the doorway. Her eyes were open, but she was out of her head a lot, so it didn't mean she was really awake. I walked over to her. She opened and closed her mouth like a fish just caught, or like she wanted to say something, only she couldn't. Her neck was so swollen it was hardly there. I felt my own throat, skinny enough to almost circle with one hand, and thought how painful it must be for her.

I don't know what made me do it, but I reached my hands out and put them against her throat. Softly, like I was holding a butterfly. I felt her warmth, a high fever they said, and was sure the cool of my hands might make her feel just that bit better. The corners of Janet's mouth stretched a little wider. Seemed like a sort of smile. Then she said, her voice all scratchy, "Thank you."

I didn't know if what I did was any help, but it surely didn't hurt her. I would've stayed, but Collins, the butler, opened the door all sudden-like. "Get away from there, Fraser!" He said it like I was touching a burning stove.

I jumped I was so scared. I'll never forget the look on Janet's face. It turned from light and calm to hopeless and scared, and her mouth closed into itself like she'd never smile again.

2

The doctor came the next day and bled her, but it didn't do a bit of good. She died just the same.

I was ever so sad about Janet. Not like I knew her well, but she was sweet and helped me learn my duties. It was different doing them all alone, not having someone to point out where I missed a speck of dust or hadn't piled the coals up so they'd catch proper.

At first I took no notice when Mavis Atkins started in on being jealous of me. I was too busy learning what to do, and then all worried about Janet. Mavis worked in the kitchen as Cook's maid, which wasn't such a good job as mine, and she was desperate to get out. She had dreams, she told me. She said, "A girl with ambition could go far in a 'ouse like ours." Mr. Abington-Smythe, the master, was in Parliament, and men came to dinner and talked about important things over brandy and cigars. Mavis wanted to be under parlormaid so she could clean up after the gents, maybe get someone to notice her.

"It ain't fair!" she said every time she saw me after I changed my position. "A smart uniform and all. I say it ain't fair!" I couldn't believe she wished for the black dress that itched so, and the white apron and cap I had to clean and starch day after day.

"They'll probably give you the position soon too," I said, trying to make her feel better. "It's a big house. They should have two parlormaids. They did, till Janet got sick." Mavis and I'd been friends when she was above me and I was just a scullery maid. We even brushed each other's hair at bedtime. Hers was light brown and straight, down below her waist. Mine was thick auburn curls that didn't seem so long because it kinked up that way.

But then Mavis said, "There's no room for another par-lormaid. Not unless you get diphtheria, like Janet." Seemed to me like she wished I would. I tried not to think anything of it, just got on with my work and hoped Mavis got on with hers.

I should have known Mavis wouldn't just let it go at that. First she stopped brushing my hair of a night. I tried to be friendly and nice, but she ignored me. She was up to some-thing, I thought. But when I discovered what, I couldn't believe she had such a mean spirit in her.

It all came out when we were getting ready for bed one night.

"Fraser!"

Mr. Collins's harsh voice yelled from right outside our bedroom door. He never talked soft and nice, but I'd not heard him so cross before. "Yes, Mr. Collins," I said, open-ing the door.

"Stand over there, Fraser." He pointed to the window. I looked at Mavis, but she wouldn't look back, so I just did as Mr. Collins said.

"Atkins, kindly show me the evidence you discovered."

Evidence? Of what? I didn't know anything then and I thought they'd gone stark mad. Mavis pointed under my bed. Mr. Collins got down on his knees, moved my valise aside, and started pulling out bits and pieces of things from

4

all over the house. He stood up with his hands full of silver and trinkets. "What do you have to say for yourself, Fraser?"

"I . . . I don't know. I never seen those things—'cept where they was s'posed to be." My mouth went dry, and I could feel the heat rising up into my face.

"I must inform the master and mistress that we have a thief in our midst. Be ready to leave in the morning."

No! I wanted to scream out that it wasn't fair. I hadn't done anything. I reached a hand toward Mavis, not threatening exactly, but she clutched her robe around her and turned her shoulder to me like she thought I was going to hit her.

"If it's all the same to you, Mr. Collins," Mavis said, her voice high and quaking, "I'd rather not stay here with Fraser."

"There's a cot by the coal hole. That'll do for you," Mr. Collins said to me.

Still not believing this was happening, I got my things. He went so fast down the stairs I could hardly keep up with him, then he pointed to the cot, with its dirty old blanket. It was where they sometimes put beggars to sleep when they knocked on the door in the midst of a storm or something.

The dust made me cough all night. I was too angry and upset to sleep, so I spent my time thinking of ways to get back at Mavis. Now I could see she must've been up to that mischief ever since Janet died. Perhaps even before, when

I first got my new position. I wanted to creep up on her while she slept and cut away a chunk of her hair that she was so proud of. Or maybe put salt in the sugar bowl, so she'd get in trouble. But it wouldn't have done any good.

The next morning they made me stand up in front of all the servants while Mr. Collins accused me and lectured everyone. My knees felt weak. I tried to say I didn't do it, but no one listened. After all, things only disappeared after I started working upstairs. I tried to tell them I'd have to be stupid to keep things I stole right where they might be found by anyone, but nobody'd let me say a word.

Only Will spoke up for me. Will was tall and straight, and he had kind eyes. He didn't treat the rest of us like we were dirt, like Mr. Collins did. Perhaps that was because he wasn't much older than us, maybe eighteen, maybe twenty, and he came from London too. He helped me lift the heavy coal buckets sometimes, and always asked after my mum and dad when I came back from my half days. He didn't have a mum and dad. They died of the cholera a few years back.

"This is just circumstance," Will said, the only one brave enough to answer Mr. Collins. "Molly's never done anything dishonest before. We should hear her side of the story."

I wanted to thank Will. I looked at him, trying to push how grateful I was through the air so he could feel it. I don't know if he did, but I saw just a bit of a smile on his face. I knew then he'd say something reassuring to me if he could get a word in.

Since Will couldn't get them to listen I thought I'd best

pluck up the courage to defend myself. "I ain't no thief!" I said, lifting my chin and staring down my nose at Mr. Collins. I'd no intention of giving Mavis the satisfaction of seeing me cry.

"See! That just proves what a devious chit she is!" Mavis practically screamed. Even Mr. Collins flinched. No one wanted to believe anything but the obvious. What a drama! After a bit I felt far away from it all, like it wasn't me they were talking about and I was looking in the window watching everyone's mouths moving and their hands and arms waving about. Mavis played shocked and innocent quite well, her eyes open wide and eyelashes fluttering. *Practicing to go on the stage*, I thought. She had apparently got over how nervous she was the night before.

I don't know what's become of her, whether she stayed on as parlormaid there in Cadogan Square or ran away herself and put her play-acting to good use on the stage. I don't know, and I've come so far myself since then that I don't much care now.

Fact is, when I think about it, in a way I owe everything to Mavis and her scheming.

Chapter 2

I soon enough found myself out on the street, with only the clothes on my back and a small bag with a few bits and pieces—a hairbrush, clean underthings, some ointment my mum made in case I got chilblains. I'd walked around London often enough on my half days, from Knightsbridge to the East End, down Whitehall across Trafalgar Square, past St. Martin-in-the-Fields and St. Paul's. I crossed over Fleet Street where the newsboys cried out the headlines—I couldn't read then, so it was only gossip and the other servants talking and what I picked up on the street that told me what was going on. Right then, the news was all about the war with Russia, in the Crimea.

I remember that day like it just happened. It was just about the end of the second week of October. The air was chilly, but I wasn't cold in the coat my mother made for me. It'd be no match for a real icy winter, though, and I knew I'd be wishing I could've stayed on at Cadogan Square and earned enough for Mum to make us all new coats that winter. As it was, I'd probably have to work in one of the dark, cold factories, feeding cloth through a sewing machine, like the girls in the house next to ours, with their pale faces and hollow eyes. No one else would hire me without a good character—now that I'd been named a thief thanks to Mavis. At the factories they didn't check. They took you if you were young and healthy enough to stand up twelve hours a day.

"You'll be lucky if they don't send the police after you," Mr. Collins said just before he shut the door behind me. That gave me a chill. It was one thing to lose my position. Another thing entirely to go to Newgate.

I turned toward home because I had nowhere else to go, and I wanted my mum to tell me I was good and everything would be all right, that Mavis would get her punishment for lying and I'd be able to get another job. My feet took steps without me even thinking about it.

I don't know exactly what made me stop and listen to the criers, waving their broadsheets about and selling them to City gents. Perhaps I was tired by the time I reached that part of town, but I stood there like a pillar, people around me busily going to offices or delivering packages. I nearly got run over by a carriage that came fast around a corner, but I jumped away just in time, splashing right in a puddle. My shoes were ruined. I didn't know where I'd get another pair.

"Scandal at war! Our brave soldiers land with no medical supplies! Doctors amputate in the field!"

I'd heard some of this belowstairs at Cadogan Square. Mr. Collins sometimes read us articles in the *Times* at tea. It sounded horrible. There was a fierce battle about a month ago. Young men far away, fighting for our queen and getting horribly wounded, and not even a bed to lie in or someone to say a kind word to them. I paused and listened, just in case there was anything new to hear.

"Party of nurses to go with Miss Nightingale! *Times* raises a thousand guineas for the cause!"

That was news. How I wished I could read and find out more. I had a penny, but with no prospects of earning so much as a farthing anytime soon, I wouldn't have spent it no matter how desperate I was to know the whole story. Besides, I'd have to get someone else to read it to me anyway. Instead I walked along slowly, hoping I might hear something more.

And I did. An old gentleman with his coat unbuttoned and a stained waistcoat showing leaned against a lampost, a copy of the paper open in front of him. A group of curious folks gathered round. I stayed at the back like I wasn't interested, but I listened anyway.

"Mr. Sidney Herbert has asked the capable Miss Florence Nightingale to assemble a team of a hundred nurses to set things right in the Crimea, where our brave soldiers who have fallen at Bulganak and at Alma have not adequate supplies and medical care to treat their wounds, slight and serious. Applications to accompany Miss Nightingale should be addressed to Mrs. Stanley of Belgrave Square. Qualified nurses only need apply. Wages and expenses will be paid."

That started everyone murmuring and talking. Some said, "I wouldn't go halfway across the world to nurse—there's enough that need it here." Others said, "Shame I'm not younger, or I'd go myself."

Me? I was thinking, hard.

The paper said that wages and expenses would be paid. And these nurses would be going away, far away. Would a body need references? But I was no qualified nurse. I'd helped my mum with the little ones, sure, and was by the midwife when my youngest sister was birthed. And there was the time I had to dress Jimmy's broken arm because we couldn't afford a surgeon to do it. And what happened with Janet. But no one would think of me, a parlormaid who'd been let go without a character, as a qualified nurse. Unless . . .

I don't quite know what got into me, but I knew then that I would do whatever it took to be one of those nurses, or even a charwoman along to do the laundry and clean the grates. At least I'd be out of London.

And besides, the closer I got to home, the less I felt I could face my mum. She was so proud when I went off to service at such a grand house. Dad could only work a little because of his bad hand that was crushed on the docks, and his wages weren't enough to take care of all eight of us. I could hear Mum's voice saying, "You saved us from the poorhouse, you 'ave, my Molly. I knew you for a good girl." Ted had started going with Dad to work on the docks, but he only earned a penny now and then because he was so young and not strong enough to lift the heavy crates. And now? What would she say now?

I stopped again. I felt like someone wrapped a band

round my chest and squeezed, and my eyes stung. I told myself it was the wind that blew off the river, cold and damp and unhealthy, stinking of dead fish and tar. But I knew different, deep inside. It was shame. I had to do something to make it better. No one would believe what I said, so I had to do something to prove it. I knew I was a good girl, that I worked hard and was willing and honest. I would show all of them at Cadogan Square. And Mum would be proud of me—even prouder than before.

Chapter 3

I was nearly home, but I turned right back toward the West End, this time walking like I meant it. Instead of being in a fog, I was in a hurry. It was late afternoon, and that time of year night fell early—hardly seemed like there was any day. By the time I got to Belgrave Square—not so far as Cadogan Square, so that and my fast pace made the walk much quicker—the lamplighters had already finished their business, and the mist was that sickly yellow color that makes me think of piss. I never liked being out at dusk.

The grand houses in Belgrave Square looked identical, and there were no tradesmen about to ask which one was Mrs. Stanley's. I walked all around the square once, peering at each door to see if I could tell anything, hoping a bobby didn't see me and think I was a thief—once in a lifetime was more than enough for me. There wasn't anything at all to tell me where Mrs. Stanley lived, though I don't know what I expected. Hardly likely they'd hang a sign or set a servant out on the street to show the way. I finally worked up enough courage to ask. I could see a light in the stairwell that led down to the kitchen floor of one house, and thought I might as well knock.

It was teatime. The irritation in the parlormaid's voice when she answered the door told me that clear enough.

" 'Scuse me, miss, but could you direct me to Mrs. Stanley's house?" I asked.

"It's number fifty-four," she said, closing the door without even a by your leave.

I soon found it, only a few houses up. I started down the steps to the kitchen and the servants' hall, then stopped. Why would I go there? I wasn't applying for service. If I was to persuade anyone I was a nurse, I'd better act like one for sure and all. That is, if I had any idea what a nurse acted like, which I didn't, but most likely not like a parlormaid.

While I stood there thinking, a woman carrying an umbrella and a black bag and wearing a close bonnet on her head come toward me from the other direction. She marched right along as if she were going to fight in the lines with the men, not nurse them. She turned her steps and climbed up to the front door of number fifty-four and pulled the bell. I could hear it tinkling down in the servants' hall, and knew pretty well how long it would take for someone to interrupt their tea and answer.

I slipped in behind the woman with the brolly so I wouldn't have a chance to back out of my crazy scheme. She turned and looked down her nose at me like she would at a dog sniffing at her skirts. I sent her my frostiest stare and lifted my chin. Lucky I'm tall for my age. I would have to pass for at least eighteen—maybe twenty, I figured.

She didn't have time to say anything to me before the butler opened the door.

"I'm here about the expedition to Turkey," she said, thrusting a sheet of paper at the bloke. Obviously she'd never been in a fine house before. Butlers are for announcing visitors, not taking papers from people who came for jobs. When he noticed me, I put on my best airs and graces, like the fine ladies use at the Abington-Smythes, and looked down at the man. It helped that he was a little shorter than I was. Didn't I get a surprise when he let us both in!

"Mrs. Stanley will be with you in a moment." I wondered if all butlers talked alike. He could've been Mr. Collins, with his posh accent.

The two of us stood in the vestibule, not talking and not looking at each other. *These Stanleys must be very wealthy,* I thought. It was a finer house than the one in Cadogan Square. The stairs were swept perfect, and not a speck of dust on anything. The windows were so clear they looked like they weren't there, and a large mirror doubled all that clean and made it huge. I was still admiring the servants' work when an old lady opened the door to the parlor—or it might've been a morning room—and asked the lady I'd followed in to step inside.

To me, she said, "Please take a seat if you wish," and swept her hand toward a silk-covered bench that ran along one wall of the vestibule.

I perched on the edge of it once the door closed, but when I heard footsteps coming up from the kitchens I stood up quick. It felt wrong to be on such a fine bit of furniture, and besides, if I stood nearby I could hear muffled voices behind the closed door. I strained to catch what they were saying, but only a few words made it through. "Qualifications," was one, and it sent my heart sinking into my boots. Another word I heard was "mature." Didn't do me a bit of good if that was what they wanted. One voice was sharper and harder than the others. While I waited, I tried to imagine what the lady who belonged to that voice would look like, and conjured up an image of an old crone with a long, curved beak of a nose, her hair all gray and wiry, with a high-necked gown fastened with a hair brooch. *This Miss Nightingale must be an old spinster,* I thought.

After a bit the door opened and the lady with the paper came out. Her face was in a scowl. She yanked the front door open without waiting for anyone to do it for her, slamming it behind her.

"Please come in, dear," the old lady with the kind face said to me.

Three people sat at a table that'd obviously been moved into the room for the purpose, since it wasn't what you'd normally find in a morning room. They each had papers in front of them, and untidy stacks of even more paper were on the floor too. The chairs and sofas had all been moved to the side, and a single straight-back chair sat in front of them. I thought sitting there might be what it was like to be up before a magistrate, and I started to sweat a little. The memory of Mr. Collins's threat was too fresh in my ears. I was relieved not to see the witch I imagined among them, though.

"This is Mrs. Stanley," the old lady said, pointing to the younger lady who sat at the table next to an old man. "And this is my husband, Mr. Bracebridge." She must have seen the question in my eyes, because she added, "Miss Nightingale has asked for our help in finding nurses for her expedition. She has much to do. Mr. Bracebridge and I will accompany her to Turkey."

She motioned me to sit in the chair.

"Have you brought your references? What are your qualifications?" Mrs. Stanley began questioning me without even asking my name, with the same loud, sharp voice I'd heard on the other side of the door—only now I could feel it right inside my ears.

"I . . . I'm afraid I haven't brought any with me. You see, I just heard when I was in the City, and I wanted to come right away." By comparison my voice came out small and whiny. They'd see right through me, I was sure, but I couldn't think what else to say.

"Perhaps you could begin by telling us about your nursing experience?" That was Mr. Bracebridge. He had a kind face, like his wife, with wrinkles that came from smiling.

"Mostly . . . I've nursed in domestic circumstances." At least I wasn't lying outright.

"Never in a hospital?" Mrs. Stanley said. "I'm afraid that

won't do at all. Miss Nightingale was very insistent that only experienced hospital nurses were to be taken. Besides, you look too young."

She sat back in her chair and nodded to Mrs. Bracebridge. My interview was over.

"I'm sorry, dear. There are so many applicants, and all of them very qualified."

"But you don't understand! I'm a very good nurse. I'm meant to be one, I'm certain, and those poor boys, wounded out in the field. Please, please take me! I think I could've cured Janet of her diphtheria, if only they had let me tend to her more." I don't know what made me beg. I wouldn't ever have begged for a parlormaid's position. But something about this adventure, the whole idea of going off and doing something different—it suddenly seemed as if I would die if I couldn't go.

"Truly, I am sorry." Mrs. Bracebridge took hold of my arm, gentle but firm, and I stood up. Mrs. Stanley rifled through papers and Mr. Bracebridge just looked down at the table, tapping his pen. I saw there was nothing else I could do.

I held out my hand to Mrs. Bracebridge to say good-bye and I had an idea all of a sudden. "Thank you for your time, Mrs. Bracebridge," I said. "My heart will be with the party that goes. When is it?"

"We leave Folkestone for Boulogne on October twenty-first."

"I shall be thinking of you. God go with you."

God and me, I thought. If I couldn't get there honestly, I'd find another way. And I thought I might know someone who could help me—if he would.

Before I lost courage, I continued west toward Cadogan Square. Will had whispered just as I left that I was to come to him if there was something I needed. And I needed somewhere to stay for a week or so and a way to get to Folkestone after that. There was another thing, too, that I realized I would have to face: I'd have to have my letters. I'd learned the ABCs when I was just a wee thing, but my dad didn't see that it was fit for me to spend time learning to read and write proper once I was big enough to help with the chores and cooking. Not with all the young ones at home needing caring for. I always meant to learn anyway. Now I'd have to.

Chapter 4

I knew it for a dangerous folly to show my face at the Abington-Smythes. Mr. Collins said he'd summon the police if I dared. But I couldn't see any other way. I went by the back road, down the alley that led to the mews. There was an entrance there the servants used if they came back late and wanted to sneak in without Mr. Collins knowing. It led directly into the pantry, and no one in the servants' hall or the butler's office could see you.

The servants' tea would just be ending and Cook'd be getting supper ready for upstairs. I had to catch Will before he went to the master's room to bring his sherry and help him dress. I figured that Mavis, who no doubt had stepped straight into my shoes as parlormaid, would be up tending the drawing room fire and helping to prepare the dining room.

I let myself into the dark, cool room, hung with hams and cheeses, dozens of eggs in trays on the shelves, and preserves in jars all labeled. The sight made me realize I was ever so hungry, but I didn't have time to think about it. I heard Cook in the kitchen ordering someone around—not Mavis, I hoped!—and waited for the sound of Will's steps coming toward the back stairs that led up to the bedrooms.

I timed it just right. The smart *click-clack* of his polished shoes came nearer. An instant before he got there, I opened the door.

At first he looked startled, then pleased, then a cloud passed over his eyes. "What are you doing here?" he whispered, pushing me back into the pantry and closing the door behind us.

"You said if I needed anything . . ."

"Yes, but they'll hand you over to the police if they find you," he said. He took my shoulders and turned me toward him. "What is it, Molly? What can I do for you?"

"Do you really believe I'm innocent, or were you just saying it to be nice?" I asked. I needed to know if he really trusted me.

"Of course I believe you! You're just not the type. I can see it in your eyes." He smiled. I liked when he smiled at me. His whole face looked happy and it made me want to smile too.

"Then I have to ask you something," I said. I had to trust him; I had no choice. He could have just ignored me, told me he had to get on with his duties, but that wasn't Will. He had a heart big enough for the likes of me. "I need a place to stay, Will," I said, deciding I wouldn't put everything on him all at once, but take it in steps.

"What about home? Your mum and dad and brothers and sisters?"

He said it so sincerely. His eyes were a clear, honest blue that always gave me a little start in my stomach when I looked into them direct. So it pained me to know I'd have to lie a little at first. "I—I just can't face them."

He let his breath out in a sharp sigh. "I know it's been a blow to you." He thought for a moment, then said, "My sister lives in Marylebone with her husband." He took a piece of paper and a pencil out of his pocket and scribbled a note. "Here. Give this to her. She'll put you up for a couple of nights. She's a good soul."

"I'll help her clean and such," I said after he told me her address. "I can't thank you enough, Will." I meant it, so I looked right at him.

This time he turned his eyes away. "You'll have to take an omnibus to get there. It's a long way."

I nodded, knowing I'd walk. "Thanks, Will."

"Go to the pantry and get me half a dozen eggs!" Cook's voice broke through our hushed conversation, and I heard footsteps coming toward us.

"Go now!" Will said, and before I knew it he'd pulled me to him and kissed me quickly on the forehead.

I ran back out the way I came, my feet so light I couldn't feel the ground. I didn't know for sure whether it was because Will had found me a place to stay or because of the warm spot on my forehead where he had kissed me, but it reached right down inside me so I didn't feel the chill all the way to Marylebone.

⸺∞⸺

It was after seven by the time I knocked on the door of the small house in the north of London where Will's sister lived. In no time a woman who looked like Will but with gray eyes opened the door. A little tyke clung to her leg, and I could see she was far along in the family way with another. Her forehead creased in a frown.

"Who is it, Luce?" came a man's voice in a room behind her.

"Dunno!" she called back.

"I'm Molly," I said, and handed her the note from Will. I could smell the remains of their tea—mutton stew, I thought—and when my stomach growled I was certain she could hear it. She read the note quickly, looking not very pleased.

"I'm so sorry," I said. "Only I didn't have nowheres else to go. I can clean and help with your boy, and I won't stay long."

Her face relaxed into a smile just like Will's. "Come in. If Will says it's important, I'm sure it is. I'm Lucy, this is Arthur." She patted her boy on his curly head. As we passed through into the small parlor she said, "And this is my husband, Jim."

I curtsied to him. "Pleased to meet you."

"See how thoughtful Will is!" Lucy said to her husband

in a tone that reminded me of how Mum talked to Dad when he came home from the pub and she wanted him to go to bed without beating any of us. Jim was seated in the only soft chair. Two other chairs were wood, and there was a bench and a table too. The fire crackled along, and my fingers began to thaw out. "He's sent a girl to help me while I'm so big, to get the house cleaned up and all for the baby."

"We can't afford no serving wench." Jim stared at me, disapproving.

"Oh, you don't need to pay me wages," I said. "I'll work just for a bed and a bit of food."

Jim turned away and shrugged, tapping his unlit pipe in his hand. There was no smell of tobacco in the room, which made me think it was a while since he could afford any.

"Come along into the kitchen, then I'll get you settled." Lucy led me to a room off the parlor, the only other one on ground level. A narrow stairway led to the upper floor. "Have you eaten any tea?" she asked. I could have kissed her.

"Not a bite since breakfast, ma'am," I said.

"Call me Lucy. Here's some stew left over, and a potato." She dished me out a generous dollop. I wanted to say I wouldn't take that much, but I was so hungry I could've eaten the wooden spoon. "Soon's you're done I'll take you upstairs. You'll share a room with Arthur—hardly more than a closet, I'm afraid. Tomorrow you can tell me what this is all about."

I wondered if kindness is something that runs in families. So many of the people I'd met up with were cold and hard, only concerned about their own selves. Like Mavis. And Mr. Collins. Today Will risked his position to help me, and his sister, who I could see couldn't afford another mouth to feed, took me in, no questions. My eyes overflowed with tears before I could stop them.

"There now, Molly. You're safe here."

I knew I was. For a bit, anyway. In a few days, I'd leave that safe hiding place and take a crazy chance for something that would change my life forever.

Chapter 5

On the fourth night of my stay with Lucy and her family, she came in and woke me up after midnight.

"I'm sorry, Molly, but I think the baby's coming." She doubled over right then. I took the lamp out of her hand so she wouldn't drop it.

"Where's Jim?" I asked.

"He's taken little Arthur to his mum's. They'll both stay there tonight. This is no time for men."

I took her hand and led her back into her bedroom. In spite of the fact I'd helped the midwife when my little sister Ann was born, I couldn't recall exactly how it was done.

"I know what to do. I'll tell you," Lucy said, reading the doubt in my face.

"Have you sent for the midwife?" I hoped I'd soon have a helping hand.

"Can't afford one." Lucy's breath was squeezed. Another sharp pain welled up and sweat broke out on her forehead in beads that looked like crystals in the light of the oil lamp.

As soon as the cramp passed I helped her onto her bed. With the next pain, I let her squeeze my hand. It was all I could think to do. She didn't make a sound, only breathed real fast.

Once the pain slacked off again, she said, "Fetch a basin of water and a clean towel. And you'll need a knife and a length of string. Get the sharpest one from the kitchen. You'll find the twine by the stove."

I did as she told me. Everything was right where she said it would be. I took a deep breath and climbed the narrow stairs with all the tools of birthing.

After that there was only Lucy, me, and the pain for five long hours. In between pains she tried to talk to me. I told her she didn't have to, but I guess it helped take her mind off things.

"How is the reading going?" she asked. With all her other kindnesses, Lucy had taken time to help me learn how to put the letters I knew together into words, but I still struggled.

"All right. But I don't think I'll be ready in time."

"Ready for what?"

I forgot I'd not told her my plan. Since I'd been there I helped her clean and cook and take care of Arthur. And in whatever spare time there was she taught me, patient and slow. I didn't even have time to explain it all to Will when he came yesterday on his half day. The worst was that I needed to borrow money from him to get myself to Folkestone so I could catch up with the nurses.

"Aarrghhhh!" Lucy's scream startled me out of my thoughts. "I don't know what's happening. I think it's too soon. Molly, help me!"

She let out a sound like a cat being swung by its tail. I looked at her hard, swollen belly, wishing I could take the pain away from her. Then I remembered how Janet seemed soothed when I put my hands on her neck. "It's all right, Lucy," I said. Then I laid my hands on her belly, gentle and calm.

Her breathing slowed, and the sharp sounds she made settled down to a whimper, then faded away. "What did you do? How did you warm your hands so?" she whispered.

"Hush. Everything's all right now," I said. She closed her eyes, and I think she might've slept a few minutes. That was good. She needed her strength.

My arms had just started aching from holding them on Lucy's belly when all at once I felt a hard, strong cramp grip her. Lucy pushed herself up again.

The pains came back stronger than ever. I began to be afraid for her. I kept mopping her brow and feeling where the baby was when her belly wasn't tight as a copper kettle. I'd not done that part for my mother. The midwife took over when it was so near to time. Now it was just me to do it all.

"It's . . . going . . . to be . . . soon," Lucy panted. "It's all right now. I'm ready. Get the water and the knife. Where's the string?" I showed her. "Mind you tie it tight before you cut."

She started pushing. "Best get down where you can help it out," she said, nodding toward her feet.

I should've been embarrassed, I supposed, but it was what I had to do, for Lucy. It wasn't long before I could see the baby's head.

"The baby's coming!" I cried. I looked up and saw a fleeting smile on Lucy's face before she began to bear down again.

Then, after two more pushes, so sudden I could've dropped the poor mite, the little baby girl came slipping out of Lucy. She was squirming but not making any sound.

"Now tie!"

My fingers trembled as I tried, as fast as I could, to knot the string around the cord that still stretched into Lucy.

"Now cut! Quickly!"

I was too careful at first, but soon Lucy's fear made me cut fast.

"Let me have my baby," she said.

I gave her to Lucy. She held her upside down by the ankles and patted the tiny creature's bottom. Her little mouth opened, and a pinched but lusty cry emerged. "She's alive! She's all right. We did it!" I jumped up, nearly upsetting the basin of water.

Lucy clutched her baby to her for a moment, then handed her to me. "I'm too tired. You bathe her."

Careful and gentle, I sponged the infant down, then wrapped her in the receiving blanket that was ready in the bassinette next to the bed. Lucy'd fallen asleep, her face drawn but healthy looking. The baby began to cry again. Lucy's eyes opened. She smiled and put out her arms. Soon the baby was nursing and making sweet, contented sounds.

I stood and the room swayed a little. I steadied myself, realizing that there hadn't been any time that night where I felt I couldn't do it. Even when Lucy was near fainting with pain I kept my head. *I could be a nurse, for good and all*, I thought. And there was that time when my hands calmed Lucy, when I laid them on her belly and they made the pain fade away. It reminded me of how I helped Janet. Only this time it turned out just the opposite.

Of course, nursing at war would be more concerned with death than new life, but right then, although I was completely done in, I felt high and happy. "I'll tidy up here. You rest."

By the time Jim returned that evening, Lucy looked well and the baby was by turns eating, sleeping, and messing her linens. How Lucy would ever manage on her own when I wasn't there I couldn't say. And with Arthur to tend as well. But there was no way I could stay. I had to earn money, not just my keep. I had to do something that would allow me to hold my head up when I walked through the door into my mother's house.

My mother. All the time I thought of her. How were the little ones doing? Was everyone well? I suddenly ached to see them, to tell my mum what I'd just done for Lucy. But I couldn't. Not yet.

We were expecting Will the next day; he had a half day and had promised to come. I knew he'd want to spend most of his time talking to his sister and fussing over the baby. But I needed to talk to him too, alone. I was glad, then, that the baby was asleep when he came in.

"I have something to do in the kitchen," Lucy said, smiling at Will. Jim was working in the market stall his father owned, so Will and I had the parlor to ourselves.

I turned to him and started in quick. No sense waiting. It would have to come out sooner or later. "I have to—," but I couldn't go on. The words stuck in my throat. How could I ask him for more than he'd already done?

Will took my hand in both of his. Those eyes stared into mine until I had to look away. "What is it, Molly? You can tell me. Do you want to go home to your mother?"

I almost said yes, but that would've been weak. "No! No, that's not it at all. Only I have a plan and I still need your help." I took a deep breath and then told him everything as quickly as I could.

He let go of my hand and sat down on one of the wooden chairs, nodding as he listened to all I said. When I finished, he said, "Are you sure that's what you want, Molly?"

I was sure, but his question made me think all over again. "What else can I do? A factory job is no life at all and not much money. And you know no one will ever take me on in service after being dismissed from the Abington-Smythes." I wished I could tell him about Janet and Lucy, and how when I put my hands on them it made the pain go away a little. But I wasn't sure of myself. Not yet.

"What's next?" he asked, his voice dipping down at the end like it wasn't really a question, but a sort of wondering out loud. I'd hoped he'd be glad for me, excited, like I was, but instead he seemed disappointed.

"I need to get to Folkestone by the day after tomorrow."

I didn't say a thing about money, but he reached into his pocket and pulled out a pouch. "I was going to give my sister a little extra. But I imagine I can spare some of that for you. This should be enough to get you to Folkestone. I'm sorry I can't do more."

He handed me the pouch without looking at me. I took it and his hand in mine. "Will, there's no one kinder than you. I swear I will pay you back."

He looked up then. Maybe I imagined it, but I thought there was a sparkle in his eyes, like tears that wouldn't fall. "I'll make sure of it, Molly, one way or another." His words sounded harsh but his tone was soft, and I knew he meant it kindly. "Tell my sister I'll come back Sunday," he said, giving my hand a squeeze and standing. He pulled me up with him and we stood there, so close but not touching. I could feel something warm coming from his heart, reaching out to mine. Was it pain? Or something else? I wanted to put my hands on his chest. I wanted to share whatever was in his heart. I looked up at him. He leaned down and very gently, more like a breath than a kiss, touched his lips to mine.

Before I could say another word, he put his hat on and took his coat from the peg and walked out the door. I clutched the pouch, feeling the weight of coins. I held my future there. But I was cold, like someone just tossed a bucket of water on the parlor fire, and I almost ran out the door to follow Will, to tell him to come back, to take his money. But I didn't.

I was sorry to leave Lucy. I wanted to do something nice for her, so I scrubbed the house top to bottom the day before I left.

"The coach to Folkestone leaves at seven," she said as I stood on her doorstep early in the morning on October 20, the mist still coating everything in dreary droplets.

I wasn't one to show my feelings much—working in service taught you it wasn't safe—but I couldn't help hugging Lucy close to me. "I've never met people as friendly as you and Will," I said. "I wish I could stay and go at the same time."

"It's all right, Molly. You did so much for me while you were here, you can't imagine. You have a special gift. Just be sure to write to us." By "us" I knew she didn't mean her and Jim. I knew she included Will in that. She gave me a sheaf of coarse paper and a pencil. My reading and writing were coming along, enough to send a word or two. She'd taken care to write the direction on the top sheet so I could copy it.

"Of course."

The time had come. I had to turn away and take my first steps to the future. I went off toward the south without looking back.

Chapter 6

I didn't expect it to be so easy to get on a coach. All it took was a few shillings. Maybe that was because I asked for the cheapest fare and found myself sitting on the top, shivering in the drizzle that had begun to fall. As a result, I still had some money left from what Will gave me. Even with that, I feared what was left wouldn't be enough for a ticket on the Boulogne Packet.

Dawn made the gray sky pale when we left Charing Cross and set off over the river. The horses' breath puffed out in little clouds as they clopped first over cobbles, then echoed on the wooden planks of the bridge, and after that thudded in the packed mud of country roads. I'd never been outside of London, so in spite of almost no sleep and my stomach tied in a knot, I just kept drinking in the sight of rolling fields with hedgerows cutting them up into neat parcels, brown now and dead after the harvest, stubble showing where hay had grown. At least I thought it was hay, for all I knew about farming. Whatever it was, the air smelled clean and earthy, not sooty like London. The wind up top made it too noisy to talk, and I was glad. I just kept my eyes turned away from the others up there with me, all men.

We drew into Folkestone late in the afternoon, my backside bruised from bumping on the wood plank seat. The man who sat next to me hopped down and lifted me off like I was a sack of potatoes, but then set me gently on my feet and tipped his hat to me.

I took my valise and set out to find the docks. Folkestone was so small I could walk across it in a half hour. Just a little ways in I saw the tops of the masts bobbing up and down on the waves and set my course toward them.

The channel was chopped up with whitecaps. *Must be a rough journey across*, I thought. I couldn't see to the other side. To France. If all went like I hoped, I'd be in a foreign country soon. Someplace where they didn't speak the Queen's English. I shivered, though the rain had stopped.

I strolled back and forth on the docks like someone taking the air, while really looking for a place I could buy a ticket. All I saw were dock workers, though. I watched them bend and lift, muscles tensing and sweat streaking their cheeks, even though it was cold enough that I could have worn an extra cloak and been grateful for it. *Boulogne Star.* I made out "Star" and guessed the first word, since she was the only boat that wasn't a fishing boat, with deck chairs and a cabin where passengers could sit.

What if I couldn't get a ticket? If there were none left? Or if they were more costly than the few shillings I had in my pocket? I had to suss out if I could get aboard some other way.

Where we lived in the East End, near the docks, I used to play with my brother Ted before the littlest one came along and I had to stay home and help. We'd go and see if we could sneak aboard the finest and biggest ship, and usually we managed it. We pretended we were going to sail off to the South Seas, but of course we never did. As soon as we heard the sailors cry that the tide was on the turn, we'd get off as quick as we got on, sometimes by swinging from a rope to the dock, sometimes we'd just scamper down the gangplank when no one was minding us. There were always children running around on the docks in London, begging or playing or thieving.

Not here, though. What I saw of the town was neat and quiet. No one was begging or thieving that I could see, not even on the docks. And there was only one narrow gangplank leading to the deck. It'd be hard to pass unnoticed. I put my best face on and walked right up to a man on the dock; he was official looking, with a uniform, but not a policeman. I thought he might tell me about the fare for the packet.

"Beg pardon, sir," I said, and I added a little curtsy just for good measure. "Can you tell me where I might purchase a ticket on the packet boat to Boulogne?"

"Fancy a jaunt to France, eh?" he said. He smiled with his lips closed. I stared right back at him and waited for his answer. "The purser'll be coming by soon. You can get your ticket from him. If you've got six shillings, that is." He turned his back on me when a gent walked up to him and asked him a question.

How did I know what a purser looked like? It didn't make a bit of difference though. I only had two and six left. I couldn't buy a ticket. I'd have to think of another way.

I was no longer a little urchin who could squeeze by everyone quick and invisible. Some of the dock workers stared at me as I walked, one or two calling out things I wouldn't repeat to my mum. I ignored them and pretended I was going into the town. Back to the train station. Perhaps I'd meet the train Miss Nightingale and her nurses were on.

I joined a queue of people at a kiosk. When it was my turn I said, "Excuse me, but what time's the train from London?"

"From London? Don't get in until morning," he said and looked behind me to the next person, dismissing me before I'd even stepped aside.

Morning! What would I do with myself all night? I didn't have money for lodgings. And after dark they probably locked up people just wandering around. It was that kind of town. Like the nicer areas in London. So now I'd have to find someplace I could hide, somewhere to put myself out of view all night, and where I'd be safe too.

As I suspected, even though Folkestone was a prospering town, the harbor had its secrets. I wasn't the only one lurking there waiting for daily business to stop. There were lots of nooks to tuck myself away behind crates and great coils of rope. I just hoped the weather wouldn't turn against me, or some thief set on me. Little chance of that, since anyone with something worth stealing would likely have a room at the inn. No, my only difficulty would be managing to keep dry all night long and still look decent in the morning.

So, stomach rumbling and hands now numb from cold, I wandered until the to-ing and fro-ing stopped and the dock workers went home, then found a corner to hide myself in and tried to sleep, sitting on a crate with my back against some sacks of grain.

—⟨∞∞⟩—

The train's whistle woke me. My back and neck ached. I wiped a little drool from the corners of my mouth and stretched, straightening my clothes. At least I was dry. And no one made off with my valise—which had nothing valuable in it anyway, but I'd seem even odder aboard a packet with no luggage.

I hurried to the station, arriving just in time to see the London train come steaming in, great puffs billowing from the smokestack in the front. The whistle blew again and again so loud I had to cover my ears.

As soon as the train screeched to a stop everyone flew into a tizzy. Porters and vendors bumped into me, all crowding up at once to help passengers with their luggage or sell them cockles and tea if they were continuing on to France. I wished I could make myself invisible in the crowd so I could watch for the group of women to get off the train. I assumed it would be a large number and easy to see. The newspaper said a hundred would go.

The first-class compartment emptied. Only eight people got out, dressed very fine and one lady carrying a small dog with a squashed-in face. At the same time, all manner of men and women tumbled out of the third-class carriages, some smoking pipes or carrying bundles tied up with paper and string on their shoulders. Still no one who looked anything like a nurse, and no Mrs. Bracebridge.

It was beginning to look like I would have to walk all the way back to London because I didn't have enough for a coach when a second-class carriage door opened, and I recognized the gentleman who'd been introduced to me as Mr. Bracebridge getting down. He cast his eyes up and down the platform as if he was expecting someone. I turned away quickly, hoping he wouldn't recognize me, but kept sight of the carriage door out of the corner of my eye.

Soon they streamed out, one by one. There were two different sorts. One had uniforms, or something like them, like the nuns we sometimes saw in the poor neighborhoods bringing food. The others were dressed in ordinary street clothes. I counted them. Twenty-eight, not a hundred. Was one of them Miss Nightingale? Then Mrs. Bracebridge stepped down from the train, and by the way they all queued up behind to follow her, it didn't seem like any could be the lady herself. Perhaps she was one of the others I'd seen get down from the first-class compartment.

I stuck close to the nurses but out of sight, my only hope

being I could somehow blend in with the lot and sneak aboard as if I was part of the group.

They all stopped at an inn, most likely for a bite to eat. Lucky for me, they didn't stay long. In twos and threes they came out after a bit and gathered on the cobbled street where other people also stood round in groups. I kept my distance but followed them again to the docks.

Passengers already had their tickets out and were filing aboard the packet up the gangplank, all looking like they were on holiday. A man in a uniform, I guessed he was the purser, scowled at each ticket. He stopped people and looked carefully at their papers. My heart dropped like a stale roll to my stomach. How would I pass? There was no hope I'd get by unnoticed. After all this trouble, it looked as if I'd get no farther than Folkestone, and with not enough left over to make my way back to London either. I watched the nurses get their tickets out, ready to take their turn, wishing so I was one of them. I clenched my jaw to stop the tears I feared might start any moment.

Just as I was about to give up hope, a fat man wearing a sash like he was the mayor or something came bustling up to Mrs. Bracebridge with a handful of police officers scurrying behind to keep up. At first I thought the whole crowd of nurses would be arrested.

"Are you Mrs. Nightingale?" he asked Mrs. Bracebridge in a booming voice.

"No, I am afraid *Miss* Nightingale has gone ahead from Dover."

The broad smile on the man's face faded and he started to bow and turn away.

"But these are her nurses, whom I am to accompany to Turkey," Mrs. Bracebridge added, touching his arm to stop him. His smile full of teeth returned and he kissed Mrs. Bracebridge's hand.

By this time a small band had formed. A cornet, a clarinet, and an accordion. At a signal from the mayor—or whatever he was—they struck up "The Girl I Left Behind Me." Everyone watched the nurses. Even the sailors and dock workers stopped what they were doing and swayed a little to the music.

My blood of a sudden rushed into my fingers and toes. Here was my chance! Before I lost my nerve, I slipped up the gangplank, all the while sure the whole crowd would see me and I'd be stopped and thrown in gaol. But I made it to the deck. Then, instead of hiding like I would have done when I was younger, I sauntered past the other passengers like I belonged there, forcing myself to move slowly. I even leaned on the rail looking down at the fuss on the dock. I had to be calm, but my heart thumped. I gripped the rail so no one would see how my hands shook.

The mayor made a short speech—time was getting on and the boat had to sail—and then all the nurses and the Bracebridges climbed aboard.

What next? I had got on the packet, but the hardest part was still ahead of me. How would I convince Mrs. Bracebridge to let me go along with them as if it was always the plan?

As soon as we were far enough away from the shore, and the wind picked up and the waves began to rock us, I looked for her, hoping she'd not gone below with so many of the others to escape the bitter cold.

I found Mrs. Bracebridge sitting toward the stern in a sheltered place, her eyes closed. She looked very tired. I felt bad that I was going to trouble her but I had no choice, now I'd got this far. "Excuse me, Mrs. Bracebridge." I hoped my voice didn't quake too much.

She looked up, startled. She shaded her eyes from the sun and narrowed them before talking. "Do I know you?"

"We met at Mrs. Stanley's house. My name is Molly Fraser."

"Molly Fraser . . . yes, I remember. You weren't qualified. How do you come to be on this boat?"

"The truth is, I was waiting for you, ma'am. See, I don't half want to be a nurse and go with your lot to Turkey." Now that I'd got it out, everything was in her hands. She had a kind face. I kept my eyes fixed on her, hoping she'd see how desperate I was and how much I meant what I said.

The frown on her brow creased deeper. "But I explained to you that Miss Nightingale requested only trained, mature nurses."

I'd practiced what I was going to say to her over and over to myself, but now that it came out it all sounded hollow and flat. "I learn things fast. I know I can prove myself. I know about healing. Please just give me a chance." I talked too fast. My lips felt like India rubber.

"It's not my decision to make," she said.

"But Miss Nightingale trusted you to choose the other nurses, didn't she?"

She let out a short laugh. "Yes, but if I bring her an inexperienced girl, what will she think then?"

"If you don't tell her, she won't know. I'm here now and I went to a great deal of trouble to get here. Won't you please just let me try?" I was afraid I might cry if I went on. I was so tired after my night on the docks and all the planning and hoping of the last few weeks.

She sat silent for a moment, looking out over the water. I could almost hear her tossing the idea back and forth in her mind. What would she decide?

"Do you realize that you have taken a terrible risk? I could have you arrested by the purser as a stowaway—unless you have a ticket? Not to mention that you need a passport once we arrive in France."

I shook my head. "No, I don't have neither one of them."

She was silent again. She put two fingers to her forehead and rubbed it a little, like it would help her think. At last she folded her hands in her lap. She looked steadily at me. "All right, Molly. I won't turn you over to the authorities. But this deception does not add to your scanty recommendations. You will have to prove yourself or you will be sent home. We shall have to see to the passport in Paris. But it will be up to Miss Nightingale whether you may continue with us to Turkey. And you must obey me and Miss Nightingale in everything. This is not a pleasure trip. I doubt you can truly

44

know what you are signing up for. Not a wisp of that beautiful hair must show beneath your cap. If you so much as look at a wounded soldier with those big gray eyes, I'll send you packing even if Miss Nightingale doesn't notice. And if she agrees to keep you, you mustn't expect the same wages the trained nurses will receive."

She meant to discourage me. But I was so happy I could've thrown my arms around her. I didn't though. I didn't want to do anything that might make her doubt me. Instead I tried to keep a straight face and control the trembling that I thought might overpower me at any time. "You won't be sorry, I promise." I put out my hand to shake hers. She took it and smiled.

Chapter 7

I don't know what Mrs. Bracebridge said to the others, but they accepted me quickly enough. Most of them were older, well past the age of marrying. Except one.

"My name's Emma. Emma Bigelow. I'm not half glad to see someone who isn't a sour old puss or spends her time on her knees praying."

Emma was pretty—or she would've been if there wasn't a scar across her upper lip, a white line that cut from the outside of her nose to the corner of her mouth, which kept her from smiling on that side. But she had big eyes that were a nice, golden brown color and went with her light brown hair. Almost the color Mavis's was, only with threads of blond in it.

"I'm Molly Fraser," I said, leaving it up to her if she wanted to keep talking.

"Still, you're young to be a nurse. Where was you nursing?"

I wished I didn't have to answer her, because it'd be a lie.

I made like I just wanted to stroll along a little, leading us away from the other nurses.

"I've only done a little nursing," I said quietly.

"Oh! Well, then . . ." A spark of interest lit up her eyes. "I can tell you some about nursing in an hospital. It's easy, but you got to have a strong stomach." She looped her arm through mine and nattered on in my ear all the way across the channel.

When we got on the train to Paris in Boulogne, she sat next to me like we were old friends. She kept telling me stories about assisting with operations in the hospital she worked in up north, she didn't say exactly where.

"There was this doctor, see, he was too drunk to stitch up the poor old fella, so I took the needle myself and did it. And it was a neater job than ever he would've done, you can be sure!"

Something told me I should take everything Emma said to me with a pinch of salt. I noticed she told her stories when the others weren't listening, when they were belowdecks on the packet or asleep in their seats on the train. And her London accent was as thick as mine, so she couldn't have been in the north for long. I didn't question her close, though. I had my own secrets to keep, so I figured it wouldn't do much harm to let her have hers.

We didn't clap eyes on Miss Nightingale until we arrived in Paris. We were to stay one day there, in a convent on an island in the middle of the Seine—a river not half as big as the Thames, not even deep enough for ships, so everything had to come in by barge. And it was green and stinking too.

There were ten nurses already there, Catholic nuns, Mrs. Bracebridge said, who would go on to Turkey with us. Their leader was called Mother Bermondsey.

"Let's bunk next to each other," Emma said, putting her arm through mine as if we'd been friends for ever such a long time.

"Put your bags down and come into the chapel," Mrs. Bracebridge said to all of us. "Miss Nightingale would like to speak to you."

I should've been shaking in my shoes about meeting Miss Nightingale, but by then I was so curious to see this famous lady that I put on my bravest face and decided to take whatever was coming. I didn't have a choice, after all. I hoped Mrs. Bracebridge wouldn't say anything about how I came to be among them. Still, I stayed near the back, which wasn't hard with all the others trying to get as near as possible to Miss Nightingale, probably to impress her or make her notice them at least.

You could've knocked me over with a feather when she came in. She was beautiful. And young. And tall! Taller than I was by an inch or two at least. Unlike the other nurses, she didn't wear a plain dress but had on silk and full petticoats, with ruffles and lace. I guessed she was a proper lady. She looked nothing like someone who was about to be up to her elbows in blood and stench. The only difference betwixt her and any other rich lady was her hair: it was simpler, just pulled back with no curls or loops of braids.

"She could've married, they say," Emma whispered, giving me a little pinch.

"Why didn't she?" I asked. But Miss Nightingale began to speak, so we all quieted down.

"Nurses and sisters, I thank you for undertaking this hazardous task, for leaving the comfort of your homes or convents in England to become a part of this noble group, who will do much to enhance the comfort of our sick and wounded soldiers.

"But we must all tread very, very carefully. Mrs. Bracebridge will give each of you a paper to sign with strict rules of conduct. I am glad to see that most of you are of a steady age and disposition. However . . ."

I could've sworn she looked directly at me and Emma. I tried to shrink back into myself, make myself invisible.

". . . I will not tolerate any flirtation or inappropriate behavior around the men, who will be frightened and lonely and much in need of comfort."

One or two of the other nurses stared at us as well, the older ones mainly.

"Also not to be tolerated is inebriation in any form and to any degree. It leads to disorderly conduct and inhibits the proper carrying out of your duties. You are required to maintain your personal hygiene at all times. I have seen to the design of uniforms, and those of you who are not otherwise uniformed will be equipped with them while we are here in Paris. We have the greater part of our journey yet to undertake. The way you comport yourselves, your dedication to the task that lies ahead, will be under my scrutiny, I assure you.

"Are there any questions?"

Miss Nightingale might've been lecturing new servants. I didn't mind, but some of the others looked cross. But she, being so young and all, would have to be strong with us or the older ones might not pay her any heed.

One of the nuns raised her hand. I don't know how she dared! "Shouldn't we ask God's blessing on our journey?" she asked. The other nuns smiled and nodded.

Miss Nightingale flicked her eyes toward Mrs. Bracebridge so fast I wondered if anyone else noticed. "Religion is a personal matter. We have among us those who are of the Church of England, those who attend chapel, and those who profess the Catholic faith. I advise you to ask whatever blessings you prefer—in private."

She left me wondering what she really thought, which I suppose was on purpose.

"We shall enjoy a light supper in the refectory. Tomorrow you have some time to explore Paris if you'd like, in groups of three or more, between the hours of ten in the morning and four o'clock in the afternoon, as I have some business to attend to. We depart on the train for Lyons the day after that, and will take a boat down the Rhône to Avignon, whence we again board a train to Marseille. All the details are on the papers Mrs. Bracebridge will distribute. Thank you."

She turned to Mrs. Bracebridge, who stood by her all meek and quiet. They started talking. I couldn't take my eyes off the two of them, heads together. Miss Nightingale ran her finger down the list of names and shook her head. Mrs. Bracebridge whispered and pointed with her. I itched to know what they were saying. They got to the bottom of the list and Miss Nightingale frowned. I wished I could hear. She said something fast to Mrs. Bracebridge. Then what I dreaded the most happened: Mrs. Bracebridge looked toward me. I think I must have blushed red as a beet. Miss Nightingale looked at me for no more than a second, turned back to Mrs. Bracebridge, then walked quickly out of the room.

"Come along, I'm starving," Emma said, pulling my arm. "Won't be nothing left if we wait much longer."

I was concentrating so hard on Miss Nightingale that I didn't notice the other nurses leave the room, so there were only a few of us left. I turned to go with Emma, but Mrs. Bracebridge caught up with me. *Please, no,* I thought, then steeled myself. *This is it. I'll be sent home for sure.*

"Miss Nightingale would like to speak with you as soon as you've finished your supper," Mrs. Bracebridge said. No doubt I looked how I felt, because she added, "You're not in trouble, not yet at least. I kept most of your secret. But she has some questions."

I expected she had questions.

The smell of good food floated out of the refectory, but my throat was too tight to even swallow a bite. I tried but only pushed the food around on my plate.

"Mind if I finish that?" Emma said, looking at the sausage I'd nibbled at.

"Suit yourself," I said.

I hardly remembered anything about that meal or anything Emma was chattering on about. I nodded now and again, but her voice just rose and fell and made no sense. I would have to face Miss Nightingale and convince her she should let me go on with them to Turkey. I had no trouble picturing her turning me out on my ear and could practically feel the stares of the other nurses as I left them and got back on a train for Boulogne.

As everyone stood from the long table to go back to their rooms, Mrs. Bracebridge came over to me. "Come, Molly, you can join the others in a moment."

I followed her, feeling the way I used to feel when I knew I'd been bad and my mum was taking me in to my dad for a beating. Only worse, if that was possible, because I didn't know what to expect.

Miss Nightingale sat in a private room near a blazing fire. She had a small table pulled up in front of her, covered with papers in different piles. She didn't look up when Mrs. Bracebridge brought me in.

"Please be seated—Molly Fraser, is it?—I'll be with you in just a moment." She pointed the quill of her pen toward the chair in front of the table but didn't take her eyes off the papers.

"Would you like me to stay?" Mrs. Bracebridge asked,

putting her gnarled hand softly on Miss Nightingale's shoulder. I hoped for yes.

"No. I'm sure you're tired, dear." She looked up at last, smiling warmly in the old lady's direction. The change in Miss Nightingale made my heart leap a little. Her face looked kind. Maybe she would understand about me after all, let me continue on to Turkey with them in spite of how I got there.

Her pen scratching was loud in the empty room. After what seemed forever she pushed her papers aside and lifted her eyes, taking me in with a piercing glance. "Now, Miss Fraser. Your name was not on the list I was originally sent by Mrs. Stanley and Mrs. Bracebridge. I'm prepared to think the best of you, but I believe you should explain yourself to me."

More lies?

No. I couldn't lie to Miss Nightingale. Looking at her there, a beautiful lady who could probably have anything she wanted but chose to go and nurse common soldiers for the good of the country, I couldn't think of telling her tales. The difference between us was enormous—the scrappy, low life I was running away from and the fire that burned in her eyes, staring straight at me—what business did I have to be there? So I told her my story, all of it, from beginning to end, about service and Will Parker and Lucy's baby. About helping my mum care for the little ones in the East End. About wanting to find a way to prove myself, to make my mum proud of me again.

"Well, Molly," she said when I was finished, "it seems

you've got quite a determined spirit. That's no substitute for training, however. And your youth is without doubt a deterrent to effective nursing. How old are you?" She leaned back a little in her chair and dipped her chin so the angle of her eyes changed and threw me a little off my guard.

"Nineteen." I said it before I had a chance to think about it. Maybe she knew it for a lie but to my relief she didn't question it.

"My instructions to Mrs. Stanley were not to consider anyone under the age of twenty-four."

I studied my hands clutching each other in my lap. This was the moment. The end of the road for me. I'd go back to London to God knew what, my mother forever ashamed of me for something I didn't do. But then I remembered that Emma wasn't over twenty-four, at least she didn't look it, and somehow she was here.

"You mustn't expect to do anything but assist the other nurses, and you will have to be trained on the job. If you put your mind to it, however, and don't get distracted, I have a feeling you might become a good nurse. But that's up to you. And at the first sign of any familiarity with any man— soldier, surgeon, or servant—you will be sent home."

I couldn't believe it. She wasn't going to send me away! I looked at her. She had on her stern, all-business face, but I thought I saw just a hint of the kindness she showed to Mrs. Bracebridge tugging at the corners of her mouth.

"Thank you," I said. My heart swelled up in my chest and stopped my throat.

"You may go. But I would like to take you with me tomorrow on a few errands. I may need your help." She stood, scraping her chair back.

She could have ordered me to stick my hands into the fire that blazed at her feet and I would've done it. I curtsied to her and made my way back to the dormitory, flying with joy.

Chapter 8

Mrs. Bracebridge woke me before dawn the next morning. "Miss Nightingale would like you to go with her to the Hôtel Dieu."

I was too tired to ask questions, especially why we'd be going to a hotel at that hour. I dressed as fast as I could and soon found myself hurrying along the still-dark streets of Paris, trying to keep up with Miss Nightingale.

"The Hôtel Dieu is a hospital, where they are working hard to improve conditions," Miss Nightingale said to me as we walked. "There's something I want you to see there."

Oh, so that was it. The hospital wasn't very far from where we were staying. A nun greeted us, welcoming Miss Nightingale like an old friend. They spoke French to each other. My amazement at Miss Nightingale grew.

The smell indoors was strong but not dirty. Something stung my eyes and they teared a little.

"That's chloride of lime," Miss Nightingale said, switching back to English for me. "You must become accustomed

```
THE UNIVERSITY OF CALGARY BOOKSTORE
          2500 UNIVERSITY DRIVE NW.
          CALGARY, ALBERTA  T2N 1N4
       403-220-5937   1-877-220-5937
          WWW.CALGARYBOOKSTORE.CA
              GST #108102864

SALE                001 011 RC-3120481
CASHIER: 137            12/04/14 10:37

01 CARDS/INDEX ASST 3 X 5 10
     601008  10323410      1 T     1.99*
        Less $0.49 Sale         -0.49
02 CARDS/INDEX ASST 3 X 5 10
     601008  10323410      1 T     1.99*
        Less $0.49 Sale         -0.49
03 PEN BALLPOINT BLACK MEDIU
     601031  10475041      1 T     0.99*
        Less $0.24 Sale         -0.24
04 SALE SALE / $3.00 SALE BO
     559990  11013303      1 T     3.00

                    Subtotal      6.75
                    5% GST        0.34
                               --------
       Items     4  Total        7.09
                               --------
VISA                             7.09
Acct: ************7181
   Auth Cd: 040055
   Term ID: 66239130

              Change Due         0.00

        14 DAY RETURN POLICY
   MUST HAVE THIS ORIGINAL RECEIPT
      SHOP ONLINE 24HRS A DAY
        CALGARYBOOKSTORE.CA
```

Apple products purchased at the Microstore are not returnable.

The Bookstore retains the right to refuse any refund.
Photo ID required at time of refund.

View our complete refund policy at:
www.calgarybookstore.ca

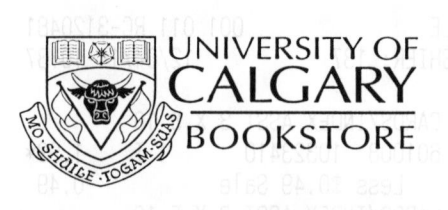

University of Calgary Bookstore Refund Policy

Refunds accepted within
14 days of purchase.
Must have original sales receipt.
Refunds must be credited in the same
form as the purchase was made.

Books must be in MINT condition.
Clothing products must not be
washed or worn and in original
condition with tags intact.

No refunds on sale items,
special orders, calculators, batteries,
access codes, e-book, jump books,
medical or personal care products.

All Microstore returns must be in original
package, in original condition and are
subject to a 15% restocking fee.

Licences, opened, sale products and
Apple products purchased at the
Microstore are not returnable.

to that smell because we will use it a great deal in Turkey. I have come here to find out where the Sisters of Mercy get their supplies so we may purchase some and bring them with us. And also to show you what you might expect and give you one final chance to return to London. At my expense, of course."

We had reached a large closed door with enormous hinges on it. The sister who accompanied us said something else in French to Miss Nightingale. She nodded. They both looked at me before the sister opened the door. I expected it to creak like some ancient entrance to a dungeon, it looked so like one. But it swung out quiet and smooth. Just inside the door hung some heavy aprons. Miss Nightingale put one on and handed one to me.

The stench hit me so hard I caught my breath. Something in that room smelled even stronger than the chloride of lime. I put my hand over my mouth and swallowed back the bile that flooded it.

"The surgeon is preparing to amputate this man's leg; it is gangrenous," the sister said in English, her accent so strong I hardly understood her.

We stepped forward and around a curtain. Behind it a man lay on a table, one leg covered by a sheet, the other out plain as day. From the knee down his leg was black and swollen. It seemed to be in shadow, like Janet's neck before she died. The surgeon, whose back was to us as he arranged some very sharp and pointed instruments on a table, turned, holding a saw and a curved knife. Three nuns and a man in monk's robes I'd not noticed before came forward and stood on either side of the table. The monk and two nuns held the man's body down so he couldn't move. The third nun stood by the doctor with a cloth in her hand.

"He has been given chloroform, but only a little. Our supply is very limited. Most of it is with our army in Turkey," the nun whispered.

I didn't know then what chloroform was. I was still hardly awake, and everything seemed odd and like a dream.

"First, the surgeon must ensure that the fellow does not bleed to death," Miss Nightingale whispered to me. "So he cuts through the skin and muscles and finds the arteries and veins and ties them off."

That was not so very different from tying the cord when Lucy's baby was born. I watched, but we were too far away to see much.

"Will we have to cut off legs?" I asked, suddenly worried that was why she brought me to the hospital with her.

"No!" she whispered harshly. "But we may have to stand by and assist, as that nurse is doing."

The man's eyes rolled open and he started moving his head from side to side. "*Ah! Ah! Merde! Ça me blesse trop!*" He began to scream and struggle. His leg twitched. The monk gripped it hard to hold it still. His pain must have been far worse than Lucy's. No gentle touch would make that go away.

The nuns and monk held him fast. The doctor continued what he was doing as if he were carving a Sunday roast, now slicing hard through the skin and muscles. The man suddenly stopped struggling and the leg lay still.

"Is he dead?" I asked, although he didn't look it. I remembered them carrying Janet's body out of the house, and her skin was gray—almost purple.

"He probably fainted from the pain," Miss Nightingale said.

I nodded and watched the nuns holding him to see what they did. One of them had her hand on his forehead. I wondered if he could feel her soft touch, even though he'd fainted dead away. She looked up and saw me staring at her. She nodded just a little. She understood about touching, how it could help. Her hand was soothing him, making him feel better, less afraid, like mine did with Janet and Lucy.

All this distracted me from what the surgeon was doing but now I had to watch. He'd carved through all the soft bits and reached the bone. The sawing was loud and rasping, like going through a piece of hard wood. Before long the blackened leg lay on the ground. Blood flowed out of it, as well as other liquids that looked and smelled putrid.

"Now he will sew up the wound, and if the fellow does not die of shock, he will get a wooden leg and live on. How do you feel?"

I looked up at her. "I feel sorry for him. But I believe he'll live." I think I was still too dazed to take in everything I'd just seen.

She cocked her head to the side. "What makes you say that?"

"I . . . I don't know," I said, realizing I'd said something I maybe shouldn't.

"You're a strong girl, Molly," Miss Nightingale said. We turned to go out, leaving our aprons on the pegs where we got them.

A moment after we left, one of the nurses who had been helping the surgeon came out with something wrapped in a bloody sheet. I saw the sole of the man's black foot as she walked off down the hall. I don't know why, but something about that, the leg going away from him forever, a dead thing no longer any use to anyone, broke down the calm I felt while I watched the operation.

"Excuse me, Miss Nightingale, but . . ." I couldn't finish my sentence before retching.

Her cool, soft hands stroked my hair away from my face as I lost what little I'd eaten. "It's all right, Molly. Perfectly natural. I did the same the first time I saw someone lose a limb. But you will see many more horrific sights in Turkey, and if you feel you won't be able to manage, now is the time to tell me."

My stomach calmed. Would I be able to stand it? I didn't really know. If I could see a person's pain so clear and obvious, how would I bear it? Perhaps I'd get used to it, maybe even be able to help, maybe learn how to do more than just soothe with a gentle touch. And I would have a chance to do something, to go somewhere. What would I do if I went back to London now? Probably starve. At the very least, be an embarrassment to my mum. "No, I still want to go. I think I'll be all right."

"Come with me then. You'll need a passport and clothing like the others. Then I shall want you to help me do some shopping."

Shopping? "What will you buy?" I imagined gowns and hats, and thought it very strange of her to outfit herself just to work in a hospital.

"Some small stoves. A quantity of chloride of lime. Linens. Since you were a parlormaid, I thought you might know the best stoves and bed linens to get; ones that would stand up to hard use."

Miss Nightingale was asking for my help. How could this be? I felt better right away. And she was right, I did know a thing or two that could be useful. We climbed into the Paris version of a cab, a small open carriage with one horse pulling it, and went off to take care of all the errands.

"Well, so aren't we the lucky one!" Emma sat on her cot with her feet up, repacking her case.

"What do you mean?"

"Going off all day with Miss Nightingale. I 'spect you're too good for the rest of us."

"I had to get a passport and warm clothes," I said. "It was Mrs. Bracebridge's idea." I don't know why I added that.

"Just so long as you don't put on no airs. Nursing's nursing."

I didn't feel much like talking to Emma. I had so much to think about and only one person I ached to share it with.

I took the pencil and paper Lucy gave me out of my trunk. I wanted to tell Will all about what had happened in the last two days, but my spelling was so terrible. Would he laugh at me?

I sat for a long time staring at that blank sheet of paper.

"Are you just going to look at it or write something on it?" Emma got up off her cot and flopped down next to me on mine.

"I've never wrote a letter before," I said, immediately worrying I had told her too much.

"Never been away from home? This is a fine place to be for the first time! Well, just start. You'll find what to say easy enough."

Of course she thought I would write to my mum. And then I thought I really ought to. She might be worried. Especially because, by my count, the day before would've been my half day, and I wouldn't have come home with wages for her. I wondered if she'd sent Ted to look for me and what they told him at Cadogan Square. Or maybe Will thought to let them know I was gone away and not to worry about me. Still, she'd have to have someone read the letter for her, since she wasn't so good at reading and Dad couldn't read at all. I'd take the trouble when I had something to really tell her and trust that they found out enough not to be off their heads with worry.

Emma soon got bored with watching me just sit there and went back to her packing. I saw her tuck a small tin flask in the middle of all her clothes. Several of the other nurses had them too. I'd seen them drinking from them when they thought no one was looking on the train. Maybe that was why Miss Nightingale made such a fuss about drunkenness. By the time the dinner bell rang, I'd written to Will what I could:

Dear Will,
    Riting from Paris. We go to turkey to-morro. Ill be a nerse! Thanks for yore help. I think of you. Rite to me at Scutari. Plese tell my mum I'm alive and well.
                                Yore frend,
                                Molly

The papers Mrs. Bracebridge gave us had the direction where our family could send letters. Will told me to write to him at Lucy's, and I suddenly realized why. No one would think I was writing a man friend. I folded and sealed the letter, then gave it to Mrs. Bracebridge to post, part of me wishing I could curl up tiny and go where that letter would go, just to see Will and Lucy again.

Chapter 9

The trip from Paris was a bit tedious. Nothing to do but stare out the train windows at dreary scenery that didn't look so different from England—except once in a while there was a castle on a hill. Some of the other nurses played cards. The nuns prayed a lot. I was too shy, knowing that I'd be sent packing for any wrong step, to get acquainted with anyone besides Emma.

Emma. There was something about her. She was always ready with a quick word, a funny quip to make me laugh. Maybe it was because of her scar, but even when she was laughing her eyes didn't look really happy. Instead of lighting up all merry like Will's did, they went hard, like crystals.

"'Ere, Moll," she said after a long silence between stops on the train. "What you think about them nuns what are coming with us? There's three different kinds. I always thought nuns was nuns."

"I've been wondering the same thing. Do you s'pose we dare ask them?"

One of the sisters walked by just as I said it. "Ask us what?" she said.

"We was wondering why you all aren't dressed the same," Emma asked, brazen as anything.

"That's because we belong to different houses, or orders. Those over there, with the black habits, are from Norwood. The ones next to them are from Bermondsey. They're both Catholic. I and my other Sellonite sisters are Anglican."

She smiled and stared straight at us, as if she expected another question. "I see," I said. "I didn't know there was such a thing as Anglican nuns."

"We're more Sisters of Mercy than nuns." She nodded to us and continued on to join the other Sellonites. That was the last time any of them spoke to us until we boarded the steamer at Marseille. And we didn't do that till after we took a smaller steamer down the Rhône River and got on another train at Avignon.

Marseille was a busy port town, more like London than Folkestone was. I recognized the lowlifes around the docks, and even though they spoke in French the rough voices could've been just the same as the ones I was accustomed to hearing in the East End. I'd no doubt they were turning the air blue with their cursing and would've made us blush if we could've understood them.

"Well," Mrs. Bracebridge said as we all gathered with our valises waiting to board the *Vectis*, "That other nurse, Mrs. Wilson, was supposed to meet us in Paris. I thought perhaps she'd catch up with us on the train since I told her our route, but there's still no sign of her."

Mrs. Bracebridge handed us our tickets as she spoke. I didn't know there was a nurse missing. Maybe she wouldn't come, and it'd be good that I was there to make up the numbers.

"I'm dreading this voyage," she continued. "The Mediterranean is always rough this time of year." Miss Nightingale, who seemed solid and sure in Paris, had turned so pale I could nearly see the bones beneath her skin.

"Excuse me!"

A woman, round in body and with at least two chins, wearing a hat with a feather that stuck up in the air and quivered as she marched toward us, burst into our group and scattered us, making straight for Miss Nightingale.

"Blimey! What you s'pose she's going to do?" Emma said. I shrugged, turning with all the others to stare straight at her. She looked like a great parrot come to light on a dead tree she seemed so out of place.

"Mrs. Wilson, at your service. I have been on this train the whole time and cannot understand why I did not encounter you, Miss Nightingale."

Mrs. Wilson had a loud voice and was trying to make it sound posh.

"I'm sure I would have noticed you in the second-class carriage," Miss Nightingale said, making one or two of the nurses stifle giggles. "However, the main point is that you have joined us at last. You will be able to change into your uniform once we board the steamer."

"Why, there's the answer to the mystery! I didn't see you because I was in the first-class carriage, which I naturally assumed was where you would be."

Every one of us froze. The look on Miss Nightingale's face was thunderous. I thought for sure she'd explode at any moment, but instead she simply turned away. "I see the purser, and the gangplank is down. Let us climb aboard."

We formed an orderly queue, Emma and me at the end. This time, instead of having to sneak my way onto the boat, I had all my papers ready for the purser, who frowned at them and then waved me on.

Everyone mostly went down to the cabin where we would sleep, but I wanted to wander around the deck. I'd not gone far when the sound of voices, their owners hidden by some barrels and ropes, stopped me.

"You understand, Mrs. Wilson, that we cannot support payment of your first-class fare. We are going to nurse the common soldiers, in the pay of the British government." Miss Nightingale's clipped, precise voice was unmistakable.

"You think I came just for your paltry ten shillings a week?" Mrs. Wilson said. I nearly gasped. Ten shillings a week were riches by most people's standards. Who would have the nerve to speak to Miss Nightingale like that? "Now that my husband is no more—God rest his soul—I intend to make my fortune nursing a nobleman and thought I'd find him in Turkey as much as anywhere else."

"I see. We have a difference of intent, Mrs. Wilson. However, as you are here and have been highly recommended by those I respect, I will allow you to come to Turkey and expect you to carry out your duties professionally."

I quickly went back the way I came, hoping Miss Nightingale didn't see me. It seemed more people were like Mavis than I thought, especially women. I suppose I shouldn't have been so shocked. What else was there for us to do? Anything that wasn't illegal paid barely enough to live on. Lots of girls tried for a rich husband any way they could.

The *Vectis*, although larger than the river steamer we'd been on, was small by ocean-going standards; I could walk round the deck in just a few minutes and there were only a few places for passengers. Our cabin had shelves along the sides, which they told us were the bunks where we'd sleep. Miss Nightingale and the Bracebridges had quarters somewhere else on board. A few doctors, Emma told me— though how she knew I didn't dare ask—had the cabin in the stern.

I leaned on the rail and watched the dockworkers load all the supplies Miss Nightingale bought in France. They stowed them away quick as could be and it was still more than an hour before they had finished.

As the engines were fired up and we prepared to set sail, I turned my attention to the men on deck. Since this was a steamer, the usual scurrying around throwing ropes and hauling sails was replaced by shoveling coal. It didn't take so many sailors to get up a head of steam as it did to hoist four masts of canvas. Some of them had little to do, only walking the deck, looking out to sea. Still, they seemed edgy to me. I couldn't tell why. I didn't see anything but calm, flat water with a dark line of clouds at the horizon.

Watching the work made me think of Dad and the boys. I wondered if any of the younger ones had started going to watch and learn the ropes. I knew Mum would miss my wages. I hoped it wouldn't make Dad cross, the way he was before I got my first position, when sometimes he'd come home drunk and make Mum cry. She'd try to keep him away from us then, and my stomach clenched, remembering his eyes hard and cruel and him coming after me with his belt. "It's your fault! Damn useless children!" he'd say. But only when he was drunk. Sober, he loved us all, and in his heart I knew he wouldn't hurt us on purpose in any way that would last longer than a bruise. Worst I ever got was a welt that I felt for a month.

The engines began to huff and puff and clouds of steam rose up from the chimneys on the boat. The horn blew so loud it made me jump. People standing on the dock waved and smiled. The sailors just carried on, but every now and then one of them looked out to sea, like he could see something there I couldn't.

Getting out on the water made me forget everything. We weren't long away from the harbor before all sign of land disappeared. I felt like I was nowhere and everywhere, going neither here nor there, just sitting on the back of the world with it all spread out around me.

It was strange to let my fancy wander. Before, I never had time where I wasn't doing anything, where I could just let my mind think what it wanted to without having to rush to get a chore finished before it was time for the next one. I had no idea how long I sat like that.

However long it was, it was still daylight when a thin line of clouds spread out over the sky turning everything above us dark gray and the waves kicked up to where white froth capped their tops. They got bigger and bigger, splashing up almost to the rail, and then the rain and thunder and lightning started. Of course. That's why the sailors were all so uneasy. They knew a storm was blowing up.

"Come below out of the rain, you daft child!" Emma's voice screamed out from the entrance to our cabin, near the top of the stairs—more like a ladder, really—that led down belowdecks to our bunks.

I had been so caught up in watching the men rush about closing hatches and fastening down anything that might move that I didn't really notice until then how bad the storm had got. Now the deck was slippery and wet. I started to shiver, and my hands were numb from cold and wet. Slipping them off the smooth wooden rail, I steadied myself.

I took a deep breath. I tried to judge when the waves would settle a bit so I could dash across the distance to the hatch. Emma's eyes were wide and her face had no color. "Come soon or I'll close the door!" she screamed.

Please, I thought, *I can do it. It's not so far to the hatch. I just have to let go and run.*

A big wave hit the *Vectis* and for an instant I stared down into the black, cold water, so deep and empty. I thought how much easier it would be just to let go. Then my mum and dad would never know about everything that happened at the Abington-Smythes.

The moment passed quickly and we were righted. My heart calmed a bit, as if contemplating death, made everything else seem easy. A lull in the waves came, and I breathed slow and deep, then let go of the rail, and ran.

Emma was still at the hatch, and she reached out her arms for me. I almost made it to her, but a powerful gust of wind and a wave hit at the same time, sending me sliding back across the slick deck. I couldn't get my footing, and something told me to crouch down low and cover my head.

Emma shrieked so loud it pierced right through a thunderclap, and before I knew it a pair of strong hands had me by the arms. Next I was lifted off my feet, scooped up and carried to the hatch.

I thought it must be one of the sailors, but when I looked up and saw the man's smooth, pale face I knew it wasn't. As soon as I was far enough down the steps my rescuer slammed the hatch closed behind me. My legs shook and I slid down the stairs on buckets of water that had washed in already in that short time.

"I thought you was dead for sure!" Emma cried and held me close to her.

71

"I did too. I'm ever so sorry; I didn't notice the storm coming."

Emma's hug was warm—like she had a fever. When she let go of me I felt cold. I wanted to put my hand out and touch her, keep that connection between us that made me feel everything would be all right, but I knew she'd think it strange of me.

"It ain't been so quiet down here, neither," Emma said once she'd calmed a bit, smoothing down her skirt and hair—such a funny thing to do with everything rolling all over the place. "Looks like you an' me an' one or two of the nuns are about the only ones what aren't sick from the storm," she said, sweeping her arm around at the bunks.

I could hardly believe what I saw. Almost every bunk was full with a green-faced, retching nurse or Sister of Mercy. Two of the Sellonites looked well enough, though: their leader, Mrs. Langston, and the one called Sister Sarah Anne who spoke to us on the train.

"Where are Miss Nightingale and the Bracebridges?"

"They took ill too. Miss Nightingale disappeared to her cabin soon as we left port!"

Miss Nightingale was ill like the others? She seemed so strong until now, just like what they said about her in the *Times* and the *Morning Chronicle*. I wished I dared to go to her. But it was clear we'd have our hands full looking after our own.

"I'm not half freezing," I said.

"I think you can wear your other clothes. No one's like

to notice in this blow." We had been told that we were supposed to wear our nurses' uniforms at all times. It wasn't a very nice uniform, and mine didn't fit properly—it was too big and too short. Black serge, a coarse apron, and a sash with SCUTARI HOSPITAL embroidered on it. And a cap hid all our hair, like the nuns'. Though I worried about disobeying, I saw no sense in making myself ill before we even reached Turkey by sitting in my cold, wet clothes. I quickly slipped out of my uniform and into dry togs.

That's when the gale really began, and I was glad I'd got myself belowdecks. The boat started pitching and lurching, the wood creaking like it was about to break apart. The violence of the storm made everyone retch, and there was swill all over the floor, sea water and bits of old meals. The bitter smell nearly made me sick too.

"Oh God, help me!" said one of the older nurses, Mrs. Drake, who'd been a bit frosty with me on the train and in Paris, like she knew my whole story and didn't approve. I rushed over to her. She rolled on her side. I picked up one of the tin basins the crew had left down below for that purpose and held it for her, smoothing her hair out of the way. When she'd finished her eyes were watering, and I could see she felt bad.

"It's all right," I said. "No sense worrying about something you can't do nothing about. I'll get a cloth." Most of the water in the basin they'd put out so we could wash had sloshed away and there was very little left. The drinking water was in corked vessels tied into shelves, but I didn't want to waste that on mopping foreheads. I blotted up what I could and gripped the edges of the bunks so I wouldn't topple over on my way back to Mrs. Drake.

"Oh no, here I go again." Someone else began to be sick just as I passed.

"I'll go," Emma said, and I continued on to Mrs. Drake.

The poor lady's face was a yellowish green. "Thank you," she whispered, once I finished wiping the corners of her mouth. "You're a good girl."

For a moment I got a little knot just above my stomach, not because I felt unwell, but because it was what my mum said to me just before I left on my half days to go back to the Abington-Smythes. At least here I wasn't a disappointment to anyone, not yet anyway.

"Give us a 'and here!" Emma called, breaking into my daydream.

From that moment, Emma and I, and anyone else who wasn't too ill to get up, tended to the others. I watched what the experienced nurses did and copied them.

"Molly's your name, right?" murmured Mrs. Drake after I mopped her face and fanned her a little for a second time. She closed her eyes. Maybe she would sleep.

Emma and I began to empty all of the full basins into the latrine before they tipped over and made even more of a stinking mess of the cabin. Every so often a huge wave would crash and send water pouring in through the hatch. It was covered with canvas, but water seemed to find its way around anyway, and we were up to our ankles in no time.

At some point after we'd been working for hours Emma stretched out on her own bunk. "I'm knackered!" she said to me. "Maybe they'll send some of the hands down to clean after the storm." She yawned.

I turned back to tell Emma that we couldn't wait for that to happen and had much better do it ourselves, but she was already fast asleep.

I was dead tired too, and a little before dawn I let myself lie down. I discovered then that the bunk was alive with lice and other crawling creatures. I crushed them and swatted, wanting to stay awake so I could battle them, but I couldn't keep my eyes open.

Chapter 10

The next morning the storm worsened. Up above on deck we heard awful crashes and thumps, like the whole steamer was breaking apart. The noise woke everyone up, and suddenly there was wailing and praying and crying all around.

"I'll go up and see what's the matter," Mrs. Langston said. She was one of the only ones who stayed calm. Whenever I felt myself getting panicked or feeling tired, I'd just look at her and think, *If she can manage, so can I.*

Emma and I helped her open the hatch. Water gushed down the stairs until we were up to our calves standing there, and it almost reached the bottom of the lower row of bunks. Miss Langston didn't stop, but climbed out before we could say anything to prevent her.

"Better leave the hatch open so she can get back in quick!" I yelled to Emma over the din of the waves and wind.

A huge splash came and drenched us and Sister Sarah Anne.

"Close it 'fore we all drown!" Emma screamed, trying to grab the rope to pull the hatch back into place.

I latched onto one of her arms and Sister Sarah Anne took the other. "No! Wait just a bit longer!" My heart raced too, though, and I wanted to close us up tight again, but the thought of Mrs. Langston out there stopped me.

A moment later, a soaking wet foot stepped on the top rung of the ladder. We reached up and helped Mrs. Langston back in. She tugged the rope and closed the hatch almost on her own head.

She heaved and shivered with cold. All around us the nurses and nuns were crying. Mrs. Langston held up one hand and put the other to her ribs. "Shh!" I said to everyone. I wanted to hear what she had to say.

"It's all right," she gasped. "Nothing to worry about. It sounds much worse than it is. There's some damage, but it's a good boat and we're fine, so the captain says."

I didn't know if she was telling the truth, but it was enough to quiet everyone down.

———∞———

The constant vomiting stopped by the third day, partly because although the storm continued it wasn't quite so fierce, but mainly because no one had any food left in their stomachs. I was afraid some of the worse ones might die. One or two looked so pale and thin I couldn't see how they would live. There wasn't as much for us to do with everyone mostly sleeping quietly, so Emma and I sat on our bunks and talked some.

"You weren't writing to your mum, were you?" Emma asked me later that night after we'd eaten a little supper of cold salt cod and stale bread. If I'd ever written more than one letter in my life, I might not have known what she was talking about. I wasn't sure what to say. The last thing I wanted was to tell Emma my story—even though she had already told me about her father who beat her and her mother who was always drunk, and that she'd run away when she was my age and the only job she could get that wasn't on the streets was nursing in a hospital. Something about how she told it all made it sound like a story, like even that wasn't the truth. It was the way she looked sideways during the most dramatic parts. But if she had secrets to keep, who was I to stop her?

"I was writing to a friend," I said at last. Since the envelope was directed to Lucy, I hoped she wouldn't suspect anything more.

"A man friend, I'd guess."

I tried hard not to, but the way she said it made me blush. "It's not what you think at all. Will's just a friend who helped me get to Folkestone," I said in a way that I was sure would end her line of questioning.

"Oh, don't be shy with me! I won't tell anyone."

I wasn't so sure about that. After what Mavis did to me at the Abington-Smythes, I didn't think I'd ever trust a girl again. And Miss Nightingale had made it very clear that she wouldn't tolerate any nonsense of that kind. That philandering, as she called it, would be cause for immediate dismissal. Emma could get me fired just like Mavis did. "There's nothing to tell. I just wanted to thank him and let him know I was on my way to Turkey."

We sat quiet for a minute or two, me listening to the creak of the wooden walls around us, wondering just how long they might hold up if the storm kept on, Emma picking at the damp blanket on my bunk.

She leaned in a little closer to me. "Can you keep a secret?"

I shrugged. "I expect so." No one ever asked me that, but there was plenty I knew that didn't tell anyone.

"I weren't really no nurse before I came."

That surprised me so much I almost fell off the bunk. How many of the other stories she had told were lies? "What were you then?"

She screwed her mouth up, like it had something bad tasting in it. "Nothing good. But it weren't my fault."

"Were you in service?"

She laughed silently, her shoulders shaking. "I s'pose you could call it service."

"Did you work in a great house then?"

"A house. Not so great. And they beat me if I didn't do as they said. Serious, Moll, don't you know what I'm sayin'?"

She worked in a house. A— "Oh my God!" I almost shrieked out the words. One or two of the others shifted, but no one woke.

"Shh! You're the only one what knows. I ran away. Got one of the gents to write me a reference, saying I was a nurse."

This was ten times worse than what happened to me. "How did you manage it? I've heard tales that girls who ended up in those houses were kept like slaves and never got out till they died."

"Like I said. One of the gents, he was a doctor. I just told him I'd rat on him at the hospital, and he was willing enough to write me a letter. Then we pretended like we was going out on the town for a lark, only I skipped and got myself signed up for this."

So Emma was running away too, and from something much worse than what I was running away from. "What about your mum and dad?"

"Never knew 'em. I was brought up in a orphanage, turned out to make my own way when I was thirteen. Now, I've been straight with you. What about this young man of yours?"

I sensed this time she had told me the truth. Who would make up such a thing? Nonetheless, I still wasn't ready to tell her my story. "Like I said, he's just a friend." No matter how she questioned me after that I wouldn't say more. I wouldn't tell her that every time I saw something new, or learned something by listening to Mrs. Langston or Sister Sarah Anne, who'd been trained proper as nurses, not just done it—every time something important happened, the only person I wanted to share it with was Will. I wouldn't tell her that each morning on that pitching and rolling boat I woke up feeling as though Will had just kissed me on the forehead again, and brushed my lips with his. And that sometimes, in my restless dreams, I imagined what it would feel like for Will to put his arm around my waist, or hold me close to him, or even kiss me long and hard on the lips. Then I'd wake up so suddenly with an ache right in my middle, longing to be back in London.

I imagined all that before I remembered where I was, and that I was going off on an incredible adventure with Miss Nightingale. Then the excitement of what was ahead would overcome my feelings, and I'd fall asleep again.

The storm stopped on the fourth day, and several of the others began to feel well enough to get out of bed and come up on deck with Emma and me. The sea was calm and the sky bluer than anything I'd ever seen, like it was trying to make up for treating us so badly before.

The other nurses were all a little nicer to us than they'd been at first, calling us by name, saying, "Molly, dear, could you fetch us a cup of tea?" or "Emma, give us a hand with this, will you?" I hadn't done much more than just be there— like the lowest housemaid. But I began to see that it somehow made a difference.

Mr. and Mrs. Bracebridge were up on deck too, looking not too poorly, though I guessed they'd had their bit of sickness. Mrs. Bracebridge shared a private cabin with Miss

Nightingale. I overheard Sister Sarah Anne say Miss Nightingale was violently sick. I imagined Mrs. Bracebridge had spent all her time looking after her.

"Molly, I hear you got some practice nursing in the past few days," the lady said to me after our salt cod and biscuit breakfast.

"Don't know as I'd call it that, exactly," I said. "I was just helping out."

She looked over at Mrs. Drake, who smiled at her. "That's not what I heard."

The praise made me feel strange. If being able to stand people around me who were sick and trying my best to ease them a little was nursing, then it was a powerful lot easier than being a parlormaid and I hardly deserved to be thanked for it. In any case, I was glad the storm was over, and when the sailors told us we'd be coming into the Dardanelles the next day, with port just a day or two after that, I found I was relieved. Caring for the others had distracted me. Although the storm hadn't made me ill, it did frighten me. Doing something, working, was what made the fear bearable.

Chapter 11

A very pale, rather wobbly Miss Nightingale came up on deck as we passed through a narrow channel into a wider stretch of water that was smaller than the Mediterranean. She stood a little away from us. No one dared go near her. Something in her face told us she was thinking private thoughts or maybe of someone far away. Perhaps she'd been at that place before, perhaps not alone. Mrs. Bracebridge told us that despite her seasickness, Miss Nightingale traveled a lot, even to Egypt, and that her Christian name was Florence after the city in Italy where she was born. And there were whispers among the nurses that she turned down a marriage proposal from Mr. Monckton Milnes, a very good catch.

"This passage is called the Dardanelles," Mr. Bracebridge called out to the lot of us who had come on deck to see the land so close again. "It's very famous. It was called the Hellespont by the ancients. This is where the Trojan War took place. Many ships have been wrecked here. Easy to understand, with the weather we've had!" It was still blowing hard, and some of his words were torn away by the wind. I moved a little closer so I could hear all he had to say. "It leads us to the Sea of Marmara. Our destination is to the east, at the mouth of the Bosporus, which leads to the Black Sea." Mostly everyone just nodded and leaned on the rail, maybe glad to be near shore but not so interested in the particulars of what was there. I wanted him to tell me more, not just about the water, but about the strange buildings that crowded the shore, with their odd shapes and fancy decorations like a lady's lace collar. I didn't dare ask, though, afraid the others would think I was trying to make myself special, be a pet of some sort. Emma was the one who gave me that fear, dropping hints the night before when I'd got that praise from Mrs. Bracebridge about nursing.

I couldn't help wondering what Will would make of this. I wished I could paint a picture to send to him. With my bad spelling and handwriting a letter wouldn't really say it all. Words are so different when you speak them than when you write them. What's easy and natural when you say it comes out all lumpy and awkward when you try to think it onto paper. Still, I'd have to try if I didn't want to wait until I saw Will again—if I ever did see him again. Perhaps they'd hire a new maid, and she'd be pretty and young, and Will would like her and forget all about me . . .

No use thinking about that. Here I was, so far away. Did my mum even imagine I could be where I was right then? She'd never been outside London her whole life. I hoped

Will told her what I did, where I'd gone. The next letter I wrote would be to her. The man across the street could read it for her. *She'll hardly believe it*, I thought.

And at that moment, even without seeing a penny of my wages or setting foot near the wounded British soldiers, I was glad I came, alone as I was. I would never, ever have been able to see anything like this if I'd gone to work in a dark factory. My eight shillings a week was near double what I earned as a parlormaid, and I'd be able to pay Will back and bring home money to my mum.

"I wonder what the food'll be like. My stomach won't take to strange things. Just give me plain mutton and spuds." Emma leaned next to me. It felt good to have her warmth. It was almost as cold as London there, with the stiff breeze over the water.

"We'll be in Scutari by morning," I said.

As if that amazing fact—that we would finally set foot in a place so talked about in the newspapers, a place that seemed unreal only two weeks before—was the most ordinary thing in the world, Emma ignored me and changed the subject. "I heard Mrs. Bracebridge talking to the old man. He said the captain got news by telegraph of a terrible battle, but that our boys—the cavalry, he said—was very brave. Thousands killed and wounded."

Emma's words jolted me back to thinking about the job ahead. *Thousands.* I couldn't get my mind around it. I thought of how I'd rushed about tending to twenty or so poorly women, and they were just sick in the stomach. What if there were thousands, and with mortal wounds and blood, and limbs having to be amputated like at the Hôtel Dieu in Paris? I imagined myself among them all, groans and screams coming from every direction, and me not knowing what to do or where to go first.

"What ho, Moll! You're looking a little pale. You going to go get seasick now the boat's not tossing us all over?"

"No, I'm fine," I said. No sense getting worked up. What would be, would be.

"Look at that!" Emma exclaimed.

I thought she was talking about the small sailboat off to our port side that skimmed the water, a single sailor in a cap like an upside-down red bucket flinging a net out like he was shaking a silk sheet over a bed. "Beautiful," I said.

"No, not the fisherman, silly! Look." She pointed up ahead to a fleet of British warships in the distance. "Do you s'pose they're bringing troops?"

"Dunno," I answered.

Now, seeing how far away we were from England, I had to wonder what it was that made us fight here, for land that wasn't even ours, alongside the French, no less, who used to be our sworn enemies. My dad still had nothing nice to say about the French, sometimes cursing them up and down when he'd had a skinful. I decided I'd have to ask Mrs. Bracebridge about it sometime, and kept on watching the fisherman, peaceful and calm and miles away from a war.

But I wasn't the only one watching the fisherman. The other passengers traveling on the *Vectis* had come up on deck too, and though most of them also stared and pointed at the warships, one man kept his eyes where I did. I'd not had much time to notice the other people on board with everyone being so sick, but this man was young, I might say even handsome, and his face looked kind. In fact, I could've sworn I'd seen it before. He must've felt me staring at him, because he turned and nodded to me. It only took that moment for me to recognize him. He was the one who picked me up and thrust me below out of the storm when we first set out from Marseille. I felt something hot in the middle of me, just above my stomach. Not a pain, but a warning. I feared I'd see that man again. He could be one of the doctors Emma told me about. *Why feared?* I thought. It would give me a chance to thank him for helping me.

<hr>

I could hardly sleep that last night on the boat, wondering, worrying about what was to come. I was one of the first ones ready as we arrived, on the side of the Bosporus where Istanbul sat, the west side. It was raining, hard. Not storming, the way it did when we left Marseille, but so gray everything looked hidden behind a curtain. The strange buildings that made the outline of the city so different from London were mosques, with towers called minarets. There was a huge mosque that Mrs. Bracebridge said was called the Blue Mosque. And another, called Saint Sophia, with its onion-shaped domes. It had once been a church, but long ago was turned into a mosque so the Muslims could worship there.

The buildings in Istanbul didn't look like anything I'd seen in London or even Paris.

We rocked at anchor out of the wind for some hours yet, not getting off the *Vectis* until late in the afternoon. By then the sky had cleared and the sun started to dry off the buildings, which now looked washed with gold. As soon as we got to the dock we climbed into smaller boats called caiques to cross over to Scutari, where our army was based, with its barracks and a hospital and all. The caiques were very fancy, with ends that curled up like the shoes the Turks on the piers wore, and cushions in the bottom to lie on instead of sit down. "I feel like I'm in a pasha's harem!" Emma said, flinging her arms out wide. Two other nurses, one of them Mrs. Drake, shared our boat with us. They smiled at Emma. I think everyone was happy to be off that steamer at last.

Mrs. Drake and I were almost friends toward the end of our journey. She'd taken to telling me I reminded her of a niece she had who lived in Wiltshire. "Mind you don't catch cold dipping your hands in the water like that," she said to me, almost as if she cared if I did or not. The water was cool and soft, though, so I just smiled.

At last we climbed out of the caiques onto a dock that bustled with people shouting in a language that sounded like gibberish. That struck me as terribly funny, so I was already disposed to laugh when I started trying to walk on dry land. With every step I took, it felt like the ground was in the wrong place and I couldn't judge the distance. I looked round to see if it was just me and beheld one of the funniest sights

I ever set eyes upon. All thirty-eight nurses and sisters were staggering like drunks, trying to look important and serious as we trudged up the hill to the town. I started laughing in earnest. Soon I was doubled up and laughing so hard the tears just streamed down my cheeks.

Emma was almost as bad as I was. Neither of us could stand up straight nor catch our breath from laughing. I had my arms across my middle trying to hold in my gasps. The other nurses didn't laugh, though, and despite their awkward steps, managed to get ahead of us. Mrs. Bracebridge led them toward a huge square building with rows and rows of windows. "W-wait!" I called. But the hopelessness of them hearing me only made me laugh harder.

The people around us, the locals, were got up in such strange costumes, and that struck us as funny too. The women had on full trousers with sashes and silk wrapped round their heads. They looked a little like the Morris dancers that came at Christmas, only with dark, exotic faces and mostly green or golden eyes. A few men in uniform swaggered toward us, smiles twitching at their mouths.

"Oh, look at those handsome soldiers!" Emma whispered, which struck me as even funnier than the women in trousers. "They must be French, with those blue coats," she said.

"*Quelque-chose vous amuse?*" said one of the men. I didn't understand him.

"*Nous nous excusons,*" said a woman's voice, commanding, right behind me.

I turned. It was Miss Nightingale, leaning on Mr. Brace-bridge's arm. The sight of her stern face pulled me up quick as anything. "I . . . I'm sorry, Miss Nightingale." I wiped the tears off my face.

The French soldiers turned and wandered off, but not before I saw one of them cast his eyes over Emma in an all too familiar way.

"I trust this was a momentary lapse in judgment." Miss Nightingale did not change her expression.

"It was only . . . ," Emma began but didn't finish the thought.

"We looked so funny, all wobbly on shore after the boat," I said, hoping maybe to get her to smile. I was amazed to see that Miss Nightingale looked quite clear-eyed and fresh, with roses in her cheeks, as if some magic made her well as soon as she set foot on dry land. She didn't stagger like the rest of us, either.

"Hardly a good impression to make in a strange place where we will all have to earn the respect of the men. And I mean respect, not admiration." This she said looking straight at Emma, who hardened her face. I didn't know how she dared. "You have lost the others." She turned to Mr. Brace-bridge. "I would rather have remained on board another day so they could take us around directly to the hospital. This is not seemly, walking through the town like this."

"You are still too unwell for such a walk, and all uphill." He waved a passing cart to a stop and helped Miss Nighting-gale in.

This wasn't a good start. "Come along, Emma, we'd best catch up."

"She'll get over it. We was only laughing," Emma said.

When I looked back, Miss Nightingale was settled in the cart with a blanket over her knees. "Mind you both hurry," she said as the donkey pulled the cart away.

We walked faster, now more used to the solid ground. I felt like a naughty child, but Emma kept a little swing in her walk, and I thought I saw her glancing now and then at the men standing around in their uniforms. She might not have had schooling in that "house" where she lived, but she'd learned a few things.

It didn't take us long to get to the big building, the Barrack Hospital, where everyone else stood outside a door that led into the middle of one of its longer sides.

"Someone should be here to meet us. I don't know where we're to go." Mrs. Bracebridge said.

A moment later, a man came out of the main door and walked toward us. "I'm so sorry I wasn't here the moment you arrived. Miss Nightingale has been settled in her quarters and is conferring with Dr. Menzies, the hospital superintendent. I'm to show you in. I'm Dr. Wilkinson."

Dr. Wilkinson had a lined face and a drooping mustache. His skin was yellowish and he had circles under his eyes. "Won't be much fun if they're all like that," Emma said, nudging me. I could feel the disapproving looks of the others and stayed silent.

Dr. Wilkinson led us through the door into a huge

courtyard, big enough for a whole other building to sit inside it, and then along to the left to a corner of the yard where there was a small door. He held it open for us as we entered a dark corridor. We could hear but not see men lying there. Dr. Wilkinson passed us at a smart clip and didn't wait for us to follow, but continued up two flights of stairs.

"Miss Nightingale will tell you how you're to be disposed in your quarters. I'm sorry they're not more spacious, but we're a little short of that commodity here," he said over his shoulder to us. I didn't understand that. Such an enormous building! I didn't know then that more than half of it was in desperate need of repair.

Dr. Wilkinson motioned us through a passage and into a small room that I later figured out was in one of the square towers at the corner of the building. Lying on a bed in the middle, propped up on pillows with Mrs. Bracebridge and a much older doctor next to her, was Miss Nightingale. Already she looked even better than she did when we saw her as Mr. Bracebridge helped her into the cart.

"Nurses, Sisters of Mercy, this is Dr. Menzies, whom we are bound to follow in all his instructions as this is his hospital."

The doctor bowed to us. "Welcome. I wish I could promise you an easy time here, but we are much beset by disease as well as injuries, and have all we can do to treat those we have a hope of being able to help."

"I have told Dr. Menzies that I am pleasantly surprised

at how well regulated his hospital is, having expected the worst from the reports we had."

I wondered how she had had time to come to any opinion, since she was obviously carried in from the street. But Dr. Menzies beamed. I supposed we'd find out soon enough for ourselves what the hospital was really like.

Dr. Menzies didn't stay long, and directly he'd gone, Miss Nightingale swung her feet out of bed. "I've assessed our quarters and decided where everyone is to stay," she said, looking surprisingly healthy and strong.

Strong or not, Mrs. Bracebridge took her arm to steady her, and together they showed us our rooms. The biggest one was to be a common room, where we'd have a table for meetings. The next biggest was for fourteen of us nurses. Then came the ten nuns, who would occupy the next. The eight Sellonites had the room directly above Miss Nightingale's. Six more nurses, the ones from St. John's House who were specially trained, occupied another small room.

"Beds will be brought in this evening, I have been assured," Miss Nightingale said. "Until then, there is a great deal of cleaning to do. Fraser, since you have experience in this regard, you will help me with the cleaning of our rooms. Any others who are willing can join in. We are to be furnished with mops, brushes, and soap."

Miss Nightingale took charge of everything so quickly everyone just did as she said, Bob's your uncle. Within a few minutes several ragged-looking men carrying mops, pails of soapy water, and brushes clattered into our common room.

We took off our cloaks and laid them on the low divans that were built next to the wall, but soon found out what a mistake that was.

"Aieee!" screamed one of the nurses.

A huge rat squeezed out of a hole in the wood of the divan and went running around the room. We chased it out the door but didn't know how to kill it, with no poison or traps around.

"These Turkish pallets are crawling!" said Sister Sarah Anne looking closely at the divans. Before you could say spit we grabbed our cloaks and piled them in the middle of the floor.

A few orderlies came back to help us, saying they were sent by Dr. Menzies. I'd never cleaned alongside men before. They swished the mops in the water and just sloshed it around the floor, without even getting down on their knees with the brushes. I looked at Miss Nightingale. She didn't seem too pleased either.

"Thank you, I believe we can manage," she said to the orderlies. "You undoubtedly have more important work to do." Miss Nightingale as much as pushed the men out into the corridor.

I put my back into that scrubbing. I didn't want to have lice all over me, and I sure as anything wanted to make certain Miss Nightingale saw that I could be useful. Cleaning was something I knew how to do. Mrs. Drake and Emma got right into it with me, and soon everyone else followed along with us.

With so many hands it didn't take much time till the place looked a sight better. Then the beds and linens arrived, and we each went to our assigned rooms and did our best to settle in. After that it was time to eat. The orderlies brought up some kind of stew in a huge pail and cups to slop it into. The bread they gave us was stale, but I was so hungry I didn't mind. While we ate in the common room, Miss Nightingale spoke to us.

"By now many of you may have heard of the charge at Balaclava, where our brave Light Brigade rode forth against the Russian heavy guns. These men were fearless, charging into a battle they had no hope of winning. When it was over, more than three-quarters of the brigade were killed or wounded. Dr. Menzies has had word by telegraph that ships will be arriving in the next few days bearing hundreds of casualties. We have landed just in time, it seems."

My head was filled with a vision of hundreds of handsome cavalry officers in their dashing uniforms, sabers raised, horses snorting and pounding across the barren countryside. I somehow couldn't make myself see them cut down and wounded.

Miss Nightingale left us so she could go and talk to the Sellonite sisters, who I saw clear enough were her favorites— them and the St. John's nurses. I didn't really understand why, but after a few weeks of working alongside them we all recognized they were the best, most experienced nurses. As for me—I had no notion of what was to come. I only thanked the stars that I was there and not sent home in disgrace. I would have a chance to make something of myself. The rest was in my hands.

Chapter 12

We all expected to start in on our nursing the very next day. But instead we sat in our quarters, idle.

Around noon, Mrs. Bracebridge came in. "Miss Nightingale and Dr. Menzies have to decide how to apportion the nurses to different wards. Until that time, you can all get to work sewing stump pillows for the amputees and mending clothes and uniforms for the men," she said.

"Humph!" It was Mrs. Drake. "I came out to nurse, not to be a domestic."

"And I'll tell you, this cap is nothing I ever would put on my head at home. It's a disgrace." The colorful Mrs. Wilson spoke up for the first time since we arrived—she'd been so sick on the *Vectis* that she hadn't been able to talk at all and only now looked like herself again.

Once she started, complaints from everyone rained down on poor Mrs. Bracebridge's head. She looked from one woman to another, opening her mouth to speak and shutting it again when the next one complained, until a din from the door that led to the kitchen put a stop to all the talking. A large woman, clearly English, stood there with a pot lid in one hand and a wooden spoon in the other, banging them together with all her might. When she stopped, my ears rang.

"Allow me to introduce Mrs. Clarke, Miss Nightingale's housekeeper, who came to Scutari separately with a load of supplies from England," said Mrs. Bracebridge.

"You all sound like cacklin' geese! If you think you got trouble, you should see the god-awful mess I have to deal with—meat as is so full of maggots it wants to crawl off the block. Now get to yer work and be quiet." With no more ceremony, she stomped away as suddenly as she had come, leaving silence in her wake.

Mrs. Bracebridge cleared her throat. "I'm terribly sorry. Mrs. Clarke is in charge of our household arrangements here. She's efficient, if somewhat coarse."

After that everyone took up needles and thread and did their sewing, quiet as mice.

"I sure didn't bargain on this kind of work," Emma whispered to me as she made stitches too big to keep the stuffing inside the stump pillow she was sewing. "Ruin my hands, I will."

"And nursing won't? What about all those bandages, and the laundry and such?"

"Laundry? Will we be doing laundry?"

I shrugged. I decided it would do no good to tell Emma

I'd overheard Mrs. Bracebridge talking earlier with some of the sisters about getting a building for a laundry, if it was needed.

That's all we did for near a week. We sewed and fought battles with the returning lice and rats. None of us set foot in the wards—except Miss Nightingale. Yet the wounded were so near, it was a pity. Right on the other side of the wall from us we could hear men groaning of a night. It was like no sound I'd ever heard before. Soft and pitiful, like a wind blowing from the grave. I wished we could just look in on them, maybe mop their faces or fix their pillows. But we'd been told we weren't to leave our quarters without permission.

Emma put her sewing down, stood, and stretched. "I can't stand it in here. Can't we go outside, walk in the courtyard or something?"

"Miss Nightingale told us not to," I said.

"And if she told you to climb on the sill and jump out the window would you do it?" Emma said. A few of the others chuckled. Emma went to the window and stared out for a bit but soon came back to her halfhearted needlework.

That evening Miss Nightingale called us all together, partly to let us know why we were still kept from the wards, but also I think because she wanted to tell us some things about nursing—nursing the way she thought it ought to be done. She said things at the start that got some of the older nurses' backs up, about nursing not having to do with giving medicines or bandaging wounds.

"First, and most importantly, it is essential for us to let the bodies of the sick and wounded heal themselves. And to do this they must have fresh air, warmth, and food."

"Fresh air and warmth! In this climate it's not possible. Would you have us go opening windows everywhere?" It was one of the nuns.

"Would you have the sick and wounded breathe only the air in a ward full of other sick and wounded men? It is possible to let in fresh air without giving patients a chill. Warming bottles, blankets—do we not have these tools at our disposal?"

What she said made sense to me, who didn't know any-thing about proper nursing, but I could see the looks some of the others gave her. They weren't likely to take what she said without a grain of salt.

"And food—what of food for them that can't stomach it?" Mrs. Drake asked.

"Of course they would not eat what a healthy man eats," said Miss Nightingale, "but without nourishment how can a body have the strength to heal itself? Light beef broths, softened bread—these must be fed to those not capable of a proper meal."

The more she spoke, the more unbelieving the nurses looked, as if she were speaking blasphemy against the gospel truth. Only the Sellonites and the St. John's nurses took it all in without doubting.

For me, I knew I'd rather be warm, fed, and breathing fresh air if I were sick. But so far we hadn't any chance to put Miss Nightingale's methods to the test, and there was little sign we would very soon, so what was the point?

For three more days our lives were the same. Everyone got cross. I began two more letters to Will but couldn't make out what to say. I wrote one letter to my mum, short and easy, so she wouldn't have to pay to get it read. Not that I could've made it very long anyway.

On the fourth day Miss Nightingale let us walk into town for exercise.

"Let's go together to the market!" Emma was like a bird let out of a cage, she flapped about so.

I didn't much care where we went, so long as it was out. Even the cold didn't bother me. Scutari was so different from London. There were people everywhere in colorful striped costumes. Every so often, chanting rang out through the air, and all around us people put down little rugs and bowed toward the east.

We wandered through the market, looking at the fruits and sundries. Sellers thrust their wares at us and followed us when we didn't buy them. I spent no money, in spite of the fact I could have spared a penny or two. I was saving my first week's wages to pay Will back.

When time came to return to the barracks, I was a little sorry. Emma was so disappointed she looked like she'd burst out crying any minute and went straight to her bunk without a word to anyone.

⬤⬤⬤

The next day an awful smell came in through the gaps in the windows.

"Ugh! What is that?" Emma said, pinching her nose.

The smell was so bad it made me retch. One nurse started sprinkling eau de cologne everywhere, but all it did was add a sweetness to the bad smell. We couldn't go out, and we were trapped inside with the odor. Mr. Bracebridge went off to find out the cause.

"It's the sewers," he said when he came back. "The latrines aren't deep enough, and they drain directly into the Bosporus."

"Why didn't we smell it before?" Mrs. Drake asked.

"That's because of the wind. The direction shifted and now carries the smell back inside."

"Even Miss Nightingale wouldn't want the windows open to this stink!" Mrs. Drake said, and everyone laughed.

I went over to close the one window we'd opened, hoping it would make the awful smell go away. As I fastened the latch, I stopped and stared. Our windows looked out over the Bosporus, and when it was clear we could see all the way over to Istanbul. It wasn't clear that day, but in the distance I could just make out two ships coming into port, not from the direction of the Sea of Marmara, but from the Black Sea. "Look!" I said. The others all crowded round.

"They're the ships carrying wounded from Balaclava," Mr. Bracebridge said.

We didn't move, but watched the slow dance of docking and then the horrible parade of men, some walking but wrapped in dirty, bloodied bandages, most being carried out by Turkish workers who hoisted them like meat carcasses and dropped them on the ground near the hospital. I wanted so to go out and do something, but we were caged up like a flock of black rooks, only able to squabble amongst ourselves.

The rest of the afternoon and evening we sat silently at our sewing, listening to the shouting and running about outside. When Mrs. Clarke came in with our dinner I couldn't eat a bite. But it wasn't the smell this time. It was wanting to help and feeling completely useless.

Just as we were about to get ready for bed, Miss Nightingale walked in, looking smart and purposeful. Her eyes were bright. I'd never seen her so well.

"I have good news in all this tragedy," she said. "Dr. Menzies and I have agreed on the disposition of nurses, and we are to commence our duties at dawn."

I could've whooped aloud, although why the beginning of hard, sad work should seem so exciting I didn't know. At least we'd be doing something. And getting out of those rooms that had begun to feel more like a prison than a hospital.

That night I could hardly sleep. I tossed and turned more even than when I was hiding on the docks in Folkestone. We were going to do what we'd come here for at last. Would I be able to manage? I didn't know much. *Just follow directions,* Emma said once when we were talking. I had watched a man get his leg cut off in Paris. Would this be worse? I couldn't imagine. *Give them air, keep them warm, give them nourishment.* Surely that wouldn't be too difficult?

I must have fallen asleep at some point but I felt as though I'd hardly closed my eyes when a bell woke me up. Miss Nightingale stood in the common room, dressed in a uniform just like ours—only hers was made of silk and fit her proper and without the sash—banging on a bell with a wooden spoon. I think everyone was so dazed that no one complained about the early hour.

"Sisters Sarah Anne and Elizabeth, you're to go to the sick wards and help the doctors there since you are the most experienced nurses. As to the other wards, we shall have a rotation, which I have planned. Fraser, Bigelow, Erskine, Kelly, Sharpe—come with me. Sisters Margaret, Ethelreda, and de Chantal and Mrs. Drake, Mrs. Lundy, and Mrs. Hawkins, I'll show you to the ward you will work in today as well. The rotation will be posted this evening."

It felt like freedom to walk out into the corridor that went all the way around the building, sun slanting in through windows that faced the parade ground in the middle. We didn't go into the ward right next to our room, though. Instead we went down the stairs to the ground floor where Dr. Menzies waited for us.

At first when we entered that dark, lowest floor of the hospital it was hard to make out what was there. The smell was so bad that we all covered our mouths at the same time and more than a few of us stifled retches. The stink was ten times worse than what came into our rooms up above. I didn't know it right then, but it turned out that we were very close to where the latrines emptied, right underneath the floorboards. And here that awful smell blended with other odors. Blood. Rotting flesh. Sweat. A trace of gunpowder.

"These are the men who were just admitted last night," Dr. Menzies said.

As my eyes become accustomed to the half light, I could make out shapes writhing on the floor. "Shapes" was all I could think to call them. Human bodies so mixed together and covered with blood and gore it seemed I was looking at a single creature.

"The wards are above. If you'll follow me."

We picked our way gingerly through the men on the floor to a staircase. Maybe upstairs in a proper ward there would be more order. My hopes didn't last long. I heard Miss Nightingale exclaim before I reached the top of the staircase, "But there are no beds! And the linens are filthy. The stink is abominable. What is that surgeon over there doing?"

I hardly noticed that Emma had put her arm through mine and was clinging tightly to me as we entered the ward.

It wasn't much better than the scene below, except that more of the men had bandages wrapped around them. Otherwise, their faces were just as covered in battlefield filth and they still lay on the floor or on the infested divans that lined the walls—the floor was at least cushioned with straw. We were all too horrified to move. I looked toward where Miss Nightingale pointed and saw that a surgeon and three orderlies had a man pinned down and were setting up to amputate his arm.

"Have you no operating table? No chloroform? Not even a curtain to shield the other patients from the sight?" Miss Nightingale's voice rose.

Dr. Menzies planted himself in front of her so she couldn't see the surgeon. "This is a hospital in a time of war. We do our best with what we have. We have difficulty getting our supplies. We have asked repeatedly for beds and more linens, yet they do not come." Dr. Menzies sounded angry.

"There'll be a fight for sure," Emma whispered to me.

"Might I have a word with you in your office, Dr. Menzies?" Miss Nightingale said.

The two of them went off, leaving the rest of us in the ward. A sigh went out all of a piece from us. I guess we had been holding our breath.

One or two of the men who were not unconscious or in so much pain they couldn't speak raised their heads. "I'm from Wiltshire," said one. "Any news of Wiltshire?"

Mrs. Drake went to him and knelt down beside him. "I was just in Wiltshire at the beginning of the month. The weather's already bitter." She chatted on to him about home, bits of nonsense and recollecting places they both knew.

Once that fellow spoke up, more and more of the men began to ask questions. "What's happening in London? Do you know a Mrs. Holbrook? Will you fetch me a drink of water? I'm ever so thirsty."

We soon spread out amongst the men, doling out what comfort we could. I crouched down close to one fellow who was trying to say something but could only whisper. "Can I help you?" I asked.

"You're pretty," he whispered, and tried to smile but the effort caused him pain and he closed his eyes. He was all twisted up in a dirty sheet. I tried to ease it out and straighten it. I didn't notice until then that the straw beneath him was crawling with vermin. I pulled my hands away quick. He opened his eyes. "I know I don't look so handsome right now," he managed to squeeze out. I couldn't bear to let him think it was him that made me shrink away so I stiffened my back and got on with what I was doing.

Emma was tending to the soldier next to me. She tipped up a cup of water carefully into his mouth. Most of it dribbled out the sides. He looked as though he might die at any second, he was so pale and still. "Eek!" she screamed, ripping the silence open, and dropped the cup.

"What is it?" I asked. She pointed to a large rat that ran up and down and over the men until it disappeared into a hole at the base of the wall. I looked down the long ward.

Every now and then another rat would poke its head out and run. "Blimey!" I said. "There's rats everywhere." Some of the heaving shapes I thought were men were actually rats scurrying over bodies too wounded or sick to scare them off.

Emma dug her fingers into my arm. "If this is what we're in for, I'm going home!"

"If you ain't seen rats in a hospital before, get used to it." It was Nurse Grundy. She was always pretty nice to me, but her face had gone hard and set, like there was another person she kept inside until she needed to put her on. None of the other experienced nurses had batted so much as an eyelid at the rats here, although they were afraid enough of them in our quarters.

The Sisters of Mercy spread out across the ward and went from pallet to pallet speaking to the men, touching them lightly, straightening linens. Right then I wondered if I had the courage to be like them. It didn't matter how bloody, how filthy a soldier was, they did what they could for him. It was all too much to get into my head. And these men had mostly already been operated on and were patched up and healing—or perhaps on their way to dying—so not even fresh from the battlefield.

Before I had any more time to think, Miss Nightingale came back without Dr. Menzies. "Nurses," she said, "we have work to do."

Everyone gathered again and followed Miss Nightingale. We headed to another of the corner towers. Once we got there she divided us into groups: those who would clean, those who would sew, and those who were strong enough to lift the men. Emma and I went with the cleaners, of course.

I don't know how Miss Nightingale did it, but soon we had mattress ticking and bales of straw being dumped in the empty corridors by Turkish merchants. First off after we swept the floors we had to stuff the empty mattresses that had mostly been sewn up somewhere else—did she know ahead of time about this too? Could Miss Nightingale see into the future like a gypsy? Did she buy empty mattresses and ship them over with us from France? I was too busy to do anything but wonder. Too busy to talk. My hands were quickly scraped raw by the straw, but the women who were sewing up the mattresses had it harder, their fingers pricked and bleeding trying to get the needles through the tough ticking.

"Soon enough be so much blood on these no one'll notice a drop or two of mine," said Mrs. Drake, making everyone laugh, as was her way.

As soon as we stuffed the mattresses, orderlies took them and piled them up on the floor below.

"Fraser, Bigelow, Hawkins, and Drake, come with me." I had got quite used to Miss Nightingale's commands. They didn't seem so harsh now that I saw what we were faced with. She led us down to the ward. One end of it was not yet filled with men. "You'll start cleaning here. As soon as you're done, we'll spread fresh straw and mattresses, then move the first of that lot over, working our way down as we go."

I was already shaking from the hard work. Even my first day as a parlormaid was nothing compared to this. At times

I thought I wouldn't be able to continue, and felt a lump rise up in my chest, squeezing my breath out, making me feel as though I would cry. *Don't, don't,* I told myself. I just thought about the horrible condition of the men and realized how lucky I was to be just tired, not waiting for a limb to be cut off or for my life to float away.

That first day all we did was put two hundred men on clean mattresses. I felt as if I'd climbed a mountain and hauled a ton of coal. I was almost in too much of a daze to hear my name called out as we ate our dinner in the common room.

"'Ere, Moll, you got a letter," Emma said, jolting me out of my thoughts.

"A letter?" I couldn't imagine how. I'd never had a letter before. I hoped I'd be able to read it. I stood—it took so much effort to do just that—and got my letter from Mrs. Bracebridge.

It came from England, of course. And it said my name plain as day on the envelope. Miss Molly Fraser. I put it aside and finished my dinner, right then more hungry than curious.

"Well come on," Emma said, plopping herself down next to me. "Open it!"

Having become used to doing exactly what I was told to all day long, I put my fork down and picked up the letter, sliding my finger under the seal to pop it open. The paper still felt crisp though it was dirty from its long trip from England in the hold of a packet boat.

The letter wasn't long. But I'll never forget a single word of it.

Dear Molly,

Things got bad at the Abington-Smythes after you left. I decided service wasn't for me after all. It seems they need good men to fight the Russians, and so I joined up with a regiment of foot.

That's not the only reason I did it, though. I can't stop thinking about you, wondering if you got there and are all right. If I see you again, I was wondering if you'd walk out with me, so we could talk like we used to.

I expect you've met people more interesting than me probably. But I wanted you to know. Take care of yourself.

Your friend,
Will Parker

Will was coming to the Crimea. I might see him! A familiar face. A familiar face that was very dear to me. I thought suddenly of that kiss, the one on the lips when I last saw him, at Lucy's. Would he kiss me again? I didn't know, couldn't guess, but it was enough just to imagine it. I read the letter again, this time faster since I'd already made out all the words.

Will. Coming to fight. The men in the hospital, wounded and broken, had got that way because they'd been fighting.

Others were killed. If I'd not come, it seemed Will wouldn't have either. If he got hurt, or worse—would it be my fault?

"Well, aren't you going to tell me the news?"

I had completely forgot Emma was sitting there. "It's from a friend," I said, too tired to face everything and explain it to her. I wanted to write back to Will, to let him know how much I wished I could see him, but what use would there be? He might've left even before my first letter got to him.

I don't think I dreamed at all that night. I had too many wonderful and terrible thoughts in my head.

Chapter 13

Our first week in the wards I didn't do any of what you really call nursing. Me and Emma were always the ones helping to stuff the mattresses or clean the floors—though keeping the wards clean, Miss Nightingale said, was just as important as any of the other things nurses did, because it helped the men to heal. I suppose I had no cause to complain. What did I know, after all? I was just lucky to be there.

But it wasn't easy, all the same. Seeing the wounded soldiers when they brought them in bothered me something terrible at first. It was all I could do not to cry every time. But before long I learned a trick that helped me keep apart from them, not allow myself to think about how much they must be hurting or who was back at home sleepless, waiting for news of them, good or bad. I'd set myself the task of guessing what was wrong with them, to see if I could figure out what the doctors would do. I never knew if I was right or wrong. But it made me feel like I was learning something. And it took my mind off Will.

I figured it would take Will some time to get to the Crimea. And he'd have to learn to be a soldier. They'd hardly send him off to fight without teaching him how so he'd be ready, and that would take time.

What was Will thinking right at that moment? Was he afraid? I realized I didn't know him all that well, in spite of owing him so much. All I knew was his kindness to me. No one outside my family had ever been so nice. I surely didn't want him to think I took advantage. So when I got my wages the first week, I put aside half to pay Will back. *It will take me only a few weeks to save enough,* I thought. I'd find a way to send the money to Lucy, perhaps, to keep it for him until he got back. Or maybe she should just use it, since he'd been going to give it to her that day anyway.

I was doing all right in Turkey. Earning a wage that would let me bring plenty back to Mum. But it wasn't easy work— even without nursing in the wards night and day. When it rained the water poured in on us, and we put out pots and basins to catch it and as soon as they filled we'd empty them. Other times the cold wind whistled through the gaps in the walls and the windows that didn't fit proper in their frames. It was so cold. I never felt warm.

Then one night we woke up to a terrible banging.

"It's a hurricane!" screamed Mrs. Drake, running up and down between our cots with her white nightgown flapping and nightcap half off her head. I wanted to laugh at first, then I realized the wind had whipped up so fiercely it was tearing bits of the building away and flinging them onto the ground.

"Leastways we're not on the *Vectis*," I said to Emma, pulling my covers up to my chin.

All at once there was a terrible crash above our heads, over by the tower where Miss Nightingale's and the Sellonites' rooms were. In a second we leapt out of our beds and ran as quick as we could through the common room and toward the dark corridor that led to the tower. Miss Nightingale herself stopped us. She came through soaking wet, a splintered wooden post in her hands. "The wind blew my windows in," she said. "I wonder, Molly, if you'd let me share with you for the rest of the night? You're the slimmest."

There was no question in my mind of my answer. "Of course!" I said. Everyone made their way back to their beds, one or two shooting glances that were green with envy in my direction. "You lie down and make yourself comfortable," I said. Miss Nightingale stretched out on my cot, trying to shrink herself as small as possible. But it was no use. There wasn't room for two, no matter how hard she tried. I feared I'd push her out for sure, or be pushed out myself. "If you give me one of the blankets and a pillow, I'll be just fine on the floor here."

"Oh Molly, no!"

I guessed she only called me Fraser when we were working. "Don't say another word, Miss Nightingale. I can manage." I took the blanket and pillow and lay on the hard, damp floor between Emma's bed and mine.

"Oh, I'll be just fine!" Emma whispered to me, reaching

down to give me a pinch. It wasn't hard, though, and I knew she meant it just to tease.

"Tomorrow we shall have to do something about the sick cookery," Miss Nightingale murmured, her eyes closed. I thought she must have been dreaming already.

I tried my hardest to fall asleep, but down on the floor, with the wind coming in above and whooshing into our room, I soon set up shivering and my teeth chattered so anyone could hear them. Emma touched my head.

"Come up and share with me, you daft thing," she whispered, then leaned over and took hold of my arm.

I crawled in with her. The warmth of her soon put a stop to my shaking. We curled up together. I could feel Emma's breath on my ear.

"If I tell you a secret do you promise not to say?"

I nodded.

"I'm sweet on one of the men. In the lower ward."

I craned my head around. "You mustn't be!"

"Why not? The great Miss Nightingale doesn't have charge of my heart! Besides, he was ever so brave in a battle, and isn't hurt too bad."

"But how? When?" As far as I knew, Emma was with me so much that she never had a chance to do something I didn't know about.

"Oh, I'd just take a longer route back when Miss N. sent me on an errand. And it wouldn't take me all that time to go to the latrine when I said I had to."

I shook my head. "Emma, you'll be sent home for sure.

You know what Miss Nightingale said." I don't know if it was just because I was tired and cold, but a few tears leaked down my cheeks. I wiped them away quickly.

"What's the matter? You jealous?" Emma said, nudging me with her knee.

"No, that's not it. I just don't want you to go home," I said.

We didn't talk any more after that, and I soon fell asleep, warmer than I'd been any night since we'd arrived.

I woke up sometime later, thinking it was dawn. I was in a cramp from not moving—there wasn't room enough in the cot even for Emma and me, the two smallest, to be comfortable. I looked at the windows. Still dark. Not even moonlight came through them. *Who's lit a candle?* I thought.

I lifted my head to look around. Emma squirmed and nearly pushed me off onto the floor. But it didn't matter. I saw what caused the light.

Miss Nightingale was sitting up and had put a match to the lamp by her bedside. It was one of those odd Turkish lamps with a pleated paper shade, a little greasy and dirty so the light wasn't strong. Very slowly, so she wouldn't wake anyone, she put one foot at a time out from under my blankets and slipped them into the soft shoes by the bed. She pulled her large black shawl around her and stepped gently between the cots, heading to the door that led to the wards.

What was she doing? I waited until she passed through

the door, leaving it slightly ajar behind her, then eased myself out of Emma's grasp. I had no slippers. The floor was icy under my feet.

Trying not to make a sound I walked to the door we never opened and peered through the gap Miss Nightingale had left.

There I saw her, going quietly to every bed, her lamp held high, looking to see that the men were asleep, pulling blankets up to their chins or tucking stray arms underneath the covers, like a nursemaid with young charges. I watched her slow progress to the end of the ward, fascinated by the care she took.

Before she turned and came back I stepped away from the door and got back into Emma's warm bed. No wonder Miss Nightingale was so exhausted—she spent hours every night wandering through the wards, making sure the men were safe.

———

By the time we woke up, Miss Nightingale had already gone from my bed. I made it up extra careful, not sure if the damage to her rooms would be repaired before night and she might have to sleep in my cot again. The wind still howled though not as harshly as it was screaming the night before, and the rain had let up some.

"Well, now that they have all the mattresses they need for the soldiers, at least all they can fit in the hospital, maybe we'll actually get to do some nursing." Emma and I chatted while we dressed behind one of the screens in our room.

Our breakfast—some watery porridge and tea—waited for us on the table. Mrs. Clarke made a racket in the kitchen with her pots and was muttering so loudly we could hear her out in the common room. "Wants me to do the sick cookery now! As if I don't have enough to do. These nurses are a bad lot." She went on and on. It was her way.

I looked about, checking the roster Miss Nightingale posted. We'd only been in Scutari for a few weeks and already things were much more organized—and cleaner.

Miss Nightingale came in, looking more disheartened than I'd ever seen her. "Last night's gale has been a true disaster," she said, shaking her head. "A ship containing a thousand beds, linens, clothing, a ton of sugar, a quantity of arrowroot, and numerous other vital supplies was wrecked. Half the crew is gone and there's not a hope of anything being salvaged."

"Shame!" cried Mrs. Drake, always the first to say something.

"What is worse is that we have a terrible challenge before us today." The serious look on her face got everyone's attention. "Just now, a ship has docked—or rather, limped in— bearing seven hundred and fifty wounded, and one hundred and forty-six ill. There are some cases of cholera, so the greatest attention to hygiene must be paid. We shall all need to do our best this morning to get everyone in and treated as quickly as possible. But that is not the worst of it. I have had word that another ship follows this one, with fifteen hundred men who must be accommodated in our hospital."

Fifteen hundred men? On top of the hundreds we were already expecting? How on God's earth would we do it? There was no space. Already the pallets were only eighteen inches apart from each other in every ward, and a walkway of just three feet was left to get from one end of a ward to the other.

"Fraser and Bigelow, you will help the orderlies with those who are being discharged. They will be given a suit of clothes to wear out of the hospital, and then they must bring them back to us when they have their own uniforms provided again. Mind you make that very clear. You are to keep a register of all the names and regiments of the men that leave." She gave me a tablet and a pencil to write with. "What's wrong, Fraser? Better to be seeing to those who are healing than those who may not live the day out."

I nodded, but my heart was caught up in my throat. It took me nearly an hour to write my one short letter to Will. I'd have to write fast to keep up—Miss Nightingale expected everyone to be as quick as she was at everything.

"They're waiting for you in the lower ward. On your way!"

Emma and I set off. The destruction in the rest of the hospital was even worse than in our corner. The gale had blown in windows everywhere. Orderlies swabbed the floors, but in some places the water was deep enough to slosh over our shoes. And on the ground floor the rain had made the sewers back up so the mess was all over the floors.

"Ugh! Disgusting!" Emma said. I had to tuck the paper

and pencil under my arm so I could lift my skirts out of the muck. As we passed by one broken window, a big gust came, bringing dust and dirt in. Something lodged in my eye. I put my hands over them quick, forgetting the tablet, which dropped into the stinking water.

"Oh no!" cried Emma. "It's ruined."

Thank heavens! I thought, wiping my eyes. I was saved. "Don't you think if we just tell the men to bring the clothes back they will? I'm sure they'd rather wear their uniforms."

Emma stared at me. "Is that you inside that head? What happened to Little Goody Two-Shoes?"

"We'd best hurry. They need these beds for the new ones." I ignored her. I didn't want her to know the real reason I was glad the tablet was ruined.

We rushed into the convalescent ward, where we normally weren't allowed because the men were well enough to cause trouble with a girl if they'd a mind to. Here the floor wasn't covered in filth, thank heavens. The orderlies went down the line of men yelling at the ones who just had their arms in slings or bandages round their heads, telling them they'd bloody well better get up unless they wanted to share their beds with someone whose guts had just been shot out.

Down at the far end, stacks of shirts, trousers, and jackets were roughly arranged by sizes. "Do they know what to do?" I whispered to Emma.

"Why are you whispering?" She turned and clapped her hands loudly. "Oy, mates. If the orderlies say you're to go, come see us and we'll give you a suit of clothes. You can change outside."

They must've been surprised to be ordered about by a woman. One by one they stood up and came over without a murmur. Most were all right by now, not like some I'd seen in the other wards. The ones who were the most themselves winked at us and even sometimes said, "Hello, darlin'! Where they been keepin' you?" We ignored them, just handing them a shirt and trousers and pointing to the jackets, each time telling them they were to bring the clothes back tomorrow, as soon as they had uniforms again.

Some of the men came up in clothes so tattered or ripped apart that they were nearly indecent. We weren't supposed to care, I knew, but I couldn't help blushing. And they blushed too, not looking us in the eye.

"What'll happen to them?" I asked Emma once we got a system going and settled into our job.

"The ones as are strong enough will go back and fight," she said.

Fight, to be blown apart again, I thought. What was it all for? Mr. Bracebridge told us we were pledged to help our allies, the Turks, when Russia invaded them. But I didn't know why we cared anything about the Turks. They were so far away from England, and not even Christians, most of them.

And to make matters worse, I couldn't help seeing Will in my mind. Any one of the men who might be sent back to fight could be him. A lot were plenty young enough.

"'Ere! Mind where you're going!" Emma stopped handing

out trousers and rushed over to a fellow whose head was bandaged and who staggered about, crashing into other men.

"I dunno what's the matter, miss. My head don't hurt no more. But I can't stay on my feet."

I hurried over to help Emma. The fellow was shaking and seemed like he didn't know up from down. "He shouldn't be sent out," I said. "He's still poorly."

"I'll get him to sit down," Emma said.

"Can you manage on your own for a bit?" I asked. She nodded. "I'll be back as soon as I can."

I went through the ward, past the orderlies already hard at work putting new sheets on the empty mattresses. Everyone did things as fast as ever they could, and as soon as a bed was ready they carried a wounded man in to fill it. *It's like a factory*, I thought. *Only here we stitch together people.*

"S'cuse me," I asked one of the orderlies, one who was nice to us nurses, not cross and mean, "I need to find a doctor. There's a man been discharged what shouldn't have."

He pointed to the stairs. Without thinking I ran up. I asked another orderly on the next floor the same question, and he pointed me down to the far end of the ward, where a screen hid an operation that was under way. Still no tables— they'd been on the supply ship that sank. We weren't supposed to interrupt a doctor working, so I waited. I'd not seen an operation since that day at the Hôtel Dieu. I got as near as I dared to the screens—Miss Nightingale persuaded Dr. Menzies to use them, as well as to change the sheets when new wounded came in—and listened.

"We're going to have to take your arm, soldier," the doctor said. The doctor's voice was calm and patient, and he had a slight, soft accent.

"Will it hurt?"

"Not so very much worse than it hurts already, and then it will be over. Hold him, men."

"No! No! No!" The soldier's voice rose to a girlish scream. I wanted to cover my ears but all the other wounded soldiers in their beds stared straight at me. I tried not to imagine that leg in the Hôtel Dieu in Paris, the blood and such that poured out of it. *Come back to now,* I thought. *Look at what's around you.* I made myself think about other things. What first came to mind was rats. I didn't see a single one on this floor. No food for them, I supposed, now that everything was cleaner. And then it struck me that it was generally quieter. There was no rasping of men scratching at their beards, hairy chests, arms and legs. The chloride of lime had begun to do its work. The vermin stayed away. Everyone somehow seemed healthier, less wasted. It was all because of Miss Nightingale.

I saw a soldier lying all crooked, his head about to loll off the edge of the mattress. "Let me straighten your pillow," I said. He was only just conscious, but he murmured and didn't resist when I nudged him into the center of it again. He raised two fingers on his right hand. It was a thank-you.

A moment later the doctor came out from behind the screen, his coat and hands covered in blood and his face pale. If I didn't know he was a doctor, I might have thought that was the first time he had ever amputated a limb, he looked so unwell. I thought I'd better tell him my business quickly. "There's a man—" He lifted his eyes to mine, and I stopped talking. I knew this doctor. He was the one who nodded to me on the *Vectis*, when we both looked out and saw the fishing boat. The one who helped me get out of the horrible storm our first night at sea. I thought he looked kind then, and what I heard from behind the screen sounded kind now. I cleared my throat as if I had a cough, just to give myself a little time.

"Yes?" It was a drawn-out sound, not crisp and sharp like most of the army doctors.

"Downstairs, a man is crashing about like he's still got his sea legs. I don't think he should be discharged with the others."

"I can guess the one you mean, Nurse Fraser," he said.

I was so surprised he knew my name that I almost missed what he said next.

"He's got a bad head wound, won't likely be right ever again. No one seems to know what to do with him." The doctor's face had already regained some of its color.

"Well, he can't go back and fight," I said. "He'd be a danger to our side!"

A group of orderlies had meanwhile gathered around us to listen, and all of them started laughing. I didn't mean to be funny. What if Miss Nightingale heard about this? I wasn't supposed to be on this ward anyway.

The doctor must have noticed me worrying. "You lot

should be helping bring in the wounded. Get to it!" They scurried off in their dirty uniforms, taking the smell of dried blood and old food with them. *If Miss Nightingale was in charge of them they'd be good deal more orderly*, I thought.

"Thank you," I said to the doctor, wondering how to get his attention back to the matter of the man downstairs who was stumbling about. Then I don't know what but something made me brave. "You know my name, but I don't know yours."

"Dr. Maclean. James Maclean, at your service."

He gave me the slightest bow. No one had ever bowed to me before, nor looked right at me until I thought he could see inside my head.

"I have a little brother named Jimmy," I said, not really sure why, but I had to get back to something familiar, something to anchor me. Will's blue eyes were lovely and kind, but they didn't make me feel uneasy. Dr. Maclean's brown eyes with their thick, dark lashes knocked me off balance, like the poor fellow downstairs. With Dr. Maclean, I couldn't have said what might be going through his mind. And he spoke with an accent, Scotch, I guessed. "I'd better go back downstairs," I said.

"Before the fearsome Miss Nightingale finds you up here alone with a doctor?" he said.

I looked around at all the eyes focused on us from the nearby beds. "Not exactly alone."

He laughed. "That's twice in five minutes you've made me laugh, Nurse Fraser. It's a dangerous precedent."

He gestured with a blood-covered hand for me to precede him along the narrow space between the wounded men's feet. I didn't need to be told twice, and hurried back down to where Emma was handing out clothing to soldiers, holding on to the memory of the sound of my name in Dr. Maclean's musical accent.

Chapter 14

We finished with the discharged men just in time for tea. Emma and I sat in the common room with Mrs. Drake and two others, all of us so exhausted we could hardly speak.

"Where's everyone else?" Emma asked after a bit.

"They just keep coming," said Mrs. Drake, shaking her head. "No time to take a rest."

One other, a nurse who hardly ever spoke to us, said, "So many, and so badly wounded. We wanted to stay, but Miss Nightingale is sending us back to eat in shifts."

All this had been going on while Emma and I were getting the healing soldiers fitted out with togs so they could go back to fight again. We exchanged a look. I don't even remember whether it was me or Emma who said, "We must go and help them." I couldn't bear to think that wounded soldiers might be waiting for care, and us sitting by, taking our rest.

It was definitely Emma, though, who said, "She's trying to keep us away from the men. She thinks 'cause we're young they'll get distracted or upset, and we won't be able to nurse. But that shouldn't matter. Why shouldn't a man in pain see a pretty face to comfort him? I can nurse just as well as the rest."

Emma was so worked up she had tears in her eyes. I agreed with her. It didn't seem fair. Why have us there at all if we weren't going to be any help? I'd only eaten a few bites of our supper of bread and cheese when Emma stood, grabbed my arm, and said, "Let's go, Moll. We didn't come out here to be serving maids."

I barely had time to grab my cloak off the hook before I found myself running by Emma's side through the corridor to the stairs.

Instead of stopping indoors, where the men who had already been seen by the doctors were being put on pallets prepared by the orderlies, we ran straight outside, out to where the ships docked and the wounded and sick were still being unloaded.

A clear sky and a full moon sat calm and beautiful above us. The wind didn't blow such a gale any more. Spread out over the ground all the way from the hospital to the dock were soldiers—or pieces of soldiers. Even the ones who sat up and smoked, dirty bandages on their arms or legs or wrapped round their chests, looked like something had gone missing from them, like they left a part of themselves on the battle-field. There were so many, and I knew the wards in the hospital were as full as could be. Where would all these men possibly go?

No time to wonder. "There's Miss Nightingale over there. We have to go and talk to her." This time I took hold of Emma.

"Are you completely daft? Let's just get to work. She'll only send us back."

I watched Miss Nightingale pointing and talking, keeping calm but with an edge of urgency to everything she did. *It must be hard to be her, to be expected to come to this impossible place and make everything right,* I thought. I turned back to Emma. "I don't think so. I think we have to tell her we're here." I pulled on Emma again. When she resisted, I let go and walked as quick and direct as I could, stepping around wounded men to get to where Miss Nightingale stood. She looked up as I came over, at first staring past me like I wasn't there. "We've come to help, Miss Nightingale," I said, standing my ground in front of her, hoping Emma had followed me.

"They need people to clean wounds. Not enough orderlies. Go over to Dr. Maclean and follow his instructions." She pointed to an area where a few tents had been set up closer to the hospital. Turkish soldiers carried stretchers over, not much heeding whether they bumped or jostled the men on them, only trying to get as many moved around as fast as possible.

I turned to call to Emma and found her right behind me. "Let's go."

Though he'd been bloody enough when I'd seen him earlier, I hardly recognized Dr. Maclean for the blood all over his jacket, arms, and legs. Even his shoes were covered, and he'd wiped a streak across his forehead too. As each stretcher arrived, he'd yell out, "Stump!" or "Shrapnel!" or "Dead!"—which in his accent sounded like "Daid"—and point to a tent where the stretcher should be moved.

"We're here to help," I said to him not wanting to waste any time.

He glanced up briefly. I thought I saw a moment of surprise, or something like it, in his eyes. "Nurse Bigelow, you can go over to that tent and do as Dr. Arbuthnot says. Nurse Fraser, you stay here."

I didn't dare look round at Emma, lest she guess from my face that I was glad to be by Dr. Maclean. Before I had a chance to breathe, though, the Turks brought over a man writhing in pain, hands gripping his stomach. Through the dried blood, the coarse linen scraps of bandages that must have been wrapped round him in Balaclava were still faintly visible.

"Put him right here. He shouldn't be moved anymore." Dr. Maclean knelt down beside the stretcher on the ground. "Now, my man, you have to let me see what's happened to you."

"I can't. It'll all fall out if I take my hands away." His voice was shaky and shrill, like a child afraid he'll get a beating.

"Nurse, get this man a drink and wipe off his face." As I turned to go Dr. Maclean grabbed my hand and murmured, "Distract him a little; try to get his mind off what I'm doing."

I went to the barrel of water that had been brought out

for washing and drinking and dipped one of the dirty tin cups in it. I had nothing to use to clean off the soldier's face, so I quickly tore a bit of my petticoat and soaked it in the water.

When I returned, the soldier was still clutching his stomach with surprising strength, considering how bad he was. I crouched down by his head. "Here, take a sip of water. You must be ever so thirsty." I mopped some of the dirt off his face and turned it toward me, trying to make him see me. His eyes jumped around and he blinked fast, like gnats were getting in the corners. I gently cleaned around them. "It's all right. You're safe now. Dr. Maclean's going to make you better."

"Are you an angel?" he said, finally letting his eyes rest on me. "Have I died?"

I smiled. "Not an angel. Just a nurse. And you're looking a sight better already."

I kept talking to him, low and soft. He told me where he came from, and about his mother and sisters. I could tell from the set of his shoulders, how they relaxed back to the ground, that the soldier had finally let go of his stomach, and from the activity that I sensed rather than saw I knew Dr. Maclean was doing his best to stitch him up and bandage him again. I didn't dare shift my attention away from the lad's eyes, like I was holding him in a trance that would break if I blinked. The last thing I wanted was for him to realize what was happening and reach down and get in the doctor's way.

"Will they send me home?" the soldier asked.

"I imagine you're done fighting for now," I answered. He closed his eyes and smiled, not broadly, but with such sweetness I wanted to kiss him. Then his pale face got even whiter and he went so completely loose that I thought he fell into an instant, deep sleep. I turned to Dr. Maclean. He sat up and looked at me, eyes full of sorrow.

"He's dead."

I wanted to yell out, *No! He can't be! We were just talking.* But before I could react, Dr. Maclean motioned the orderlies over and they covered the soldier with a blanket and took him away.

Chapter 15

The sun came up while we were still treating the wounded and trying to find places to fit them in the hospital. I got pretty good at telling what was wrong: a bone sticking out was a compound fracture. The stumps were easy enough to identify. Then there were bullet and bayonet wounds—lots of blood, but if the bones weren't broken and if they were only in a limb and not through the chest, not so dangerous. Those were sometimes treated right there outside, the men bandaged up and sent back to the camp where their regiments had started out before sailing across the Black Sea to fight.

Always I stayed aware of Dr. Maclean even when I wasn't looking at him. His movements were slow and careful at the same time, as if he was thinking through everything he did, trying his hardest not to make a mistake. We eventually caught up with the stream of casualties and the numbers of wounded thinned out so you could see the ground between them. Only then did I stand up straight and stretch my arms out, noticing how stiff and sore I was from holding hands, wrapping bandages, and kneeling.

Dr. Maclean had stood up as well. He didn't look at me, just stared across to the hospital ships. His face was sad and angry at the same time. The other doctors wandered aimlessly, checking bandages now and again, smoking their pipes, talking in low voices. But not Dr. Maclean.

He caught me staring at him and turned. "You must be tired, Molly. Why don't you go and get a cup of tea?" So he knew my first name too.

"Would you like me to bring you a cuppa?"

"No. I can't seem to eat or drink in this kind of situation," he said, nodding his head toward a group of doctors who were biting chunks off of loaves of bread and swigging something out of flasks. "I guess I'm just not very used to it yet."

Not used to it? He was a doctor.

"Where are you from, Molly?"

I cast a quick look round to see where Miss Nightingale was. I couldn't find her and figured she'd gone inside to help with getting the ones who'd been admitted to the hospital settled and cared for. "I'm from London. The East End."

"Where did you nurse before you came here?"

I'd been wondering when one of the doctors or patients would ask me that. I looked down at my hands, which I saw were sheathed in blood. "I never nursed anywhere before this," I said.

"Really?" He sounded almost glad. "But you're so calm

and good at it. And I thought Miss Nightingale only brought out experienced nurses."

"It's a long tale," I said, "and I'm none too proud of it. But I'm here, doing what I can."

He nodded. "My parents didn't want me to become a doctor. Someone from an old Scottish family should be in politics, or work the land, or become one of the fearsome Highland Dragoons."

"Oh, so you're Scotch!"

He smiled. "We prefer Scots, but yes."

"I like the way you talk." I didn't know what else to say.

"Is that why you look at me sometimes?"

My face and neck went hot and tingly. "I . . . I . . ."

Dr. Maclean laughed. "You see, Molly, you seem to have this talent for making me laugh. And with those auburn curls I can see peeking out from your cap I think perhaps you may have some Scottish blood in you too."

I quickly tried to tuck the ends of my hair back under my cap, wondering how much had strayed out and what a sight I must appear. "Molly! We're wanted in the hospital." I jumped at the sound of Emma's voice. I hadn't heard her coming. She gave me a curious look that said, *What do you think you're doing?*

"I'll be along. Thank you, Dr. Maclean." I don't quite know what I thanked him for, but I felt grateful to him. Grateful for treating me like I knew what I was doing, and letting me prove myself, perhaps. Grateful for talking to me. Grateful for knowing my name.

"Cor, I'm not half done in," Emma said as we walked to the hospital door.

"You have circles like coal smudges under your eyes," I said.

"And you have twinkly stars in yours." She pinched me, but I could feel her hands shaking and knew she had no more strength left than I did. "Be careful, miss. I have my eye on that one."

"What about your wounded soldier?" I asked, nudging her in the ribs.

She turned all serious. "Don't you say a word, Moll. He was one of them what we discharged today. Or rather, yesterday. He says he's going to find a way to see me."

That would be a mistake, I knew. But after that night, seeing how short life could be and how uncertain everything was, I understood why she'd risk it. I felt a tug in the center of me when I thought about the way Dr. Maclean looked into my eyes. There was an answer inside him that wasn't like anything I'd ever felt before. There was something in what we had done together that night, something terrible and important. I don't know how many of the men that passed through our hands died, if not right then, after they went to the ward. For some it was obvious they wouldn't live out the night. For others chances were they'd heal. Heal to fight again.

"You're awful quiet, Moll. What did that Dr. Maclean do to you?"

I didn't have time to answer because we'd entered the

ward. Two or three Sisters of Mercy walked calmly amongst the beds, bending down now and again to straighten a sheet or give a drink of water. Mrs. Drake stood at the foot of the stairs to the upper wards. When she saw us she called us over. "Miss Nightingale wants to see you two." She cocked her thumb toward the stairs.

"This is it," I said to Emma. "We'll get the sack. Or a drubbing at least." If Miss Nightingale had made one thing clear, it was that her orders were to be strictly obeyed, whatever we thought of them. We had most definitely disobeyed by coming out to nurse last night, when we'd never really been allowed to do it before. We'd be back to stuffing mattresses at the very least.

I saw her standing in the middle of the ward. The sun streamed in through the rows of windows in a pattern that showed floating specks of dust and made the dingy linens look almost white. Miss Nightingale, dressed all in black silk, was like a statue there, her eyes traveling up and down the rows, looking for anyone in need, watching her nurses mop brows and hold basins while men who were just coming to realize they no longer had an arm or a leg, or they'd lost the sight of an eye, choked out their despair.

We stood quiet and still, waiting for her to notice us. She did at last. She came toward us not quickly, but with purpose, the way she did everything.

"Fraser, Bigelow," she said, in a tone that I knew spelled business. "You know I have not wanted you to mix with the men in the wards. Had things been otherwise, I would not

138

have brought either of you to this place. But somehow in the rush to get here, you managed to come along.

"I have been informed that the doctors you worked with last night have expressed their satisfaction. It seems you are both natural nurses, whatever your lack of training. But this lack can be dangerous—even with talent as a substitute."

Miss Nightingale stared at us, one after the other. Standing there, I couldn't tell what she was going to do. When she reached her arms out for us, I started to shrink backward at first, expecting a cuff on the ear. But instead, she held us close for just an instant.

"You've done well," she murmured. "Don't disappoint me." Then as quickly as she'd done it, she let us go. "Go eat and rest. Come back when I send others for their turn. We'll have to work round the clock today."

No one had held me close like that since my mother, the last time I saw her before I was let go from my parlormaid position. I tried not to think about that—there was no point. She couldn't put her arms around me when I was on the other side of the world, and she wouldn't want to until I came back and showed her that I had made something of myself. Still, I was unaccountably happy that Miss Nightingale was pleased.

Whatever happened next, I felt that I'd finally accomplished something. I was a nurse. Or, if not exactly a nurse, I had a natural talent for nursing. None other than Miss Nightingale herself told me so.

That was the beginning of my real life, that night. And it

was the beginning of something else, too, something far more important in the end. I felt safe, for a minute at least. But soon the war came closer to me than I could have imagined, and the days and hours raced on so that I could hardly see my life passing as they went.

Chapter 16

We all soon learned to cope with the unpredictable schedule of battle casualties. Sometimes things would seem quiet as peacetime and there wouldn't be enough to keep us busy. Then the older nurses would get wool from the market and start knitting socks, and we'd all roll bandages and help with washing linens. Mrs. Drake told us stories, most of them funny, about her grandchildren and about nursing in London. She'd sometimes do it in a way that was meant to teach me things, without making it too obvious. In turn I'd sit patiently while she wound a ball of wool from the skein on my outstretched hands. I never knew my grandmas, but Mrs. Drake was what I always imagined they'd be like.

We took turns in the laundry, set up as I'd heard it would be in a hut outside the hospital. There was another hospital about half a mile away that we didn't know about when we first came. It was called the General Hospital, and had mostly convalescents. Only the Sisters of Mercy were sent over to work there. They didn't want more than one female nurse per ward because the men were getting healthy.

Every day it seemed Miss Nightingale found some other almost impossible challenge to overcome. The first one, after the wards were cleaned up and real beds brought in, was the food the wounded and sick were given.

"Half the time the meat is raw and the other half it is overcooked and cold. They tear their food apart with their hands because they don't have forks and knives. There are no fresh vegetables, and the bread is so hard the men can't chew it. As for sick rations . . . there are those here who seem to think that a light diet means no diet!"

I thought for a while we were all going to have to learn how to cook. But the Muslims would not allow women to prepare food for the men. Mrs. Clarke was pretty happy about that. Though we did end up with a roster for serving food. Soon enough, everyone in the hospital was given wholesome meals according to what the doctors recommended. Whole rations, half rations, quarter rations, or spoon feeding. I swear the men began to heal more quickly.

But as soon as things started to get into a pattern, like a well-run household, something else happened that upset everything.

I had come in from taking my turn in the wards, watching over men who had just had surgery to see if they were getting past the crisis and would live. A moment after I hung my cloak on the peg, I heard a disturbance at the door and the bright chatter of many women's voices, none of them familiar to me.

When the door burst open to admit another eighteen women in nurses' uniforms and ten more who were plainly Catholic nuns, my first thought was that some of us might be going home. But it had only been a few weeks, and there had been only one or two minor problems and two nurses sent away for drunkenness.

"Excuse me, girl," said the one who seemed to be in charge, "I wonder if you'd be so kind as to direct us to Miss Nightingale."

"What do you want me to tell her?" I asked.

"Tell her Miss Stanley is here, with reinforcements."

Miss Stanley? She looked a little like the Mrs. Stanley who had interviewed the nurses at Mr. Herbert's house in Belgrave Square. Probably her daughter. At this time of the morning Miss Nightingale was in her rooms, working in what she called her office. She was currently making a plan to get provisions to the hospital more quickly, so we wouldn't run out of bandages and chloride of lime. I knocked on her door. When I told her Miss Stanley was waiting for her downstairs, a shadow crossed her face.

"She also said to say she's brought reinforcements," I said.

"Reinforcements? I hope she means supplies. We don't need any more nurses. It's hard enough managing you lot as it is." She smiled at me, but not with any real mirth. The expression passed as quickly as it came, replaced by a frown that tugged at the corners of her mouth.

"I'm afraid, Miss Nightingale, she means nurses. And more nuns too."

I've never seen someone's jaw actually drop before, but Miss Nightingale's did, and her expression changed in an instant to that determined hardness I'd come to recognize any time she was going to meet with the hospital administrators about one of her plans. "I told Mr. Herbert nurses were only to come out upon my authorization! And we already have too many nuns. I promised there would be no effort at conversion in the hospitals," she muttered, marching out of her room so fast she sent three papers swirling into the air. She didn't say not to follow her, so I did—at a bit of a distance, so she wouldn't remember I was there. *This could be a very interesting meeting*, I thought.

The two women embraced like old friends. Which seemed odd, after what I had just heard Miss Nightingale say upstairs. "It's always a pleasure to see you, Mary," Miss Nightingale said. "But you needn't have taken such a task upon yourself as to rush out here. You'll see that we're managing quite well as it is."

Miss Stanley drew herself up a little. "There can surely never be enough nurses. And now I have brought you some with a higher level of education and a more reliable moral character. Sidney said you were having difficulties with some that came out with you initially."

"If I required more nurses, I certainly would have written to Mr. Herbert, who assured me that he would never take it upon himself to send anyone whom I had not personally approved."

The conversation was hotting up. The nurses—still in their winter cloaks and bonnets—began to shift from one foot to another. The one who was the head of the nuns stepped forward. "If you'll excuse me, my bishop decides what we do or do not, and I have been charged with the task of nursing the poor dying men out here." She spoke with a thick Irish accent, which I recognized immediately from having heard the Irishmen on the docks in London.

"I think you'll find that I have complete jurisdiction over the nursing in this and the General Hospital," said Miss Nightingale. "It is for me to determine who nurses or otherwise, not your bishop."

"Allow me to introduce Mother Bridgeman, superior of the nursing sisters I have brought with me," said Mary Stanley.

"Superior in religious matters does not mean superior in medical matters." Miss Nightingale's voice was rising and sharpening. Things were set on a downhill course, I could see. I decided I'd better do something to stop it, even if I risked losing some of the favor I'd won with Miss Nightingale.

"Perhaps the travelers would like some tea and to take off their cloaks," I said, walking in as if I'd not been listening to everything that had just been said.

"Yes of course, Molly. Miss Stanley and I can speak in

my office. Would you have Mrs. Clarke bring tea for everyone?"

"I shall come along as well," Mother Bridgeman said.

"That won't be necessary." Miss Nightingale dismissed her like a common servant.

And now I would have to go and wheedle Mrs. Clarke for tea. I dreaded asking her for anything. She was likely to throw something at you or let loose a string of curses if she didn't like what you said.

"Who will take our cloaks?" asked one nurse, whose genteel accent told me she wasn't of the same class as me.

Without thinking, and I suppose because I was so used to taking orders from Miss Nightingale, I began to collect all their wraps. They dropped them from around their shoulders one by one like they were about to walk into a ballroom. I saw why Miss Nightingale was so put out that they'd come.

I put the cloaks on one of the wooden divans that we'd never managed to rid of vermin, secretly wishing I could watch them all start scratching themselves when the lice began to do their damage. I went in to Mrs. Clarke.

"Miss Nightingale asked me to ask you to bring tea to our lady visitors."

"Oh, she did, eh?"

I cringed, waiting for the assault, be it words or crockery.

"Get off with ye. I'll serve 'em tea, if that's what she wants."

I didn't wait to hear any more, leaving her muttering and complaining as she put the kettle on.

The ladies had arranged themselves on all the available chairs, leaving me standing in the room. I wanted to leave but didn't know whether I should. Soon Mrs. Clarke came in with her big pot on its tilting cradle, returning a moment later with a tray of cups without saucers. The lady nurses Miss Stanley had brought stared as though they'd never seen such a thing before. I thought I'd show them how it was done and help myself, but as soon as I'd poured a cup, one of the ladies came over and reached for it without so much as a thank you. Soon I found myself pouring out for everyone. I should have taken it without being miffed, but I boiled with anger.

After they all had their tea and were settled once again on our chairs, I said, "If you require anything else, ring the bell and Mrs. Clarke will come. I must go and do my job, which is nursing." I took my cloak off the peg and left the tower, heading across the parade ground to nowhere in particular. I was on my break. I should have been resting. Instead, I decided a walk around, cold as it was, would do as well as a sit down with a cup of tea in that odd collection of would-be nurses.

I hadn't got halfway around when someone called me. "Nurse Fraser!"

I turned. It was Dr. Maclean. Out of habit, I gave a quick glance behind me to make sure Miss Nightingale hadn't come out with Miss Stanley since I last saw them. The parade ground was empty except for a few orderlies smoking. I waited for Dr. Maclean to catch up to me.

"I haven't laid eyes on you since that night when we were seeing to the casualties together." He stated it not as if it was a fact, but more like he expected things to be different. "I've been wanting to thank you. I don't think I could have done as much as I did without you to help me."

It was the first time a doctor had praised me. I smiled. "I learned so much from you that night."

"From me? I don't know how." He said it more to himself, then focused again on me. "I expect you could have done as much on your own. Maybe by the time you've been here a while you can do the surgery yourself."

Was he mocking me? Women didn't operate, and in any case, it was very different watching than wielding the knife. "No need for that with doctors like you around," I said, hoping it was the right response. "I'm really not as experienced as I should be, even just to nurse. But nothing would have prepared me for all we have to face here."

"Molly . . . I want you to understand something about me." He turned his eyes away, then lowered his voice, stepping nearer so I could hear him. It was odd, like he was talking to me but not at the same time. "I'm not a true doctor, you see, at least not quite."

His words snapped me to attention. "You? What do you mean?" It occurred to me for no more than a second that perhaps he was only as much of a doctor as I was a nurse. But that couldn't be.

"I've barely finished my training. In fact, I never did. I've never operated on a person before this, nor done anything but the most rudimentary of caring while attending the local country doctor on his rounds. That's not nearly enough here."

I wanted to tell him it was more than I had, but something stopped me. "Miss Nightingale says that a body can have the right instincts, and sometimes that makes up for less training. It seems to me, watching you, that you know what to do even if you haven't been told."

"You're a sweet girl, Molly. How old are you?"

His question caught me off guard and I answered, "Seventeen," before I remembered I was supposed to be nineteen. I covered my mouth with my hand. "Only no one knows! Miss Nightingale's nurses are supposed to be older. Please don't say!" I was so concerned with making him keep my secret that without realizing it I'd taken hold of his sleeve.

"So we both have secrets to keep. I was wondering, Molly Fraser, would you let me take you into town for tea one day, if it's quiet and we don't have to stay up all night to bring in men who are only partly put together?"

I didn't know what to say. No one ever asked me to tea before, or anywhere else for that matter. Will and I only knew each other from work, except when he came to see me at Lucy's. Sitting in a restaurant would mean someone would serve me—something I couldn't imagine. But it would never happen, nice as it sounded. We were only permitted to go into town in pairs, and only on errands. I'd done it a few times with Emma. And, of course, we weren't supposed to be friendly with any of the men or we'd be sent home. I looked up into his warm eyes. He was waiting for an answer. "I'd love to—"

"Good! Then that's settled."

I smiled. No sense trying to set him straight. *It will never happen anyway. We're too busy, and I can always say no at the time.* But I knew I didn't want to say no.

Dr. Maclean crooked his elbow out for me to take. I pretended not to notice, instead looking into the center of the parade ground and stepping just a little bit away from him. It wouldn't do for someone to see us strolling arm in arm like that. I wondered if he knew how awkward that would be.

He continued to chat as we slowly wandered around the parade ground together—I mostly let him talk about Scotland and the harsh winters there, and what it was like to have to travel to the little villages to tend to the sick.

"Couldn't you just have a surgery in a town and all those people could come to you?" I asked.

"You sound like my brother. He studied law and is going into Parliament now. He is always telling me that I should make a business of doctoring, but somehow I can't. Most of the folks I saw with the old doctor in the hamlets didn't even have a horse to ride, let alone a carriage to protect them from the weather. They'd as likely die before they reached me."

I pictured him on his horse, braving the swirling snow to bring medicine to someone sick with fever. And then I pictured myself, seated behind him on the saddle, holding his medical bag, sharing his hardship, and when the rounds were over . . .

"So, what do you think?"

I was too embarrassed to admit I hadn't been listening to what he'd just said. I opened my mouth, then shut it again.

Dr. Maclean laughed. "You were miles away, I could tell. Can't say I blame you. Things are pretty grim here. At least they are when I don't have you to keep me company." He touched my arm and stopped me, not taking his hand away, but letting his fingers drag along down to my wrist to grasp my hand.

We'd reached the entrance of the hospital. At any moment someone might come through it and see us there, my hand in his, and I didn't know how to take it away, or whether I wanted to.

"I must return to my rounds, Molly. Are you on duty?" I shook my head no. "Then adieu, until next time."

He lifted my hand, I thought perhaps to shake it. But instead, he brought it to his lips, using his thumb to draw down the cuff of my glove, and kissing the back of my wrist very softly. He slowly lowered my hand, then turned and went inside. I stood there for several minutes before going back to have my cup of tea, clutching my hands together, wondering what had just happened to make me feel so good.

Chapter 17

The lady nurses caused a terrible uproar. Miss Nightingale refused to situate them, and they had to get back on the ship that brought them. She wanted to send them away, but Miss Stanley wasn't having it. And then there was Mother Bridgeman. I overheard Miss Nightingale speaking with the other nuns in their room.

"I just don't understand it. I have offered to take four of the sisters in the Barrack Hospital and the others in the General Hospital, but Mother Brickbat will not have it. They must be all together or nothing. Then nothing it shall be."

It didn't help that we were in the midst of one of the lulls in the wounded coming through. Everyone got a little bad tempered at those times, and more of the nurses ended up drunk and we had to cover for them. Already two more had been sent home. And Miss Stanley and her ladies weren't the only ones who suffered.

"It has come to my attention," Miss Nightingale said to us one evening, "that some of my—the—regulations are not being obeyed. In particular, those having to do with fraternizing with the doctors and the patients." She cast her stern eye around at all of us. Several nurses shrank just a little, and others puffed themselves up. I felt guilty, in spite of the fact I hadn't done anything about Dr. Maclean. When I saw him in the wards I'd smile and pretend I had to hurry away so he wouldn't have a chance to ask me the question I knew I didn't have an answer for.

Still, he would keep appearing in my thoughts at the oddest times, and I found myself cradling my right wrist in my hand sometimes, feeling for the exact spot where his lips had touched it. "I am sorry to punish the innocent with the guilty, but as voluntary adherence to the rules has not had the desired effect, I shall have to insist that you remain in these quarters whenever you are not on duty in the wards, and that any entrance to the wards when your shift is not taking place will result in immediate dismissal."

A cry of protest went up from everyone. We had all got used to walking into town to buy sweets and bits of this and that, and some nurses would sneak off to the wards to have a laugh with the men that weren't too poorly. I didn't know what we'd all do with ourselves when we weren't busy. There was only so much sewing and laundry that had to be done.

But another part of me was glad we couldn't go again, after something that happened the last time Emma and me walked into town together. We were on an errand for Mrs. Drake, to get her some wool of a particular color. We did it gladly enough, preferring an excuse to go out over sitting and staring at the walls. I never learned to knit at home, and Mrs. Drake said she'd teach me if I did this for her.

"If you could have anything—and I mean anything in the world, Moll—what would it be?" Emma liked to torture me when we were out of the others' hearing by asking questions that were impossible to answer.

"Oh, I don't know. I suppose it would be money, to help my mum and dad." I couldn't think of anything else to say that wouldn't give something away that I didn't want to share. I really wanted to say that I wished I could see all the pain in the world and touch it and make it go away—but she would never understand what I meant.

"That's no fun. S'posing you didn't have to help them— that they was doing all right. Something for yourself, something silly."

"Why don't you tell me what you'd want?" That was what this game was really about. She had something in mind, I could tell.

"I'd want to be able to make myself invisible, so's I could go wherever I wanted to and no one'd see."

That was even stranger than what I really thought for myself. "Why?" I asked.

"Because then I could go find Thomas, we could be together, and I could come back and nobody would ever know I was gone."

So now she was going to ask me again to pretend she'd stopped to do some shopping and I came home with a headache, just so she could go find Thomas in his camp. I should have known. She would get me in trouble for sure.

We stopped at a market stall with baskets hung from a thin frame that held up a flimsy cloth tent. The baskets swayed in the wind, making a dry, rustling sound. It was an eerie noise, and I shivered.

"Moll?" Emma prodded me, taking hold of my shoulders and turning me toward her. I didn't want to look away from the stall. It seemed to be empty. That was odd. Merchants often reached out to draw you in, already starting to bargain until the price they originally said was halved by the time you reached the next stall and the next merchant. "Is something the matter?"

I didn't exactly feel ill, but the market suddenly seemed very far away from me. I turned back to the stall with the baskets and realized that I'd looked right past the proprietor, an old woman who sat in the back, her fingers working like the wind as she fashioned another reed basket. Her eyes were a startling jewel green and her skin was lined like old leather. She wasn't looking at what she was doing, just staring straight at me, like she knew me. She began to talk to me, but her lips didn't move. I heard the "shushing" sounds of Turkish, but somehow I understood everything she was saying, as if her words went directly into my heart.

"You have a gift. I see it in you. Rare in the West, but not unheard of. Use it well. You are a healer."

That was all she said, and as soon as she finished I was back to myself, standing next to Emma, who was shaking me.

"Molly! Molly! What's wrong?"

"Nothing. Just felt a little queer all of a sudden. I'm better now."

She let out her breath like she'd been holding it. "Phew. I thought you'd been bewitched or something. It's strange here. Let's go."

We continued on to find the wool for Mrs. Drake, and as I suspected, Emma asked me to go back without her so she could visit Thomas quickly in his camp.

"Oh no, Emma! No one will believe me again."

"You have to do this for me. He'll be shipping out soon. Just one last time?"

Of course I said yes. I wondered if Emma ever realized that she wouldn't be the only one to get into trouble if she was found out, which she was bound to be eventually.

That was a week before Miss Nightingale made her announcement about our new restrictions. The old merchant lady's words had haunted me since then, and I sometimes woke up after dreaming of her green eyes, like a tiger's, following me around the hospital.

"What am I going to do?" Emma whispered as we ate our supper in the common room that evening. "I'm supposed to meet Thomas tonight. He's off back to the front tomorrow."

So the time had really come. And instead of waiting to walk into the market, Emma decided to risk sneaking out at night. "I don't know. It's a terrible chance to take. You could lose your position."

"You've got to help me, Moll," she whispered. "I'll die if I can't give Thomas a proper good-bye tonight."

"What can I do? If you get caught, we'll both get the sack."

She leaned in close and spoke into my ear. "If you do this for me, I won't say a word about you and that Dr. Maclean."

I pulled away from her. "There's nothing to tell," I said.

"Then why did your face just go a lovely shade of red?"

Yes, why did it? "It's just that you embarrass me with your suspicions."

In spite of the fact I knew it was the wrong thing to do, I gave in and agreed to help Emma steal out that night.

We waited until everyone was asleep and Miss Nightingale had gone up to her own room. She always checked on us when we weren't doing round-the-clock shifts. It struck me that she was up above us in the tower like a hen with her chicks tucked beneath her feathers. But Emma had sprouted wings. Nothing could keep her in the coop.

"No one'll notice I'm gone if we just bunch up the blankets like I'm sleeping here still."

I didn't really think the trick would fool anyone, but I suspected that almost all the other nurses who weren't nuns or sisters had their own secrets to hide and would hardly turn Emma in. Fortunately, the weather was cold but dry. "Leave the door unlocked and don't wait up," she said, kissing me quickly on the cheek before darting off toward the tents of the army camp.

I was asleep so I didn't know what time Emma came back, but she was in her bed by morning. I had to shake her hard to get her to wake up and she yawned all through our shift at the hospital.

When I came back for tea before evening rounds, there was a letter waiting for me. I knew it could only be from one person, since my mum didn't know how to write. I'd not written to Will since that first time, knowing from his letter to me that he wouldn't be in London. At least that's what I told myself was the reason. I took the envelope off the table where messages and letters were left for us and went in to my bed to read it.

Dear Molly,

You'll never believe it. I'm here! In Scutari. I wanted to come to the hospital to see you but they said we weren't allowed to go there unless we needed to see a doctor. I'm in the camp, not too far away. We'll be shipping off to Balaclava tomorrow. I'd sure like to see you. Can you find a way?

Will

Will. Here. So near! My heart did a little bump in my chest and I started breathing a bit quicker. But a moment later icy tendrils of guilt crept through my veins. What would I say to him? To be honest with myself, I hadn't thought about him much recently. Instead, the face that floated into my mind unbidden was Dr. Maclean's. I told myself it was because of the work, because Dr. Maclean and I had shared so much lately. But I knew it wasn't as simple as that. Dr. Maclean's kind eyes and soft voice refused to leave me, even when days passed and I didn't see him. There was something in them, something a little frightening and dangerous, like they could make me do something I never thought of before.

It was different with Will. He made me feel safe. Something about him wasn't simply familiar, it was home. Yet now, after everything I'd been through and seen here in Scutari, I wasn't the same parlormaid who let someone trick her into being fired, who didn't have the courage to speak up for herself. I would have done it all so differently if I had it to do over again.

But the fact remained: Will was here. Had he changed at all since I last saw him? All at once, I pictured him in my mind, bloodied and unconscious, being triaged and treated at the Barrack Hospital. All those other young men, so many who died or were maimed for life—any one of them could be Will. This was no time to let my fancy run off with my heart. I knew then and there that I would do whatever I had to in order to see Will before he left. Emma had got away with it. She would cover for me. She would have to. I prayed there would be no ships bringing wounded and sick men to the hospital in the next day. Usually we knew by telegraph and then someone saw them far out to sea and sent word, and there had been none recently. I owed it to Will to try.

And I had his money! He would be proud of me for paying him back. Although it now seemed insignificant in a way. What would he do with money at the front? Maybe he'd be able to buy better food than what he'd get in his rations.

"Fraser, what are you doing in here all alone?"

I jumped and crumpled Will's letter in my hand. Miss Nightingale appeared from nowhere, it seemed, although she must have simply walked across from her quarters and I just didn't hear her. "I got a letter," I said. I couldn't think of anything else to tell her.

"Not bad news, I hope?" she said. She walked toward me and stood near, taking a quick glance at the watch she kept at her waist.

"No. At least, not yet."

"Not yet?" Now, instead of just that passing interest she often showed when her mind was caught up with some project, she looked into my eyes with the full force of hers. She had complicated eyes. You never knew exactly what she was thinking, or you saw in them so many different things that didn't make sense all together like that. Now whatever I'd said meant I would have to answer her.

"It's my friend Will. I used to work with him in service. He lent me the money to get to Folkestone, and now he's here, in Scutari. Going to Balaclava tomorrow, to the front."

Miss Nightingale walked closer. "Is this Will...a sweetheart of yours?"

Was he? Not really. At least, I didn't know for sure, especially now when I thought about Dr. Maclean. But he'd helped me more than a friend ever would. And he'd kissed me once. And I liked it. But did that mean he was my sweetheart?

"Molly? Are you certain everything is all right?"

"Yes. I mean, no. Will's not my sweetheart. He's just a good sort. And I'd like to pay him back the money I owe him now, just in case . . ." I couldn't finish the thought.

"Would you like permission for him to visit you here, in the common room, with a chaperone?"

I'd not even thought such a thing was possible. It would solve so many problems and make everything easy for me. "Could he?" Relief washed over me.

"Send him a note with one of the Turkish servants and tell him that he may visit at eight o'clock this evening, for one hour."

She looked at her watch again and hurried away before I had a chance to thank her. Would this start something with the others? Most of the nurses were too old to have sweethearts, although Emma had told me some of them did things with the healthier men on their rounds that made me blush to think about. Maybe having a visitor would give the others ideas, though, and we'd have all sorts of men coming in to sit and drink tea.

Whatever might happen because of it, there was no time to waste. I wrote a note as quickly as I could—my reading had got much faster, but I didn't have to write often so

I wasn't in practice—and sent one of the boys to the army camp with it. I went off to my evening shift in the strangest mood. I was happy and anxious at the same time. I wanted to see Will and yet I dreaded it. Once I gave him back his money, I wouldn't be in debt to him anymore. Or would I? I worried that Will would expect something more from me. I was afraid I'd disappoint him, just as I'd disappointed my mum. I spent the time until he came that evening wondering what I would say, how he would act. It almost spoiled the pleasure of looking forward to seeing the first familiar face in weeks.

Chapter 18

I sat with my back to the door, across the table from Mrs. Drake, whom Miss Nightingale asked to chaperone the visit. She had her knitting with her, I assumed so she'd have something else to look at besides us. Everyone seemed to think that Will and I meeting would be romantic. The more I said it wasn't so, the more they teased me.

"You just don't mind me," Mrs. Drake said. "A young girl should have beaus, even if she's a nurse with Miss Nightingale."

I started to protest again but decided not to bother when she winked at me for the tenth time that day. It was no use, and now I'd be blushing when Will arrived, which might give him the wrong idea.

So I sat there, not saying anything, just listening to the *click-click* of Mrs. Drake's knitting needles for what seemed an age. At last I heard the door open, and saw Will's arrival reflected in Mrs. Drake's face. She smiled at him. I didn't turn around until I heard his voice.

"I'm here to see Molly Fraser."

I don't know why it was his voice that first touched me. I stood up and ran to him, throwing my arms around his neck and enjoying the feeling of his strong arms squeezing me back. After a moment, when I thought maybe he would try to kiss me, I took hold of his shoulders and pushed away from him. "Let me look at you. You're just the same. Different uniform, though. I think this one suits you better." He seemed taller and straighter, and his shoulders a little broader. I didn't think he could have grown. Maybe my own memory had faded.

"You look . . . well," Will said. "I mean, very pretty but older."

"It's been hard. Come and sit with me. Fancy some tea?"

He shook his head no. He didn't sit but crushed his hat in his hands, looking at Mrs. Drake.

"Oh, this is Nurse Drake. She has to stay with us. It's a rule."

"Don't mind me," she said. "I'm just for show." She winked at me again. Now that she'd seen me greet Will so warmly the news would be all over in no time.

Will and I took two chairs a little away from Mrs. Drake. "What happened after I left? Why did you decide to join up?" I wanted him to talk about facts, solid things.

"I couldn't stand how they talked about you after you left, and that I couldn't defend you without making them think we were in on it all together. So I saw an advertisement in the paper that they needed more soldiers to fight in Russia, and I thought if you were brave enough to come, then I could be too."

I would have said that it didn't require bravery to be so far away from the front lines, but in my heart I knew it did. Bravery to watch men die, or recover as pale shadows of themselves. "I've seen many horrible things here," I said. "Promise me you'll be careful? Don't take chances you don't have to."

"Do you care what happens to me? Truly?" He reached for my hand. I didn't have the heart to pull it away, but I couldn't help feeling his touch on top of the place Dr. Maclean had kissed. I felt like a traitor.

"You know I do, Will. You're my only friend." Even as I said the words I could feel the effect they had on him.

"Friend? Is that it then? I wouldn't have done all I did for just a friend. You must know, Moll."

I took my hand away, resisting the urge to rub the spot on my wrist that now burned like a brand.

I didn't understand why I felt that way. It wasn't like Dr. Maclean had been as kind as Will, and I didn't know him, really. But I never before felt the way I did when Dr. Maclean looked at me. And a shock went right through me when he touched me. Now, I didn't dare look into Will's eyes, afraid he'd be able to read everything I was thinking and he'd hate me for it.

"I saw your mum before I left. She said to tell you she misses you, but not to worry. Young Ted has been making money at the docks." His voice was still gentle, but I could hear the longing in it, like what he was saying wasn't the same as what he meant.

And talking about my mum and Ted—it brought them right up to me like they were there, inside Will's heart. Touching him linked me to them. I reached out to him again. "Was she cross? About me going away?"

Will covered my hand with both of his. They were large and callused and warm. He smiled. "Not cross at all. She's very proud of what you're doing."

"Did you tell her—"

"No. There was no need for her to know what wasn't true anyway. But Molly, do you really just think of me as your friend?"

He leaned forward and lifted my chin so I had to look into his eyes. They were that clear, honest blue I remembered so well, a color that made me trust him, like they were letting me peer right inside his heart. And I knew they were searching mine for an answer. "I don't know," I said. "Things were so upside down when I left." It was as close to the truth as I could get.

He nodded and leaned back, relaxing his hold on me. "And you're so young."

I shook my head the tiniest bit, trying to send him a message that no one knew exactly how young I was, that Miss Nightingale thought I was at least nineteen. "Old enough to be a nurse," I said, trying to turn it into a joke.

"Not old enough to be married, though." He fixed me with his gaze again, leaning so close that he couldn't look at both my eyes at the same time but had to flick back and forth from one to the other. I had to force myself not to cast my eyes down again, to escape from the question that I knew was coming but I wasn't ready for. "When this is over, will you think about it? Will you, Moll?"

Marry Will. It was a crazy thought, half pleasing and half terrifying. Why would he want to after everything that had happened? "I don't know." I felt stupid, not able to say anything else. And I could feel Mrs. Drake listening, wondering if she'd heard it all and what she'd tell the others.

"I see." The sadness in Will's voice stabbed my heart and the eager light faded from his eyes.

"Oh, Will, you know I care about you very much, and I'm so grateful for what you did. Here." I fished in my pocket and handed him a little pouch I'd sewn with most of the money I owed him in it.

"What's this?"

He brightened up when I gave him the pouch, and I realized he must have thought I had made some kind of present for him to take to the front, some token for luck. I was suddenly ashamed and wished I'd thought of making him a handkerchief or something. "It's not all of it, but most of the money you lent me, for the train."

All at once, the door that had welcomed me through his eyes and into his heart slammed shut. I had wounded him deeply, and he'd not set a foot on a battlefield yet. He stuffed the pouch in his jacket pocket and stood.

"I have to get back to camp, Miss Fraser." He bowed to me, formal and stiff, as he used to bow to Mr. Abington-Smythe. I wanted to cry, to beg him to start his visit over again, to let me make it come out differently.

I bit my lower lip. What was I doing? This honorable young man who talked of marrying me was going off to war, and I was letting him leave without a word of encouragement. It wasn't too late, if I was brave enough.

"Will!" I called to him as he walked away. He stopped and turned. I ran to him and rose up on my tiptoes. I intended to kiss his cheek, an affectionate sign that wouldn't mean too much. But he turned and met my lips with his, trembling. I reached my arms around his neck and whispered into his ear. "I will think about it."

He gave me a smile so full of hope and love it hurt, then turned and walked out, his head high and shoulders set.

<hr />

"So," Emma said as we got ready for bed that night, "you've got two beaus, it seems."

"Don't say that! I haven't got any." Sometimes Emma's teasing really annoyed me. Especially when she was so wrong and I couldn't find any way to convince her of it.

"That's not what Mrs. Drake is telling everyone she sees. How 'poor you' sent your fiancé off to the front."

My fiancé! How would I squash that rumor? "Don't poke fun at something you don't understand. I'm just grateful to Will is all. And he is not my fiancé."

"I suppose that depends on how you show your gratitude." She nudged me with her shoulder.

"I showed it by paying him back the money he lent me so I could get to Folkestone and come here. Nothing else."

She pursed her lips into a kissing shape but didn't say anything. Just before we blew out the lamp on the table between our beds, Emma said, "You know it's just a bit of fun, Moll, don't you? I don't want you to feel hurt by what I said."

I rolled onto my side and propped my head up on my hand. "I know. But I wish you wouldn't tease sometimes. It's complicated with Will."

"Was it always? I mean, what if you hadn't met Dr. Maclean?" She leaned forward so we could talk more quietly.

"Dr. Maclean is nothing to me! He's a doctor and I'm a nurse."

"Haven't you noticed that he always manages to be in the wards when you are?"

"All of the doctors are in the wards." I rolled onto my back. Was it true, what she said? I had noticed but didn't want to make anything of it. And he always greeted me and asked me about cases.

"You may be blind, but I'm not. You watch yourself,

Miss Molly. Or you'll be the one who gets sent home for fraternizing. And I wouldn't like that one bit."

Maybe Emma said that just because if I went, she wouldn't have anyone to cover for her when she broke the rules. Even so, I was glad she said it.

Chapter 19

Our short reprieve from the shiploads of wounded didn't last long. But Miss Stanley's new nurses were still not employed.

"We expect to receive another seven hundred men by ship any day," said Miss Nightingale. "As you all know, the wards are completely full and all that are able to be discharged have been. And despite the efforts of Lady Stratford de Redcliffe, work in the wards has not progressed because the men she had hired went on strike almost immediately. Therefore, I have taken matters into my own hands and hired two hundred Turkish workmen to repair the dilapidated hospital wings, which have enough room for an additional eight hundred men."

Miss Nightingale walked up and down in front of us in the common room like she was giving orders to a battalion of soldiers. Lady Stratford de Redcliffe was another one of her personal skirmishes. She'd come from the embassy, sweeping in as if she could accomplish everything Miss Nightingale still hadn't got to. But everyone underestimated Miss

Nightingale's strength of purpose. If she couldn't do it, it couldn't be done.

"Mr. Macdonald has graciously been supplying us with much needed materials, and I have requested hair mattresses and more wooden beds. I have no intention of returning us to the task of stuffing mattresses."

A sigh of relief went round the room.

"Because I shall be much occupied with supervising the reconstruction of the dilapidated wards, I have decided that some of the new nurses, the ones who arrived without my sanction, can be employed in the hospital. In addition, a new hospital is being built a short distance away, at Koulali, and I have every hope that they will find adequate employment there once it is completed."

Although I didn't know everything that was going on, I could tell Miss Nightingale was pleased that she had stopped the others from interfering with her. Sometimes I worried that she was trying so hard to get things done that she made more enemies than she needed to. And yet she cared very much about everything and everyone. I never begrudged her for it, not like some of the others—including Emma. Thinking back to when we arrived, the hospital was now a completely different place thanks to her. Who else would have been able to bring such order to the mess? Men's wounds were now cleaned and dressings changed regularly; everyone had mattresses and most also had beds for the mattresses to lie upon; everyone got the food they were supposed to, three times a day. Even the rats obeyed her and were much less bold than they were when we first arrived. The latrines, too, had been dug deeper so the stench didn't come into the wards. She seemed to have power to do things beyond a normal lady's abilities. I adored her.

"There is another small matter that also demands our attention. That is that I have been made aware of certain needs of the soldiers' wives, who have followed their husbands to war. It seems there are a number of imminent births. I have requested a separate basement ward for the purpose of creating a lying-in hospital."

She assigned two of the older nurses to be ready to assist at births if necessary.

I supposed it must have been so she could give the lowest duties to the new nurses, but Emma and I found ourselves suddenly on shifts where we had to do more of what you'd call real nursing. And I was quite surprised that first day to find I'd been assigned to follow Dr. Maclean on his rounds in a ward that had some of the most critically injured men.

"I'm glad it's you, Molly—Nurse Fraser," he said when I arrived with an armload of towels and a basket of clean bandages.

I didn't dare really look at him. I hoped we could simply be two people working together, instead of that frightening state where we weren't quite friends, but almost something more.

"This fellow's had an amputation and we must see how his stump is healing," Dr. Maclean said, talking to me as if I were another doctor. I tried to pretend I was used to it, that there was nothing more normal to me than being on an equal footing with a medical man, and said nothing. "Kindly unwrap the wound for me, Nurse," he said.

The fellow's leg had been removed just above the knee. I folded the blanket back so it only revealed the bandaged stump and set my fingers to untying the tight knot the surgeon had made in the gauze. It was stiff with dried blood.

"Use these," Dr. Maclean said, handing me a pair of scissors with angled blades and a dull edge on one side. "They're made so you can slip them under a bandage and cut without hurting the patient."

My hands trembled a little, but I snipped the tied gauze and then unwound it. As I got closer to the wound, I could see that the blood had seeped through and I thought it might pull at the man's skin. I looked into his face.

"Don't mind, miss. You can't hurt me."

He had stubbly growth on his face and his cheeks were ashy gray. Despite what he said, I was afraid. Dr. Maclean gently took the bandage out of my hand and continued the job.

"There, it's healing well, my man," he said. "Take a look, Nurse Fraser."

He stood aside so I could see. After standing by when so many open wounds were being treated, I didn't hesitate to look. And it was a very clean-looking stump. I could see the stitches criss-crossing in the middle.

"Let's clean it off and then wrap it up again," Dr. Maclean said, handing me a soft cloth soaked in fresh water.

I gently patted the wound, cleaning away the dried blood until it looked almost like the edges of a torn sheet that had been sewed together with black thread.

"Now watch while I put a fresh bandage on."

I was so intent on what we were doing, really fascinated by seeing how a wound could heal and someone who had been badly injured could be made nearly whole again, that I didn't hear anyone walking up to us and jumped at the sound of the voice.

"Maclean! What do you think you're doing?" It was Dr. Menzies.

"I'm taking care of this man's stump, sir," Dr. Maclean said, continuing what he was doing without so much as looking round.

"Do you suppose we have an excess of bandages and can afford to wrap a perfectly good surgery more than once?"

I shrank back out of the way, leaving the two doctors near the patient. I saw that the bandage had been dirty and needed changing. Would they really have left him in his original, bloody bandage until it was time to fit him with a wooden leg?

"I'm nearly done here, then we can go and discuss this— that is, if you consider it important enough to take me off the ward where there is much to do."

The muscles in Dr. Menzies's jaw tensed. *Any minute now he's going to bellow*, I thought. But instead, he turned on the ball of his foot and marched past me, so close he brushed my skirt, without so much as a glance in my direction.

Dr. Maclean said nothing. I continued to follow him on his rounds for the next two hours. By the end, I was binding up wounds myself.

The next day I was assigned to him again. And again he took me around, showing me how to do things, letting me watch as he administered poultices, checked pulses, removed bandages, and bound them up again. Every so often he'd ask me to do something as if I'd been doing it all along.

At the end of the ward lay a man as still as death. At first I thought his soul had already fled to heaven, but Dr. Maclean took hold of the man's wrist and pressed it for a few moments.

"He's alive, but very weak. I don't know what could have happened to the fellow. I admitted him myself a few days ago with a clean bayonet wound." As he spoke he took my hand and, using his own as a guide, pressed my fingers around the soldier's wrist just as he had done before. "Feel it?"

I did. It was a soft pulsing, rather slow.

"Let's check his wound."

This fellow's injury was low in his belly. Dr. Maclean whisked the sheet off quickly, exposing the unconscious fellow's privates. I looked away quickly, but not before my cheeks burned.

"Come now, Nurse Fraser! It's only the human body." He was teasing me, but he pulled the sheet up so the soldier was partially covered. "And there's no time to be modest. Something's gone wrong with this fellow."

The wound was bandaged and it didn't look like blood

or pus seeped through it. "You unbind it while I check the rest of him."

It was different taking a bandage off the tender part of a soldier. As was the usual practice, someone had wrapped the gauze right around his back, so I could only snip through all the layers and let the orderlies—or Dr. Maclean—lift him to remove the gauze later.

It wasn't long before I revealed his scar. Most of it looked clean and was stitched up nicely. But a little bit down lower, toward his right side, looked funny. His belly was swollen around it. "Dr. Maclean, I think something's wrong here."

He left what he was doing and came right over. "You're right. There's some infection. The only thing to do, if my tutors were correct, is to open him up and drain it. The man's burning with fever and unconscious. Will you help me?"

I should have been more afraid than I was, but all I could think of then was doing something to help the suffering soldier, who'd survived a bayonet wound only to have it go septic. "I'll fetch the screen," I said, heading down to where they were kept at the end of the ward to use for surgeries.

By the time I struggled back with the folding wooden frame with fabric stretched over it, Dr. Maclean had taken a scalpel from his bag. I quickly shielded us from the view of the other patients. "Won't you need chloroform?" I asked as he put the point of the scalpel just below the wound, where the soldier's belly bulged out the most. "And a basin?"

"There's no time for chloroform," he said, "but fetch a basin, quickly!"

Again I hurried, this time to the supply cupboard, where I also grabbed a few more towels. I hoped Dr. Maclean had all he needed in his kit to stitch the fellow up again when he was done.

"Steady now. You can look away if you want to," he said. I shook my head and stayed staring at the razor-sharp blade as it pierced through the skin. The soldier gave a shudder but didn't wake up. *Thank God*, I thought.

At first, nothing happened. Then, as he stuck the blade in deeper, all manner of liquid and blood started pouring out of the slit. I tried to position the basin to catch it, but there was an awful mess. It wasn't long before the oozing stopped. Dr. Maclean straightened up. "That's not right. There should be more. How is the man's pulse, Nurse Fraser?"

I took his wrist and felt it the way Dr. Maclean had showed me. If anything, the pulse was weaker than before. "I can barely feel it."

"He'll die if we don't get to the bottom of this," Dr. Maclean said, and without hesitating he made a much longer and deeper incision with the scalpel. "That's it!" he said, sounding as if he'd discovered treasure. "The appendix. It's nearly ruptured and must be removed immediately. Use these clamps to hold the skin apart."

He gave me two instruments that looked like scissors, only they weren't sharp and when I pressed them shut they locked. Without hesitating I took each side of the new wound with the instruments, locked them, and opened up the cavity farther. Blood flowed freely. "Won't he bleed to death?" I asked.

"I have to be quick." Plunging his fingers in confidently but gently, Dr. Maclean teased something out that looked like a mottled sausage, and in seconds had cut it away. Then he mopped up as best he could. I released the clamps when he told me to. "While I hold the wound shut, get the thread and needle, the curved one, from my kit. You'll have to sew it together."

Except that I wouldn't have wanted to do the holding the way he was, I felt queasy thinking about what he was asking me to do.

I found everything he described and threaded the needle. I was about to put a knot in the end like we did for sewing stump pillows.

"Don't knot it first," he said. "Leave the end hanging and tie it tight after you've made the stitch."

With Dr. Maclean's soothing, calm voice in my ear, I put a dozen stitches in the soldier's abdomen. They weren't all the same size but they worked. The wound was closed, and the blood stopped.

Between the two of us we made short work of bandaging the fellow again. Only after we'd finished completely did I look up at Dr. Maclean. Drips of sweat still trickled down from his hairline to his chin, but he glowed. "We did it, Molly!" I tried not to notice the change from Nurse Fraser to Molly. "I've only seen that procedure done in textbooks, although it's not uncommon. Not really the kind of thing we normally have to deal with here."

I didn't want to admit that I didn't know what he meant. Whatever it was, I could see that our soldier had survived it. He was breathing slowly. I felt his pulse. It was still there, although hardly stronger than before.

"He'll have to be watched carefully. Will you check on him whenever you can? I never know where they'll make me go."

Dr. Maclean drew nearer to me until I realized we were only a breath apart from each other. His eyes shone with something—excitement, I thought, but perhaps something else. I searched them for an answer.

Suddenly, he closed the distance between us and kissed me softly on the mouth. I felt his tongue tasting my lips and teeth. I did nothing, but I didn't push him away. I was washed over with a warmth that came from deep inside me. Then he pulled away, turning to examine the patient again as if nothing had happened.

I was about to say I didn't know if my own schedule would allow me to check in on this fellow we'd just operated on, but at that moment I looked up to see the thunderous face of Miss Nightingale, holding her lamp high.

Chapter 20

"Miss Nightingale!" I was so shocked I almost yelled it out. How long had she been there? I knew I was blushing. I felt the blood beating in my veins.

Dr. Maclean continued his examination of the soldier and only turned when I said her name. He responded to her angry look with a smile. "Ah! Your Nurse Fraser has been a valuable help to me. I have just performed an appendectomy. The poor fellow would have died. Now at least there's a chance he'll make it."

Miss Nightingale did not alter her expression of fury, but she said nothing in front of Dr. Maclean except, "Nurse Fraser, your shift ended half an hour ago. If you do not return straight away to our quarters you'll miss supper." I could tell that she wanted to say a great deal more than that. I bobbed a curtsy to both of them and walked off, trying not to cower or run, both of which I dearly wanted to do.

"Where were you?" Emma said in a hoarse, indiscreet

whisper. Everyone at the dining table quieted down, no doubt so they could hear what I had to say.

"I had to help a doctor with an emergency," I said, unwilling to add any more details. No doubt it would get around quickly enough.

Emma nudged me in the ribs. By the look on her face, I could tell she thought I was dallying with Dr. Maclean, not nursing. I wanted to explain it all to her, but I knew she'd think I was only making it up, so what was the use?

The stew tasted dusty in my mouth, and I could feel every swallow trace its way down to my stomach. I hoped it wouldn't come back up the same way, which sometimes happened when I was very upset.

I don't know where Miss Nightingale went or what she did, but she didn't return until we were about to get ready to retire for the night.

"Fraser, a word," she said, not even pausing as she passed through on the way to her rooms in the tower. I didn't look at Emma, just stood and followed Miss Nightingale, whose lamp was the only illumination for the dark stairs that led up to her office.

I followed her in. "Close the door," she said. "Sit."

Could it be that she would send me home when I was just beginning to learn something?

"Tell me exactly what you did, what Dr. Maclean did, and how you came to be alone with him in that particular ward."

I wanted to say that we weren't alone, because we weren't.

But I knew that in her view the soldiers didn't count. I was the only female there. I should have realized and insisted someone else come along, but I forgot. But then there would have been no kiss . . .

And so I told her about the man's infection and how I saw the swelling below his wound. When I was describing the operation to her she leaned forward, as if she wanted to catch every word. She even interrupted to ask me questions now and again. When I'd said it all, she stayed quiet for a minute or two.

"Fraser, you have overstepped the bounds of our duties here in Scutari. We must not presume to take on the role of doctor to these patients. We are here to assist only, to nurse the patients back to health by obeying the doctors' orders."

I wanted to point out that I had been acting on a doctor's orders, but something told me she wouldn't take kindly to that observation.

"For the next week, you are not permitted on the wards. You are to help Mrs. Clarke in the kitchen and to clean our quarters. Only in the event of an emergency will I release you to perform nursing duties." She took up her pen and a pile of papers and without looking up at me said, "You may go now."

I stood, my knees barely able to support me. Not allowed on the wards! It simply wasn't fair. How would I check on that soldier? What if he died? I thought I'd left all that misjudging and mistaking behind me in London, but it appeared that people were just as quick to jump to conclusions half-way across the globe.

As soon as I entered the room Emma came running up to me through the dark dormitory, where half the beds' occupants already snored. "What happened? Tell me!"

I shook my head, threw myself down on my cot, and let the tears flow into my pillow.

The week passed more quickly than I thought it would, and without any fanfare I noticed that my name had reappeared on the roster. I wanted to go look for the man whose appendix Dr. Maclean had removed, but I knew if I did I'd risk Miss Nightingale's wrath again, and I might not be so lucky to get only a week's exile from the wards.

In fact I hardly saw Dr. Maclean, except from a distance. He always seemed to be with another doctor, although there were few enough of them to spare.

The next couple of months went on in a sort of pattern. Shiploads of wounded and sick arrived, were treated, and straggled out of the hospital by getting better or dying. The new nurses prepared to work in the new hospital in Koulali, while some of the nuns under Mother Bridgeman finally agreed to be split up and take shifts in the Barrack Hospital. Five soldiers' wives had babies, making the lying-in hospital another triumph of Miss Nightingale's.

With Mrs. Clarke to run things on a daily basis, we didn't see much of Miss Nightingale in our quarters. She was always busy doing something, and it usually involved a dispute. There was a big to-do when the nuns were accused of preaching religion to the dying men, no matter their beliefs. Then Miss Nightingale went on a tear that the doctors weren't following the rules of hygiene she'd set up, and the sick were mixed in with the wounded. Always there was an issue with supplies. They didn't arrive on time. There weren't enough of them. They were the wrong ones.

In December I got a letter from Will, who wrote me the night before he went into a big battle.

Dear Molly,

I want you to know that thinking of you, considering what I asked you, has kept me going these weeks. Tomorrow is bound to be a hot one, they say, although the winter weather is bitter and I've nearly lost a finger to frostbite. They've taught me how to use the Minié rifle. It's very accurate. As long as we have a clear shot, we can hit them before their shotguns or pistols are close to being able to reach us. Only the big guns have a longer range. There's always danger from them.

But why am I telling you this? I thought I'd reassure you if you knew I had a good rifle—and God—on my side. I expect the Russians claim God as well. It's so strange. Anyway, I just wanted to say you're a good girl and smart too, and whatever happens to me you'll be all right.

If I don't come out of this, visit Lucy. She's very fond of you.

Love,
Will

I had put Will in a little pocket of my mind before then. Suddenly he was back, a thought I couldn't ignore. It would be one of my worst nightmares to have him turn up wounded or sick at the Barrack Hospital. So many of the men were near to death by the time they got to us, the less serious ones having been treated in the field and sent back to fight as soon as they were able. The lucky ones we saw were sent only to get more care or another surgery they couldn't do on the battlefield. And what was interesting, something Sister Sarah Anne pointed out, was that the ones who had amputations right away in the field were much less likely to die than the ones who had to wait until they got to us. She thought it was because there was time for the wound to fester on the slow journey across the Black Sea. I sometimes wondered if the pain was more bearable when you saw how many didn't make it, so you stood it all the better.

Whatever it was, Emma and I checked the casualty lists every day. She looked for her Thomas, and I looked for Will. We were always relieved not to find their names there. I began to wonder after a bit why I didn't get any more letters from him if he wasn't wounded or dead. But I imagined it was hard at the front lines, and maybe they couldn't even get paper and a pencil to write with.

That December and January were awful. Not only was the weather bad in Scutari, but it seemed the army hadn't counted on how hard the winter would be in the Crimea. All the soldiers who came to us were tired and worn out as well as half frozen, so sickness and frostbite became as dangerous as the Russian guns.

"They have no warm clothing! How could the army have been so negligent?" Miss Nightingale complained to no one in particular as she took her tea, staring out the window at snow swirling in the air. We were all busy in our spare time knitting socks and mufflers for the men in the wards. Mrs. Drake taught me so I could do it well enough, but it took me longer than the others. Still, it kept my hands busy and my mind off the cold wind that whistled in through the cracks throughout the whole building. Sometimes in the morning there would be a light coating of frost on the men's blankets. The stoves in each ward were no match for that kind of cold. At least in the winter, and with the deeper latrines, the foul smell from the sewage was not so bad. And when the wind blew from the other direction we couldn't smell the corpses buried in shallow graves in the nearby cemetery—a worse smell, I thought, than the other.

One day in February, when the cold was brutal and there was no way to keep warm, Emma and I stayed close together while we checked the men's dressings to make sure they didn't need changing. I made sure, after all that happened with Dr. Maclean and the surgery, to have another nurse with me all the time.

"You remind me of my sweetheart back 'ome," leered one fellow with a stump where his hand had been. "Gi' us a kiss, for old time's sake!" Any of the men who were conscious nearby laughed or whistled.

"Fraser!"

The call came from one end of the ward, and I knew without looking that it was Miss Nightingale. She probably thought I was fraternizing when I hadn't done anything at all, it was just the way the men were. I stood straight and walked quickly with my chin up to where she stood, just as she'd taught us to do, not looking at any of the men in spite of their clucking and whistles. "Yes, Miss Nightingale?" I said.

"I would like to speak with you, along with a few of the others. Come with me."

I followed where she led, toward the stairs that went up to another of the corner towers where the doctors had their offices. What now? Was I being called up in front of the doctors for what had happened with Dr. Maclean in November? Did they think I was wrong to assist him in that surgery? We'd saved the man's life, I learned, though I never saw him again. I hadn't so much as looked at Dr. Maclean since then, and he seemed to avoid me as well. Perhaps Miss Nightingale, among her other powers, could look into our minds while we slept. I could feel my cheeks becoming hot with shame. What if she had seen the kiss and just hadn't bothered to say? *Impossible*, I thought. *She'd certainly have sent me home for that.* I made myself breathe deeply to slow the wild pounding of my heart.

We went into an office where I saw Mrs. Drake, Mrs. Langston, Sister Turnbull, Nurse Roberts, and Nurse Hawkins sitting in chairs and Dr. Menzies at a table piled high with papers. Now I was certain I was in trouble.

"Please sit over there," Miss Nightingale said, pointing to a chair next to Mrs. Drake, and took a seat herself somewhat off to the side.

"Thank you for coming, ladies," Dr. Menzies said. I could feel Miss Nightingale flinch. She had repeatedly insisted we were not ladies, but nurses. Dr. Menzies ignored her. "I have a proposition to put to you that you are free to decline, but that would greatly enhance our ability to care for the wounded before we subject them to a hazardous voyage on the Black Sea. It is the wish of Lord Raglan, commander of the army, that we open a small army hospital in the Crimea, near enough to the front for the injured to be treated quickly but not so near as to put any of you in danger."

He paused to let his words sink in. I looked toward Miss Nightingale. She sat perfectly straight in her chair, the black silk of her dress not showing the slightest crease or wear, every hair on her head so smooth it looked like a tight black cap beneath her white one. Her eyes drilled into Dr. Menzies. I couldn't tell whether she was excited or angry. She looked as though she could spring out of her seat at any moment and fly across the room.

"I have not yet selected the doctors who are to be stationed there, but Miss Nightingale has chosen you from among her staff as those most capable of enduring the hardships of the front. She will accompany you in the beginning and see to the establishment of the hospital, and then we shall decide the permanent arrangements."

I didn't understand at first that I wasn't going to get a drubbing. That actually I'd been singled out with several other nurses that I knew were good at what they did, and we were going to do something exciting and dangerous.

"I have my doubts about the wisdom of creating a field hospital. It will be impossible to run it in such a way that will promote regularity and cleanliness."

How could Miss Nightingale not want a field hospital? Sure, it wouldn't be as organized as the Barrack Hospital and the General Hospital, but treating wounds quickly might save many lives.

"Your reservations have been duly noted, and I agree with them in principle," Dr. Menzies continued. "But we cannot disregard the wishes of Lord Raglan." He turned to the rest of us. "I will give you twenty-four hours to make your decision about whether you wish to be part of this experiment or not. If you do, you will sail in three days for Balaclava."

"I need no time to decide, Dr. Menzies. I shall gladly accept the challenge." It was Mrs. Langston, head of the Sellonites. Sister Turnbull soon said the same and Mrs. Drake chimed in as well, although she looked at me first as if wondering what I would say. After that, Mrs. Roberts and Mrs. Hawkins—the other two nurses—agreed too, leaving only me.

I looked from Miss Nightingale to the others. What would she want me to do? She had clearly chosen me. But what about Emma? "I'll go too," I said. The words leapt out before I even realized what I was saying, before I had time to regret anything.

When we returned to our rooms in the hospital later that day, everyone was talking about us. Except Emma. She looked at me as if I had betrayed her. I couldn't understand why. She didn't need me there. She of all of us was capable of finding ways to have a lark in spite of the regulations and had got on well with her nursing. With her Thomas gone off to the front, I often noticed that she amused herself by flirting with some of the younger, less badly wounded men. I pointed it out to her that evening after we'd got into bed.

"That don't mean nothing," Emma said. "It's only a bit of fun for the men. Helps 'em get better faster."

"But why are you so upset? I won't stay there forever, you know. And anyway, it's just a trial, to see if it helps."

Emma rolled on her back and looked up at the cracked ceiling. "It's only—I was counting on having you here. Someone else wanting a fellow to be safe at the front. Not these old dames or them religious, holier-than-spit nuns and sisters. And there's sure to be more work to do when you're gone."

I decided it wasn't worth mentioning that since the wards had been cleaned up and everything put on a more regular footing by Miss Nightingale there wasn't so much to do.

Even the wives seemed to have obliged us by not giving birth lately. There was something else bothering her, but she didn't want to tell me. I figured I'd find it out eventually.

We stopped talking when Miss Nightingale and two of the Sellonite sisters returned from their evening rounds. The sisters climbed immediately up to their room. Miss Nightingale, I knew, would spend several hours yet writing letters; requests for supplies, trying to get Miss Stanley's nurses out of her hospital, trying to convince everyone else to agree with her ideas of what was necessary and proper. Mrs. Bracebridge brought her new candles every evening, and Mrs. Clarke had complained about the amount of oil she burned up in her lamps. There was no doubt in my mind that the Barrack Hospital was Miss Nightingale's, whatever Dr. Menzies liked to think.

It wasn't until everything was quiet that I thought about that other party that would go to Balaclava, those who Dr. Menzies hadn't chosen yet. Which doctors would they select to come with us? We might work with the regimental doctors who were already there, who were used to operating in trenches with bullets flying overhead. I'd heard about them from some of the men in our hospital. *Please, God,* I prayed as I felt my eyes closing in spite of the excitement, *don't let it be Dr. Maclean who comes with us.* I meant it, in my head. But my heart did a little flutter inside me as I said the name to myself, and I knew I secretly hoped for the opposite.

Another change. Another sea voyage. And who knew what we'd find on the other side? Will was there somewhere. Perhaps I would see him. Another good reason for Dr. Maclean to stay in Scutari.

Chapter 21

The time passed very quickly. The day before we were to leave, Emma and I watched from our window as the Turkish dockworkers took crates out to the ship, where it rocked at anchor in the port. Salt pork. Bandages. Arrowroot. "Won't hardly be room for you," she said, one of the few times she acknowledged that I was going instead of maintaining a determined silence about it.

When the day arrived, we gathered with our valises—none of us had much to take, only a uniform to wear and a few personal things—before walking in twos to the dock.

"Where's Emma?" I asked Mrs. Drake.

"Dunno," she answered. "She's an odd one, that. I would've thought she'd be here to say good-bye, being your particular friend and all."

I didn't say anything, but my eyes ached with the threat of tears. I knew she didn't want me to go, but how could she not even come down to the dock to say good-bye, like everyone else? Aside from Will and Ted, Emma was the closest thing I'd ever had to a friend.

I decided I would write her a letter. That would please her. With no family back home she never got letters. She'd not even received one from her Thomas since he'd gone to the front.

Every once in a while as we walked through the town— past the market where I'd seen the old lady whose words I imagined speaking in my head and where Emma used to get me to cover for her when she went to see Thomas—I looked around, just to see if she might come running after us, perhaps regretting that she didn't wish me luck. But there was no one. Just the usual traffic of Turkish matrons going to and from the market with their baskets.

I was so caught up with wondering about Emma that I almost didn't notice Dr. Maclean standing in the stern of the ship, smoking his pipe. I caught sight of him just before I took the first step off the gangplank and onto the deck, nearly losing my footing.

He turned, as though he could feel me looking at him, and I turned away as soon as he saw me. But it wasn't soon enough to stop my heart from racing.

I would have to stay out of his way, make sure he didn't smile and wave at me, or Miss Nightingale would be furious. I knew the best way would be to stay as much as I could in our cabin below. He would never go there.

But I didn't want to close myself up in the little room

that'd no doubt be crawling with vermin and stinking of old rum. I liked to be on deck where I could feel the wind and look out over the waves, even though last time it had been so frightening. The time holed up in the cabin stuck in my mind even more; the smell of it, and not knowing what was happening outside. At least for this voyage all the nurses except Miss Nightingale claimed to be good sailors, so with luck I wouldn't spend my time mopping up vomit.

I stayed out as long as I could and watched Scutari and Istanbul disappear behind us. Dr. Maclean went below, I was relieved to see, but also disappointed. Perhaps I had offended him by not nodding to him or saying hello. But I couldn't. Surely he'd understand that.

After not more than a quarter of an hour my fingers got so cold I worried I'd get frostbite, so I made my way to the hatch that led down to the cabins.

"Pssst!"

I thought it was the ship's cat hissing at me, so I kept walking.

"Pssst! Molly!"

No. Not a cat. I turned around, looking to see where the voice came from. The wind, the ship creaking, and the sails flapping put up quite a din of their own. And at first I didn't see anyone.

"Over 'ere!"

Then I spotted something. A hand, poking out from under a tarpaulin covering one of the lifeboats that were lashed to the deck. A hand I recognized. I quickly glanced round. The sailors were all busy with the tasks of managing the sails and navigating us out into the open sea, and I was the only passenger that hadn't yet gone below out of the cold. Except for Emma, who'd managed to get herself into the lifeboat without anyone knowing.

"What are you doing here?" I had to speak loudly enough for Emma to hear me but didn't want to alert any of the sailors to the fact that we had a stowaway. Meanwhile I untied one or two of the ropes that held the tarp down so I could see her. She was wearing her nurse's uniform and had even brought her valise.

"You think I was goin' to let you go off all on yer own to see my Thomas and maybe flirt with him?"

I knew she was just joking. She wanted to see Thomas. That was her reason. I didn't know why I hadn't thought of it before, it was so obvious. That explained why she was so mad at me when she found out I was going. "Emma, why didn't you say?" I asked. "It's going to be dangerous, and you won't probably run into Thomas anyway in Balaclava. He might be miles away."

"I have to see him. I just have to."

Tears sprang to Emma's eyes. "Emma, what's wrong?" It wasn't like her to cry so easily.

"You wouldn't understand."

"Well, whatever it is, you can't stay here for three days. You'll freeze to death. You'll have to come below and own up."

She looked down. "Miss Nightingale won't half be cross."

197

If she was just cross, Emma would be lucky. Fortunately, not even Miss Nightingale would throw someone overboard because she disobeyed her. "I'll try to make things right with her. She might be too sick to care right now, anyway."

I helped Emma crawl out of the lifeboat and straighten her uniform, then we went down to the cabin. When the two of us walked in, Mrs. Langston's mouth opened wide.

"At the last minute Miss Nightingale asked Emma to come along," I said. With Miss Nightingale in her cabin and not likely to come out for a while, I decided it would be better to lie just a little. How bad was it, after all, that Emma was there? There were plenty of nurses at the Barrack Hospital to manage, even if another few hundred wounded arrived. And things had slowed down a lot lately anyhow. We were in the middle of the Siege of Sebastopol, or so I'd heard. That meant a lot of waiting and hiding in trenches for the men, and not too many actual battles. More men came back sick with dysentery and low fevers than wounded.

We had a quiet sail across the Black Sea. No storms. It wasn't icy—the water was too salty for that. Just cold, so we stayed mostly in our stuffy cabin. I was glad Emma came in the end. We played cards and guessing games to pass the time. The others mostly read. Mrs. Langston and the other Sellonite sister prayed a lot and talked about nursing. Mrs. Drake, once she got over her disapproving looks at Emma, spent her time knitting and sleeping. I only saw Dr. Maclean once, when we went up on deck for a breath of air on a day when the wind died down a little. Something made me turn toward the stern and I saw him there, staring in my direction, smoking his pipe. He raised his hand to wave, but I turned away, just like last time. It would be folly to be friendly with him. Still, it pained me not to let him see that I knew he was there, and that I was mostly glad to see him. It would be much simpler if he paid no attention to me at all.

We didn't see Miss Nightingale until we got to the peninsula, the Crimea. This was the place all the fighting was for, so Mrs. Langston told us. We needed to beat the Russians back, not let them get a foothold past their borders. I asked her why.

"It's very complicated. As far as I understand, things are balanced now, with England, France, and Austria powerful in the west of Europe, and Russia in the east. We don't want Russia to get too powerful, especially if she unites with Austria. It's a way of keeping the peace all over Europe."

"So we are at war so we may have peace?" I asked, still not understanding.

"In a sense."

I didn't ask her anything more after that. It all seemed pointless. So many already dead or maimed, and it wasn't even England we were fighting over. But as we approached shore we would see where the battles were firsthand. Everyone came on deck for that. It was a sight I'll never forget.

"Look at all them ships!" Emma exclaimed. I made sure she was on the side of me that was away from Miss Nightingale, who stood farther down the deck. But everyone was so amazed by the sight of all the British, French, and Turkish ships carpeting the sea, bobbing up and down at anchor or slowly moving closer or farther away from shore, that I'd have been surprised if anyone noticed her.

"Why don't they sail into the harbor and attack Sebastopol from the water?" I wondered aloud. The city came right down to the water, like Istanbul did, and from what little I knew it looked easy to attack that way. But the British and French ships were all clustered at the mouth of the harbor, like an invisible fence kept them away.

Mrs. Langston answered. "The Russians sank several of their warships on purpose, just over there"—she pointed to the harbor—"so our fleets couldn't pass."

Of course. There was a fence after all. A lethal trap under the water.

But not all of the vessels gathered around us were warships. One not far off—close enough for me to make out the women in deck chairs with binoculars, staring at the shore—would've looked like a pleasure ship in any other place. Banners flew from the masts, and I could see waiters serving wine in tall glasses to the ladies sitting on deck in their furs.

Nurse Drake was on my other side. "They've come to watch the lovely war," she said. "See our brave men fight and get killed."

If they never got closer than they were then to the battles, it might seem glorious, I thought. They wouldn't see the fear and pain on the men's faces, just where they moved, like the painted lead soldiers rich children played with. The red coats of the

British brightened up the gray countryside. Every now and then a puff of white smoke would come from above Sebastopol, followed by a distant boom. Like fireworks during the day, but instead they were guns. I saw up close what they did to soldiers, and it wasn't glorious or pretty. I wanted someone to commandeer that sightseeing ship for a few hundred sick and wounded, and then see how thrilling the fine ladies thought it all was!

We had to sail around a small spit of land to get to Balaclava, a village on the other side of the hills that protected Sebastopol. We were able to dock at a sheltered harbor, but when the gangplank was lowered and the sailors scrambled down to help fasten ropes to the pier they sank ankle deep in mud. We could hear the squelching and sucking from on deck, not to mention the foul mouths of the men as they began to unload in the muck. How would we get through it ourselves?

The buildings by the dock were half fallen down, made of wood and stone with thatched roofs. Bony, underfed cows and oxen watched what went on around them with no apparent interest. Dock workers started laying planks over the mud so the passengers could walk up to where the ground was less muddy, though I couldn't see that it would help much, and so I wandered to the other side of the ship to see what was there while we waited to go on shore.

There was nothing more than barren earth patched with snow, climbing into the hills that rose between Balaclava and Sebastopol. Dotted around everywhere were round tents, in rows and groups, in any spare bit of ground near the town. With just a stretch of canvas and a pole to hold them up in the middle, the tents couldn't have provided more than the barest shelter against the winter cold. Here and there amongst them was a wooden hut with a chimney, so no doubt at least a stove inside. And soldiers wandered everywhere. Some were in smart uniforms, looking like they were on their way somewhere in a hurry. Others dragged themselves around, dirty and ragged, like they couldn't find a place to stop and rest. Most of them had long, bushy beards. I guessed they didn't have water and soap for shaving.

Beyond the camps, the houses in the town seemed to be thrown against the hillside, clinging however they could, only a few fitted with roofs that looked as though they wouldn't let in a steady rain.

The narrow harbor was dotted with smaller boats going in and out, dodging obstacles in the water. At first I thought it was just odd bits of wood from fallen-down buildings. But it didn't take long for me to see how wrong I was. Horse carcasses, sewage, dead fish, and things too rotten to identify. I suppose I'd got so used to the smell of death and illness that I hardly noticed how it hung over Balaclava.

The red coats of the officers and the highlanders' kilts were the only colors I could see in that brown and dreary place. It made Scutari seem lively and thriving by comparison.

"Come, nurses!" Miss Nightingale called us all to gather and disembark at the same time. Emma stood behind me, looking down. But it was no use.

Miss Nightingale's eyes rested on Emma, their expression impossible to read, but the corners of her mouth turned down just enough for me to know that she wasn't pleased at all about this added body. She must have felt me staring at her, because next she looked at me. Our eyes met, and I saw a hard, accusing expression. I immediately felt hurt. It was like the Abington-Smythes all over again. She probably assumed Emma and I plotted together. How would I convince her that it wasn't true without betraying my friend?

"Miss Nightingale! We are so grateful for the help of your nurses." A man in the uniform of the army medical department met us as we stepped on the planks quickly before they too sank in the mud and made our way up to drier ground. He talked to her the whole walk to our quarters, on the other side of the town.

Our "quarters" consisted of a large tent with wooden sides and a stove in the middle. There were cots set up inside, but that was all. The stove hadn't been lit.

"The field hospital building is completed, but we are still constructing huts outside of it for the nurses. When they are finished your nurses will have adequate—if not luxurious—accommodation." He looked at us, silently counting. "Seven nurses. I confess I had hoped for one or two more. A woman's touch can do more to heal than all the medical arts."

"My understanding is that the field hospital will treat the

most critical cases and those deemed to be slight enough that they could return to the battle. In which case, a woman's touch could make little difference, and might even prove less efficacious than your medical arts."

I had got used to Miss Nightingale's way of knocking people off their guard, especially men. And I knew the doctor had—without intending to—touched on the one subject that disturbed her most about women nursing soldiers. Still, I had to stifle a laugh at the look of shock that crossed his face.

We had a meal of sorts outside, some kind of watery stew in tin cups. I was hungry enough that I didn't mind. And it was better than what the men were eating—uncooked salt pork with sugar on it. I'd never seen such a vast crowd of soldiers in my life. They didn't act like the ones in Scutari, the ones who were well, that is. They stared at us, but not with any kind of real interest. Even the ones who had clean uniforms looked exhausted, as if just picking up their feet to walk was more than they had strength for.

All the while we sat chatting idly, I wondered when the reckoning would come about Emma. Miss Nightingale didn't meet my eyes when I looked at her. She was no doubt thinking of other things, as usual.

But as soon as we'd finished our supper and were about to settle in our temporary lodgings, Miss Nightingale called to us. We stopped. The others continued on, probably thinking one or both of us was going to be sent away.

"Well, Nurse Fraser. It seems your example has been followed—with or without your sanction."

I opened my mouth to say something but Emma stopped me. "It was without, Miss Nightingale. Molly 'ere—Nurse Fraser, I mean—didn't know nothing." I was grateful to Emma for that. She didn't have to take all the blame. I was the one who kept her out of Miss Nightingale's sight on board and lied to the other nurses.

"Nonetheless, I believe I know what brought you here. I have taken the trouble to ascertain that your young soldier is far off in the trenches and not easily reached. So your journey was wasted, if that was your intent."

How could she have known which soldier it was that Emma was carrying on with? My surprise must have shown in my face.

"You nurses think you have secrets from me, but you don't. You know I've sent home a dozen women of greater years and more experience than you—mostly for drunkenness and incompetence, but some for flirtation. If I hear of any doings with either of the young soldiers you are both acquainted with, you shall not only return to Scutari immediately but be sent back to London on the next available steamer. Is that understood?"

I was ashamed. Not so much because she assumed I was there to see Will, but because I was glad she'd not mentioned Dr. Maclean. Was I becoming devious? What did I mean, "becoming"? It was deception that had got me there in the first place. I'd no right to expect anything but suspicion from Miss Nightingale.

"Well, could've been worse," Emma said as she walked with me to the tent we shared with the other nurses.

It could have been worse, but I had a funny feeling that wasn't the end of everything. I knew Emma, and nothing would stop her from doing whatever she could to find her Thomas once she'd set her mind on it.

The other nurses had already undressed and pulled their blankets up as far as they could, trying to get warm. And no wonder. The wind blew right through the canvas. The stove was no match for it, smoking a lot and heating a little. Emma and I hopped out of our clothes fast and got under the covers before you could say spit. I shivered and rubbed my feet against each other, but they were still frozen through.

"I'm ready to go and hammer in the nails myself to get those huts built!" Emma exclaimed through her chattering teeth. I would have laughed except the same thought had occurred to me too. I didn't know how we'd be able to dress wounds if our fingers were stiff as ice.

"Emma," I said. "I was that cross at you for hiding away like that."

"I know, Moll. But you'll understand soon, I promise."

"Whyever you did it . . . I'm not half glad you're here now. I missed you as soon as we set sail."

At first Emma said nothing. Then after a bit I heard a sniff, and she reached her hand out from under her blankets to me. I reached back and held her hand tight. Whatever it made Miss Nightingale think about me, having Emma there made all the difference.

And I thought it was probably a good thing I was there too, to stop her from being too rash about her Thomas. But just then, I didn't care. We were in the back of beyond, but we were together.

Chapter 22

Unlike when we first came to Scutari, the very next day we got to work in the field hospital. It was a different sort of place, with a different rhythm of working, than the hospital I was used to—the wounded came in alone or in twos or threes, not in hundreds. And most of the men were sick. Some had lost fingers from frostbite. A good many had low fevers. One or two had their wives with them even here, and they sat by their husbands' bedside and knitted or mopped their brows. These men were lucky to have someone who cared about them by their side. They were like safe little islands in the midst of a stormy sea.

I was curious about the wives. What would make them come? They lived on board ships full of vermin, coming ashore when there was a battle or some action. I saw several of them that first day mounted on horses, their dresses dirty and torn, going off to get as near as they dared to where their husbands were fighting. These were not like the fine ladies on the ship with their spy glasses, drinking wine. They knew what fighting meant, that one day their husbands might not come home, or come home no longer the same men. One of them came into the field hospital to be treated herself, with a graze from a bullet on her arm. I thought that if the army would let women fight, they would do well and be as brave as anyone, especially if they had charge of protecting their own.

The wives weren't the only women in the camps, though. Over a ways from the British tents was a very orderly place where the French had their own camp and hospital, with a whole flock of Sisters of Mercy as nurses. Those weren't too surprising to see, but I was amazed one day when I saw several other women, not in nuns' habits but in uniforms. Their uniforms weren't exactly like the men's, but versions of them, with skirts that ended just below their knees and breeches the rest of the way. They even had swords slung at their sides and ribbons of rank.

"Who do you s'pose they are?" I asked Emma on our way to the field hospital our second day there. She just shrugged. I stopped and stared.

A lady rode up on a horse. Not one of the raggedy women, but well dressed and clean, in a very nice black riding habit. "They're vivandières," she said, pointing with her riding crop. "They serve wine and food to the men in the French army. It's their job."

I curtsied. "Thank you, ma'am."

"I see you're with Miss Nightingale," she said. "I have the advantage. Nothing so interesting happens here without everyone in town knowing. Allow me to introduce myself. I'm Mrs. Duberly—most everyone calls me Fanny. My husband, Captain Duberly, is paymaster of the Eighth Royal Irish Hussars." She touched her riding crop to the brim of her hat. "I'm afraid I can't stay to chat but I'm certain we'll meet again."

She wheeled her horse around, spurred him into a canter and was soon out of sight.

"I didn't expect to see ladies here at all," Emma said. "There's more English and French ones here than in Scutari, what with the 'veevondeers' and all."

"We'd better be going," I said and pulled her along toward the field hospital. "In Miss Nightingale's view, there's only one role for women in a place like this."

∞∞∞

When we got to the hospital, several new patients had been admitted, one a sick soldier being tended by his wife. "You'd think they'd want to stay in England with friends and family, safe from bullets and cannonballs." I said.

"I understand why they're here," Emma said. "I'd go wherever my Thomas went if I thought I could protect him. Like that Mrs. Duberly we met." She put her hand on her stomach. "Listen, Moll." She turned to me with a quick look round to make sure no one was listening. "You got to help me find him. I have to speak to him. Soon!"

She squeezed my arm so hard it hurt. "What is it?" I asked. But Nurse Roberts walked in then and Emma didn't answer.

It took me until we were getting ready for bed that night to figure it out. I don't know why I'd not seen it before. The signs were there plain as day. I watched Emma after I lay down on my cot. She moved slowly and deliberately, not seeming as if she was really there at all. Her mind was far away, in time and place. I'd seen that look in other women's faces, starting with my mum and Lucy.

Emma wanted her Thomas because she was pregnant. Not married, but pregnant nonetheless. If Miss Nightingale found out, she'd be packed off home and maybe never see him again.

I made her tell me the next day at a quiet moment, when we had our tea break. "Are you sure?" I asked her first of all.

"As sure as a girl can be," she said. Her eyes had that faraway look in them, a softness that wasn't like the Emma I knew.

"How could you let it happen? I thought you had . . . experience."

"Even them what has experience gets into trouble. But I'm not going to go to no witch to have it dug out of me. I love Thomas. I want 'is child."

"What if you can't find him? What if something worse happens? What then?" I knew she didn't want to think about those things, but she had to. Emma was the sort who would do something right at the moment she wanted to, without thinking of the consequences—good or bad.

She put her hands over her ears. "That's not possible. I

got myself here. That was the hardest part. Now all we need's a chaplain."

"But first you have to find Thomas. And Emma, I know you're sure of him, but what if he isn't—"

"No! He loves me. He said so before he left. And he made promises. The kind of promises a gentleman don't go back on."

Well, if she had a promise from him that was something. But war had such a strange effect on everyone. The men we saw here and at Scutari had pieces missing inside them. Like the constant hardship, the guns with their deadly cargoes that hit willy-nilly made them shut down and live from moment to moment. Thomas might easily have made promises when he was getting well and far away from the fighting. And he might just as easily not see the future as something much to think about while he faced the possibility of death every day.

The fact didn't change, though, that Emma was going to have his baby, and it would be better for all of them if they could be married.

I wanted to help Emma but I didn't know how. I told myself that was the only reason I went to find Dr. Maclean at the end of that day. I'd caught sight of him only once since we'd landed in the Crimea, just after we got on shore. I looked away from him, just like I had on the ship. I figured there'd be plenty of opportunities to talk to him once we were settled, back in the routine of hospital work.

But I never saw him in the hospital. I couldn't think

where he went. Then I heard something about doctors going right up to the front lines, and it frightened me.

I summoned my courage and went up to one of the orderlies. "We brought some doctors with us from Scutari," I said to him. "But I don't see them in the hospital. Do you know where they are?"

The orderly first shrugged and started to turn away. "Dunno. Got things to do."

I caught his sleeve. He turned back to me, this time with a faint spark of interest in his eyes. I was ashamed of myself, but I figured the only way I would get an answer would be to make him think there was something in it for him. I opened my eyes wide and stared into his—bloodshot and yellowish as they were. "Please. It's important that I find out."

"Well, Miss . . ." He wanted me to tell him my name, but I pretended I didn't understand. "Well, some of the doctors went up to the heights, to be near the trenches in reach of the Malakoff and the Redan and other Russian positions. There's sickness up there, and more wounded. I heard at least one of the new doctors was with them."

"Thank you," I said and smiled. He tried to grab for me but I was fast and hurried out of the hospital to the nurses' hut.

Dr. Maclean had gone to the front lines, to the trenches. I was certain of it. We couldn't see them from Balaclava, but they weren't above ten miles away. Each day, troops mustered and started the climb to go and relieve those who had been there for five days. The ones who returned were barely able to stand. After so much time crouched in the mud and with no hot food, it was a long way to walk.

But, I thought, *it wasn't so long on a horse.* There were plenty of horses in Balaclava, but most of them were as sick and tired as the men returning from the trenches. We nurses didn't have need of horses, though. We could walk easily enough anywhere to get provisions, the only difficulty being the mud. Besides, Miss Nightingale kept as close a watch as ever on us here. And we were busy. Not the relentless, round-the-clock busy we'd sometimes be in Scutari when a ship carrying hundreds of wounded docked, but busy every day, all day long. I supposed that was more what it was like in a hospital back home, which seemed odd to me. It just didn't feel right that more wounded didn't come to the hospital nearest the fighting. Where did they go?

One older soldier who came in with a broken arm but was otherwise in good health was very nice to me. "What's a sweet young girl like you doing in this godforsaken place?" he asked as I fixed his sling. And he didn't ask it like some of the other men, who said such things with desire in their eyes.

"Oh, it's a way to make something of myself," I said.

"Being a wife and mother isn't enough?"

I shrugged. "I s'pose it would be, but not yet."

"Just be a good girl and don't get into trouble. There's plenty here would lead you astray if they had a chance." He smiled. "I have a daughter about your age. She's in Shropshire with her mum."

We chatted like this until I finished my work, then, since he'd been so nice, I got bold and decided to ask him some things. "I'm surprised we don't get more patients in the hospital," I said as I tidied up the bandages and scissors. "I see lots of men walking around who are wounded, and they never come in here. Where do they get their bandages and such?"

"Humph," he grunted. "There's some as prefer to go to Mother Seacole for doctoring."

"Mother Seacole? Who's she?" I pictured a nun in a convent, those being the only women I'd been accustomed to hearing called "Mother" anything.

"Ach, don't you worry about her. She's a harmless old crone from the islands, with healing hands. Some men swear she makes them better just by touching them. I think it's all a load of rot. The doctors here have none too good reputations, or had, that is, before we found out Miss Nightingale was coming with her nurses."

He meant it as a compliment, but I'd stopped listening to him after he said what he did about Mother Seacole healing with her hands. I knew what the soldiers meant. My fingers began to tingle just thinking about it. I needed to find this lady and talk to her. Something told me that Miss Nightingale would more than disapprove, though. Nursing was a matter of organization and discipline, of keeping the men clean, giving them fresh air, and feeding them properly, not touching them with some kind of healing power. She didn't even hold with what the nuns amongst us said, that sickness was God's way of testing us and that faith had a lot to do with making the men recover.

Whatever it cost in Miss Nightingale's trust in me, I knew I would break the rules here in Balaclava for two reasons, mayhap related to each other. Emma needed help finding Thomas. And I must talk to Mother Seacole, someone who might understand the way I felt about nursing—which was something like Miss Nightingale's way, but not entirely.

First, though, there was the problem of a horse. A horse and someone to take us to the trenches on the heights. It would take time. We had to make sure everyone trusted us before we did something that might destroy that trust forever.

I knew then that what Emma and I did would throw away my opportunity with Miss Nightingale, that she would never give me a recommendation that would help me get a position as a nurse back in London. I'd be in the same situation I was before I came. No better off, and no one would want me.

But whatever I told myself, I couldn't leave Emma to sort out her own troubles. She was my friend. Funny that she could end up doing for me what Mavis had done months ago, and Mavis was not my friend. I was beginning to wonder how a body could ever get ahead, acting on what a conscience said was right—which I saw wasn't always what everyone else saw as right.

Once I decided, though, there would be no turning back. I'd see about getting the horse. That would be difficult enough. After we got to the trenches, we'd have to act fast. I hoped a chaplain would be easy to find up there. If not, our adventure would be wasted and we'd both be sacked for nothing.

Chapter 23

Miss Nightingale didn't stay in our hut with us. She was a guest in the commander's house, a famous lady everyone wanted to see. She spent her days talking with people and inspecting things in the hospital, checking in on what we were doing every now and then. It turned out lucky for us, really. She was so busy it seemed like we were left to our own more, not so watched over. But the hospital was smaller, and with only seven nurses, we spent more time in each other's company, so I suppose we kept our eyes on one another more.

Still, we generally divided into our groups as we did at Scutari. The Sellonites were pleasant enough but kept to themselves. The three older nurses—Mrs. Roberts, Mrs. Drake, and Mrs. Hawkins—sat around and did their knitting in the evening. Emma and I played cards and told secrets when we weren't on the wards or running errands.

That had pretty much fallen to us to do—run errands

and fetch things in town. I suppose it was only natural, since we were the youngest and healthiest. Nurse Drake complained that her chest hurt now and again, and Nurse Roberts had a slight limp. Mrs. Langston and Sister Trumbull were so skilled that they had the longest shifts and were always in demand.

So about three weeks after we arrived, I found myself sent down to the dock to wait for a shipment of chloride of lime and tell them where to bring it. Most of it was to go to the field hospital, but some was to be packed in small parcels and taken up to the doctors near the trenches. I thought this might be my chance to see about how to get a horse, or find some other way to get us up to the front lines. Emma and I had pooled our wages, hoping it would be enough to persuade someone to let us have a healthy mount for just a night, or to lead us there so we'd be safer.

Nothing had changed at the landing place since I was there last. It was just as muddy, cold, and stinking. The ship that docked had a different name, but it might as well have been exactly the same for all I could tell. The day was clearer, though, and I could see far out to the warships bobbing up and down in the waves. I was staring at them, wondering about the sailors on them, when someone tapped me on the shoulder. I turned quickly and pulled my cloak closed, thinking it might be a beggar.

"I didn't mean to frighten you, Molly."

My heart leapt and my face felt hot. "Dr. Maclean! I thought you were at the front lines."

"Would you rather I was? Or is it out of sight, out of mind?" He smiled just a little, but it softened his face so that I wanted to put my hand on his cheek. His eyes looked hollow, and his cheekbones stood out above his beard—a new beard, not long, but needing a trim. "I was up with the men in the trenches, but they sent me down for a little rest and to pick up some supplies."

He didn't say anything more. I thought he was waiting for me to speak. What would I say? *Lovely day? Good to see you looking so well? Are you getting enough to eat?* Everything that went through my mind felt empty and stupid, until I blurted out, "What's it like there?" I instantly wished I'd said something different.

"Oh, it's . . . You can't possibly know how good it is to see you," he said, looking out at the sea instead of at me. "So many . . . But that's not important. What brings you to the dock?"

"I'm to instruct them about what to do with the chloride of lime."

"Then we're here on the same errand. I'm bringing some back with me to the trenches."

"When? I mean, how soon?" I hated myself for thinking it, but something told me Dr. Maclean would be willing to help me—and Emma.

"Tomorrow night. Will you have dinner with me tonight,

Molly?" He suddenly swung me around toward him and looked straight into my eyes. I recognized those warm, brown pools that looked so deep, but something had changed in them. Last time I saw Dr. Maclean, the glint in the corners always used to mean he was about to smile or laugh. Now it looked more like tears might come. "I can try," I said, knowing I'd think of something, and that Emma would help me.

"Oy! Where's all this going?" We were both startled by the dock man's voice. Quickly I told the rough-looking chap to load up the cart and take it to the hospital, and Dr. Maclean took his few parcels in a satchel that he slung over his back.

"Is that enough?" I asked.

"I just need it to clean the table I use. If I had to do the whole outside, there wouldn't be enough in the entire world." He smiled then, looking more like the friendly Dr. Maclean I knew from Scutari.

He turned from me, calling over his shoulder, "Meet me by Major Rowling's hut at seven."

Seeing him walk off like that, his shoulders sagging and feet barely lifting off the ground, I don't think I would have recognized Dr. Maclean if I hadn't seen his face and heard his voice.

I shook my head. He was still the same person. And I had agreed to meet him. Why? We nurses always had our supper together. But that was at six. I could go and sit with him. I didn't have to eat.

When I got back to the hospital with the shipment, Emma was there. "Miss Nightingale's been in a fit of temper about you taking so long to bring the chloride of lime," she said, helping as we showed the orderlies where to put the sacks—one in each ward, and the remainder in the broom cupboard.

"I may have found us a way to get to Thomas," I said under my breath to her as we hurried along to resume our work on the wards.

"Tell me!" Emma whispered.

"Later," I said. Miss Nightingale stood at the entrance to the ward I was to work on, a ward filled with the most hopeless cases we had, too ill to transport back to Scutari. The only thing we could do was make them comfortable, write letters home for them, and be there when they closed their eyes at last.

"Good afternoon, Miss Nightingale," I said.

"Fraser, it took far too long for you to fetch the chloride of lime from the dock. Is there something you wish to tell me?"

"N-no, ma'am," I said.

"It's a strain, working on this ward, is it not?"

I sighed. "I only wish there was something I could do for them."

She didn't say anything but looked over her shoulder into the dimness, shades having been drawn to keep the strong sun out. Soft moans came from one or two of the beds.

Otherwise everything inside was silent. "No wonder you looked for a way to be gone from here a while. I think you need a rest. It may not be as busy here, but there is something about being so near the front, about seeing the men about to go off, and then coming back injured or sick or hollow." She stared into the distance. I knew exactly what she meant. The only thing I didn't know was how to show her that I understood.

I reached my hand out and touched hers. "I know."

She quickly squeezed my hand then let go of it. "Why don't you take the afternoon off, Fraser? I'll stay in this ward. I'm tired of arguing and making arrangements. I need to remind myself why I'm here, why it's all worthwhile in the end. Or why we need to do a better job next time."

"Yes, Miss Nightingale," I said, and curtsied. Little did she know how I would spend my time. Hardly resting. I would go to look for Dr. Maclean. That way I could avoid having to find a way to sneak out later and could still lay the groundwork for Emma's and my plan.

~⚬⚬⚬~

I found him sitting on a rock, a ways up the hill, neither in the town nor in the camps. He stared out over the sea again. I wanted to know what he was thinking but I didn't want to bother him. I waited. He leaned forward and rested his forehead on his palm. It looked like he really didn't want to be disturbed. I'd wait a bit, then come back. I turned, not making a sound.

"Is that you, Molly?" He said it without changing his pose.

"Yes. I was looking for you."

"To tell me that you won't meet me this evening? Did the formidable Miss Nightingale forbid it?" He swiveled around on the rock, his hands on both knees.

"I didn't tell her. She gave me the afternoon off. But I shouldn't meet you later anyway." I walked over to him. "Is there room on that rock for me?" He moved over a little. "I need to ask you a favor. I'm sorry, I know I shouldn't, but I don't know another body to go to."

Instantly his far-off expression changed and he focused hard on me. His face was so near the steam from his breath touched my cheek. I had to concentrate on breathing slowly to remember what I'd come to say. "Well, it's really not for me. It's for Emma—Nurse Bigelow." I took off one glove and started twisting it in my hands. "You see, she has a young man, a soldier, and he's in the trenches, and she really needs to find him, right away."

"Is she pregnant?" he asked, not sounding horrified or anything.

"How did you know?"

"I can imagine few other reasons why a young girl surrounded by men would go to such lengths to seek out a particular one, whom she can't have had much opportunity to get to know."

"Well, she's in love with him, and so is he with her. They want to get married."

"They?" he asked. "Or she?"

My cheeks burned. I only had Emma's word, after all. "She says . . . he made promises."

"Miss Molly," Dr. Maclean said, moving so that his arm was behind me, just touching my back. "A man will promise a girl anything in the heat of the moment."

I didn't know exactly what the "heat of the moment" would be, having never been in that kind of moment in my life. But I didn't want to talk about that with Dr. Maclean. "Nevertheless, she needs to see him, whatever happens."

"And you need me to take her there? To the trenches? How will she get back?"

This was the hard part. We both had to go. It was the plan. "Well, in fact, I thought I'd go with her, so we could come back together." By now my glove was tied in a knot and I started trying to unpick it so I could put it back on my cold hand.

"You'd do that? For your friend?"

I didn't dare look at him. Perhaps he thought I was foolish. At times I thought so myself. Why would I throw everything away for Emma? Especially now that I didn't have to find Dr. Maclean, he was right here. "I can't just leave her to it." I knew right then, aside from what Emma needed from me, just finding Dr. Maclean again would never be enough.

"All right. I'll help you. But I mean you, Molly, not

Emma. She's foolish to get herself into such a predicament. Let's see if we can do this without compromising your future."

He explained he could get an extra donkey to take supplies up. He'd ask for some things from the hospital and get us to bring them to him tomorrow. Then Emma and I would go back, go to bed, and sneak out together to meet him above the camp. There was a chaplain up there who would know where to find Thomas, and most likely could take us to him.

"You do realize that I could be disciplined for this if anyone found out," he said, once we'd made all our plans.

"Then why do it?" I asked, throwing his own question back at him.

"Do you know why they sent me here?" he asked. I shook my head no. "They found out—or guessed, anyway—after we took that soldier's appendix out, that I wasn't everything I claimed to be."

"But . . . you saved that man's life!" I was confused. He *was* a doctor. He'd proved it.

"I told you I only had one year of medical training. After my father refused to pay for more, I studied on my own whenever I could. But I'm not really qualified. And that's all they care about."

"But you're good at it!" I said. "You do just as well—maybe better—than the other doctors I've seen."

He smiled at me, but it wasn't his usual broad, friendly

smile. "You say that, in your position as an extensively experienced nurse."

His words stung. I turned away.

"I didn't mean that, Molly. You're very capable, you know I think so."

"Is that why you're willing to help me?"

"It's not the only reason."

"Why then?"

His face became serious again, his eyes sparkling in the corners as if his feelings might leak out at any moment. "You really don't know? I thought we settled that in Scutari." He leaned toward me. For some reason, all I could think of was the horrible smell of the harbor there, the mud and filth everywhere, and how different it was from the way Dr. Maclean smelled. His breath had the faintest hint of pipe tobacco on it, and his skin smelled like cold air and gunpowder. His lips touched mine.

"James!"

Dr. Maclean sat up quickly and moved the arm that had crept around my waist so that it looked as though he'd just been scratching his head. I stood.

"There you are. You're wanted to settle a wager in the captain's tent." An officer, looking too clean and neat in his uniform, with the white straps crossing his breast and a short cloak pinned across one shoulder, stopped just below where we'd been talking, huffing and winded from the climb.

"Just coming, Philip." Dr. Maclean stood and faced me. "Remember the list for the hospital. I'll call for the items tomorrow." Without a good-bye, as if I really was a messenger there for the purpose of taking his instructions, he jogged off down the hill and went away with the young officer.

Chapter 24

As soon as Emma and I had a moment alone I told her the plan.

"You're a brick, Moll!" she said and threw her arms around me. I pushed her off, glancing around to make sure no one saw us who might suspect we were plotting something together. In truth, as soon as I left Dr. Maclean I started having doubts. So much at stake, for all of us. The one with the most to lose, I thought, was Dr. Maclean. Or maybe it was me. Emma had already lost the most important thing she had, so it wouldn't matter to her one way or the other. In fact, she was the only one who could really come out ahead in all this.

But I'd done it, made the plan, and now I had to stick to it.

The next day dragged on and on, and I was so jumpy I kept dropping things in the wards, just when I was trying to be as quiet and invisible as I could. It was my turn to clean out the closet where we kept the bandages and such, with scissors and cotton batting and all. Somehow I managed to catch my sleeve on one of the scissors, and when I moved, the whole tray crashed to the ground. I jumped out of the way just in time to avoid being stabbed in the leg.

"Got your monthly, Nurse Fraser?" Mrs. Drake asked quietly. She was just passing by on her way to one of the sick wards.

"No, nothing like that. Just clumsy," I said. "How's your chest pain?"

"Oh, it comes and goes. I expect it's nothing."

She left me to pick up the mess I'd created.

Neither Emma nor I could eat much that evening. Of course, Emma had trouble keeping anything down and had almost run out of ways to hide it when she had to go and vomit. I wondered if any of the other nurses guessed or if they were too wrapped up in their own concerns to bother about it. Ever since I knew, it seemed so obvious.

We went to bed as usual and waited for the others to start snoring, which never took very long. We were on our feet all day, and sleep comes easily when you're that tired. Emma and I did as we planned, lumping up cushions and blankets to make it look like we were still there. I slipped out without taking anything, but to my surprise, Emma had her valise. As soon as we were where no one would hear us, I asked, "What'd you bring that for?"

"You don't think I'm coming back here after Thomas and me are married, do you?"

I didn't ask her more. There wasn't time.

We hurried through the dark streets, skirts picked up to

avoid the mud, and reached the camps. In the moonlight they looked almost lovely, the round, white tents scattered in a sort of pattern here and there. I'd never been out so late in Turkey, and it made me feel free, like no one was watching me for once.

Dr. Maclean was waiting for us where he said he would be. He had the promised donkey, as well as a second horse. "We'll go faster on the horses. I'm afraid you'll have to ride astride, but no one will see you. The donkey can trot behind. Both horses are needed up top, so he'll carry the two of you back."

Emma left her case behind a rock. Dr. Maclean first helped me up and then settled Emma behind me. His hands were strong. My skirts hiked up because of having to put my legs over the saddle on either side, and he gently tugged them down to cover as much as possible, touching my calf softly. It sent a thrill right up to my stomach.

I watched him swing himself up on the horse with ease. The packages of supplies were already loaded on the donkey so we started up the hill right away. It wasn't steep at first, but soon I was glad we weren't walking, seeing how the track wound around and the side of the hill sheared away. We climbed higher and higher. I could see Balaclava from time to time below us, a few campfires amongst the tents surrounding the town, and lamps here and there where men were drinking late.

"What regiment is your young man fighting with, Nurse Bigelow?"

"The Nineteenth," she said. Then after a minute, "What's that?"

Emma pointed to a large metal machine on the side of the road at Kadikoy, the only little village between Balaclava and the front lines. And village was a generous name: I counted three houses, which were more like huts, and all dark as if no one lived there.

"It's a stationary engine," Dr. Maclean answered. "It's used to bring guns and ammunition up to the trenches."

"How do the men get their food?" I asked, realizing as we went up and saw how rough the ground was, with deep ravines and no trees or shelter anywhere, that it would be hard to carry anything.

"They have to bring their rations themselves. A week's worth at a time. And whatever water they can carry, in case the reservoir the army dug has frozen over. And then they have to find their own fuel for a fire to cook it."

That and fight too, I thought. They must wonder what they're doing here. So far away from home, and not even fighting over English soil. For all the explanations, I still couldn't see it. Why did it matter to us if the Russians had charge of the holy lands?

Out in the dark, quiet night, Dr. Maclean's voice sounded echoing and hollow, near and far away at the same time, and barely more real than my own thoughts. I shivered, only partly because the higher we climbed, the colder it got. We were passing over ground that had seen battles, disease, and death. Perhaps it was because I was tired and also afraid, doing something I knew was wrong, but as we climbed, I began to hear whispers.

"What did you say?" I said to Emma over my shoulder.

"Nothing! It's too cold to talk."

But as we rose, the whispers grew louder. Nothing distinct at first, then soft, desperate cries of "Help!" "I'm shot!" "My leg. I can't feel it!" and more such murmurings. I shook my head. Were the whispers coming from inside me, or outside, all around us? Did Emma and Dr. Maclean hear them? "Please . . . help . . . I can't go on . . ." The whispers continued, talking directly to me.

Then I saw it, up ahead. A low, green glow, stretching right across the top of the hill in front of us. But it wasn't a steady glow, like you might see if there were lights. It flickered, glowing brighter and fainter in points. My horse stopped and whinnied.

"What's the matter?" Dr. Maclean turned his horse with the donkey in tow and came back to us.

I couldn't answer him. The whispers were now so loud and overlapping each other that they became an unceasing hiss that hurt my ears. I put my hands over them and shut my eyes. "Help!" I said, but my voice came out hoarse.

Before I knew it, Dr. Maclean had taken me down from the horse and was carrying me across the ground. The whispers quieted. I opened my eyes. His forehead was creased in worry and he walked quickly toward something. I looked ahead and saw a wooden hut with a smoldering campfire in front of it. A sign hung over the door with the apothecary's symbol painted on it. *What an odd place for a dispensary*, I thought, *not in town or close to the lines.* By the time we reached it I was more curious than frightened by what I had just seen and heard.

At the door, Dr. Maclean set me down on my feet gently, as if he was afraid I'd topple over. "I'm all right now," I said. "I don't know what came over me so sudden like." He kept hold of my shoulders anyway, and I didn't stop him.

As if she knew she was wanted without us having to knock, an old woman opened the door and stepped right up to me. She put her hand on my forehead, then looked at Dr. Maclean. "What are you doing hereabouts with a young lady—two young ladies?" By now Emma had led both horses and the donkey to where we stood. "On your way up to the trenches?"

She took my arm and led me through the door into her hut, where she struck a match and lit a lamp.

The hut was much bigger than it seemed from the outside, and on shelves I could see medical supplies and other things that would be the envy of our field hospital as well as brandy, cigars, and other items. She saw me staring. "I don't have to deal with the British bureaucracy to get my supplies. I just use cash. Works every time."

"Blimey!" said Emma, standing right behind me.

"Let me introduce my good friend, Mother Seacole," Dr. Maclean said. "This is Nurse Fraser and Nurse Bigelow."

I curtsied. "How d'you do." Then I really looked at her for the first time. I'd never seen a woman with such dark skin, not as dark as the Nubian slaves some of the Turks had in Scutari, but too dark to be just sunburned. I tried not to stare.

"Here with Miss Nightingale, I gather. Come, sit down, child." She led me to a bench, knelt in front of me, and took hold of both my hands, examining my face and eyes as if she could see something there that wasn't on the surface. After a moment she sat back on her heels and said, "Ah."

"What is it?" Emma asked.

"I couldn't exactly say," Mother Seacole said. "You've had a turn. I've seen it happen with sensitive souls. There's something about a battlefield that gets under the skin. It can be hard to fathom."

"I just . . . I heard something. And saw something."

"No matter, child. This is a horrible, sad place. I do what I can for the men, but there are many restless spirits who died here unnecessarily. I'd have gladly given my soul to Miss Nightingale if she'd have had me, but her supporters didn't approve. The War Office didn't approve either. So my British friends helped me out, and here I am."

Emma and Dr. Maclean just stared at both of us. Emma as if we were stark raving mad, Dr. Maclean with a soft, sorrowing look.

"We have a ways to go yet, and I'm much better," I said, beginning to feel foolish for causing such a to-do.

"Wait!" Mother Seacole said. "I have something for you that might help if you get that way again." She went to a locked cupboard, fished a key out of a hidden pocket in her dress, and opened it. She brought me a sachet of something on a string and placed it round my neck. "It's mandrake root. I won't go into all the legends, but I find a good sniff gets me out of my unpleasant moods and back to the present in a jiffy."

I'm not the sort who lays myself open to people easily, but something about Mother Seacole made me throw my arms around her neck and give her a squeeze, just like she was my own mother back in the East End. She squeezed me too and patted me on the back. "If you can get away, come and see me whenever you like. I could use some help, especially when the shells have been flying from the Redan."

We left. She stood in her doorway, her large person blocking out almost all the light from the lamp inside. I patted the sachet she gave me. Miss Nightingale definitely wouldn't approve. But there was no more whispering now.

Chapter 25

Our stop cost us about half an hour on a night where we could hardly afford to lose a minute. As we continued to climb to the British offensive positions, the ground became rougher and rougher. Our horse stumbled more than once in holes that were hard to see in the pale moonlight.

"We've pushed them back a little, but sometimes the shells still reach this far," Dr. Maclean said, pointing to a deep dent he steered his horse around. "It's worse up ahead. We'll go to the hospital tent first, leave the animals, then the rest will have to be on foot."

We continued on in silence for a while. Ahead I could hear the low murmur of people resting—not sleeping, but I guessed taking advantage of a few hours when they didn't have to be on their guard.

The hospital tent wasn't much—just a bigger version of the tents down below. And they didn't have many supplies either, not like in Mother Seacole's dispensary. About half a dozen wounded men lay on the ground, groaning.

"Did you bring more bandages? Any chloroform?" A doctor I didn't know came forward from the darkness at the back of the tent. He was much older than Dr. Maclean. He glanced at us. "I thought Miss Nightingale didn't want her nurses at the front lines."

"She doesn't. These two came up out of their own desire to be of some help. They'd like to see the chaplain. Is he about?"

The two of them unloaded the donkey with hardly a sound and spoke in hushed, hurried sentences. Even their motions were quick and efficient. The other doctor, named Dr. Hastings, said the chaplain was with the Eighty-eighth, where four men had died that day of dysentery.

"They're over by the Redan," Dr. Maclean said, using the same clipped, quiet tone with us he had used with the doctor. "We'll have to be quick." He saluted Dr. Hastings and motioned us to follow him.

The closer we came to the trenches, the harder it was for me to breathe. It wasn't just the smell—thousands of men who hadn't washed for days, and the stink of rot and blood—it was something else, something even more powerful than the sights and sounds that almost overcame me farther down the hill. I felt like something was crushing my heart, like I was the earth and the weight of all these soldiers was on top of me. I tried not to let on that anything was bothering me. I caused enough trouble earlier, and now we were so close. Emma looked worried but excited. I just concentrated on making my heart slow down and putting one foot in front of the other so I could keep up with Dr. Maclean.

We walked for a good half hour before we reached the British guns. They were like big ugly pots angled upward behind built-up earth with brick reinforcing it. I could see that the enemy would only know their locations by the plumes of smoke that came out when they were fired. But at night, the guns remained silent. Gunners leaned against the sides of the gun carriage, smoking pipes or sleeping. They'd stacked the cannonballs up in a grid, ready to be fed into the barrels of the big guns. I wondered what was in them—canister? The enemy soldiers would be just as badly wounded as ours.

A short way down from the guns a group of soldiers sat clustered around the chaplain. Their faces were all fixed on his, like he held the answer to some huge question. It seemed small and stupid to go and interrupt him for our concerns. We didn't belong here. Not in our dresses and gloves, thinking about life. Up here, the business was survival or death. I think even Emma realized that. I saw her clutching her stomach, like she wanted to protect what was inside her from feeling this place.

The chaplain saw us, made the sign of the cross to his audience, stood, and came over. "Dr. Maclean." He put out his hand and they shook. "Do you need me in the hospital tent?"

"No, thankfully. I wondered if you knew where we could find a soldier in the Nineteenth, named . . ." He turned to Emma.

"Thomas. Thomas Mitchell, from London." She spoke so softly I hardly recognized her voice. Not like the Emma I knew. I wondered if she was sorry we'd come.

"What is it you want him for, young lady?" the chaplain asked.

"I . . . I need to talk to him." She looked down at her feet.

"Is this something that's going to upset him? Now is not the time to go telling men bad news. Bad news can get them killed when the sun comes up."

Emma looked to me for help. I spoke up. "It's not bad news. It's the best kind of news. Only Emma needs his help with something." I drew the chaplain away from Emma, who looked more and more like she would cry.

"Oh, I see," he said. "That's why you've looked for me first. Well . . ." He folded his arms across his chest. "My duty is to the men here, keeping them safe. If it seems Thomas Mitchell isn't ready to do what your friend wants him to do, I won't force him. Is she prepared for that?"

I knew she wasn't. But we'd come this far and we had to find Thomas. "I'm sure of her." It didn't mean anything really, but the chaplain took it as a yes.

"Follow me."

We started off. Dr. Maclean hung back. I looked over my shoulder at him. I wanted to beg him to come along with us, but I didn't know why. He wouldn't be any help with Thomas and Emma.

"We have to keep behind the hills or crouch low. Even at night, the Russians will sometimes take a shot."

Emma gripped my arm. "It's all right. Just do as the chaplain says." I let her cling to me even though it made it harder to move as quickly as we ought. But that wasn't all. As we approached the men in the trenches, the weight pressed harder and harder on my heart, so it felt like to burst. But I had to go on. I put the mandrake sachet to my nose. It gave off a moldy, earthy smell, and made me feel calmer. I blessed Mother Seacole.

Soon there were no more hillocks or earthworks to hide behind, and ahead I could see the dark, wide ditches that must be trenches. "Get down, flat, and wait for me here," the chaplain said. I pulled Emma down beside me. Rocks and roots pressed into us, and the ground was icy cold but at least not snow covered. The chaplain crouched as low as he could and ran like an animal on all fours across the flat area to the trenches. Soon he disappeared over the lip of one. Would he come back or just leave us here? The only choice we had was to wait.

It seemed like hours. Emma shivered, I hoped only from the cold. But at last a shape crawled over the top of a trench, a ways down from where the chaplain went in, and moved toward us, low to the ground.

"It's Thomas!" Emma whispered to me, pointing. I saw the chaplain bringing someone back with him. *Thank God*, I thought, and promised I'd really pray when we went to church on Sunday. "Look, Moll, someone else is coming." Emma dug her fingers into my arm as she said it.

I saw him too. Yet another soldier had come out and the

two soldiers and the chaplain were doing that same low scuttle toward us. It was only a minute before they were there, and I knew right away who the second soldier was. Will.

"Quickly. Over here." The chaplain led us behind the nearest earthworks where we could stand up and face each other.

"Em!" Thomas whispered, and wrapped his arms around her. "Why'd you come up here? It's so dangerous!"

"Well . . . You see . . ." I'd never seen Emma short of a quick answer before.

"Let's all move away, shall we?" said the chaplain. Once we were a polite distance off and I saw that Emma had started talking to Thomas, the chaplain said, "So, you two know each other too?"

Until then I avoided meeting Will's eyes. I could see he was changed. Very thin, and his happy, trusting eyes were less easy to read. Or perhaps it was just the moonlight. "You look well, Moll." He reached out his hand and touched my cheek. Why hadn't I thought about the possibility I'd see him if I came up here?

"So do you," I lied. "Are you eating?"

The chaplain walked away as though he had business over by another earthworks.

"It ain't half hard up here. I 'aven't slept for three days." He'd let himself slip back into the old East End accent, not keeping up the polished ways he learned in Cadogan Square, I noticed.

"I'm so sorry. I wish I could help."

"You could! You really could, Molly." He moved closer to me. I didn't want to shrink away. Not just because it would have hurt him, but because I really didn't want to. I wanted to comfort Will, my only friend besides Emma, who'd had such a hard time since I saw him last. And he was my only link with home too. He took hold of my shoulders. "You remember what I asked you, before I left?"

I couldn't help but remember, even though I tried not to think about it most of the time. I just didn't know if I felt like that about Will. And when Dr. Maclean was close, something else happened to me, like it never did even this close to Will. Still, I let him get nearer, till there was almost no distance between us. He kissed my cheek, then pressed his against mine and spoke in my ear. "The chaplain's here. Marry me, Moll. To give me something to live for. I know we're meant for each other."

He slipped his arms around my waist. I felt the roughness of his uniform, the buckles and buttons, pressing up against me. It was safe in his arms. He'd helped me, he cared for me. He would always take care of me, I knew, be kind and never hurt me. What else was there for me? Once Miss Nightingale found out what Emma and I had done up there, we'd be out for sure. I turned my face to his and kissed him lightly on the lips.

The chaplain cleared his throat. I jumped away.

Will stood next to me and put a hand on my waist like

he was claiming me for his own. "Chaplain, I wonder if I could trouble you for a few minutes of your services." He made his voice all proper again.

"You too? I'd better see what's going on over the other side."

In the confusion of everything, I'd almost forgot about Emma. I looked for her now. She and Thomas stood two feet apart from each other, both looking down at the ground. This wasn't good. What would she do? I clenched my hands together while I watched the chaplain talking to them. Then all three came over to us.

"Seems like we have two weddings to celebrate tonight," he said, not looking pleased. "We can do them at the same time, if you'll just stand here. But I'll need a witness."

He turned, and out of the shadows walked Dr. Maclean. My heart froze.

Chapter 26

He wouldn't look at me. I suddenly felt how very cold it was up there. My feet were numb, my fingers were numb, my mind was numb. What was I doing?

The chaplain started right in before I could say a word.

"Do you, Thomas, take Emma to be your lawful wedded wife?" He stopped. Wasn't there more? It would all be over too fast. I needed time to think!

Thomas sighed, then looked long at Emma. "I guess . . . yes, I do."

"That doesn't sound like you're very certain, Thomas."

Emma's eyes were round and scared. I was just glad for a little delay, so I could think. I glanced over at Dr. Maclean, and was startled to see him staring—no, glaring—straight at me. Was he angry? Did he expect something from me? But I meant him to. I knew that. And now I wanted him to be standing where Will was. But I didn't want to hurt Will. How I wished I could close my eyes and be back in the hut in Balaclava, where none of this was real.

"Thomas, it'll be all right," Emma's voice quaked. "You'll see. We'll do well together."

She reached her hand out to him. He took it in both of his, then clutched it to his heart. "I know. I know." He was crying. Tears streamed through the dirt caked on his face, which I could see much better now. The sky was getting light in the east. "Only, I didn't expect . . ." He sniffed hard. "Carry on, vicar," he said, attempting a smile. The relief on Emma's face made me want to cry too.

The chaplain finished his very short service, and Emma and Thomas held each other close. I hoped they would be all right. It was such an odd way to come to this, and yet it was no stranger than many, I supposed. Will took hold of my hand. I had to fight the urge to pull it away from him. What could I do? It would crush him to tell him now, here, that I didn't want to marry him, or at least that I wasn't certain about anything.

"Do you, William, take Molly to be your lawful wedded wife?"

"I—"

Will was interrupted by a *boom* so loud I felt it inside my ears, coming from behind us over the earthworks.

"Watch out!" It was Dr. Maclean. Before I could think, he ran toward us, pushing us down hard. I landed on my hand with my wrist bent back and felt something snap. But I didn't have time to think about it because another boom came, as loud as the first.

"Those bloody Russkies! It's not even dawn." Thomas

jumped up and away from Emma, who reached out for him. "Gotta get back to me mates." He took off across the open ground, zigzagging and crouched, hands over his head.

"Thomas, no!" Emma screamed out, but it was too late. Just before he reached the relative safety of the trench, another shell fell a few feet away from him, exploding into fragments. He lay still on the ground. "Thomas!" Emma jumped up and started to run toward him. Will grabbed hold of her. She fought with all her might. "Let me go! He needs me! I must help him!"

The chaplain clasped his hands together and closed his eyes. I looked at Dr. Maclean. He didn't hesitate, but took off at a run to reach Thomas where he lay.

"No!" I cried. The chaplain shot out one hand and held me back. He was quicker and stronger than I guessed he'd be. I could feel the tears on my face.

Although the shells were coming fast in a great bombardment, miraculously Dr. Maclean reached Thomas. I saw him scream something toward the trenches, and a moment later two men came out with a stretcher. With stops to duck and cover their heads, they managed to get Thomas on the canvas strung between two long poles.

"Molly."

It was Will. In my anxiety I had almost forgotten he was there. I turned to him. His eyes were full of sadness. "Why didn't you say?"

Say what exactly? When I wasn't even sure myself. "I don't know, Will. I don't know anything."

In that moment where I turned my attention away from Dr. Maclean and the two men carrying Thomas on the stretcher, another shell landed, just on the other side of the earthworks where we stood. Emma ran to me and clutched me, sobbing. "What will I do? What if he's dead?"

I couldn't say anything. I feared the worst, but that was unthinkable. While we stood there, the two men bearing the stretcher with Thomas on it came around to the protected side of the earthworks. His eyes were closed, but he didn't have the pallor of death. Nonetheless, his legs were twisted in unnatural positions and I feared many of the bones were shattered. I kept Emma's face turned away, but I'd already seen enough wounds to know that these were serious, and that his legs likely would both be taken off. He might live, but he would never be able to walk. Would that be living?

Emma must have sensed me staring at him because she broke free of me, looked at Thomas, and screamed. She flew to his side. "Get him to the hospital. Quick!" Emma took off her cloak and laid it over Thomas. Where was Dr. Maclean? I ran to where I could get a better view of the stretch of ground from the trenches to the earthworks, the space where Thomas had fallen.

"Don't go any nearer, Molly!" Will said.

But I didn't pay any attention. I saw him. He was clutching his side and limping toward us. I ran out to him, let him put his other arm over my shoulders and took his weight.

A moment later Will was there, propping him up from the other side. Together we walked him the ten or so yards to safety.

"I'll have to operate on that young man," Dr. Maclean said, his teeth clenched.

"You're hurt," I said. "Let the other doctors do it. You need help."

"No!" he yelled. He took his arm off my shoulders. "Not from you." He turned to Will. "Or you."

The chaplain came over. "I'll see he gets to the hospital tent."

I watched the two of them make their way slowly over the rough ground, down to where the hospital tent was now clearly outlined against the rising sun.

"I have to go back," I said.

Will nodded. "It's over, isn't it?"

I didn't want to say yes, but mostly because I never thought it had begun—whatever it was he wanted to be between us. Everything was so strange, so mixed up. "I don't know, Will. I don't know anything."

"This place changes you. It makes things clearer."

Did it? Not for me. Everything was cloudier and murkier than ever. I didn't even know now what the day would bring. At least, beyond me facing Miss Nightingale with the truth of everything that happened that night.

"I'll be seeing you, Moll," Will said, then turned away. The bombardment had let up. Later I found out that after they fired all their guns, they had to reload. I watched Will walk slowly back across the open ground, now chopped up fresh from the shells that had hit there in the last hour.

I turned and went down to get the donkey and ride back to Balaclava alone.

Chapter 27

When I reached the hospital tent there was lots of activity. Thomas and Dr. Maclean weren't the only ones wounded in that early bombardment. There were some killed too. Their bodies lay in a row, covered with whatever dirty cloth could be found.

Some of the less badly wounded sat or stood outside the hospital tent, smoking if they could, holding bleeding arms or gingerly touching quickly patched up faces and heads. Those able to walk without too much trouble headed down the hill, I guessed to Mother Seacole's, where they could get clean bandages and probably some whisky to dull the pain.

"Nurse! Come lend a hand!"

It was Dr. Hastings who, with two other doctors I didn't recognize, was going from soldier to wounded soldier, checking them and triaging. I knew I should get back as soon as I could, but there was a good deal of work to be done here, and we weren't so busy down in Balaclava. I fell in behind the doctor, helping the men who needed it into the tent, where they mostly had to sit on the ground since there were only one or two beds.

Thomas lay on one of them with Emma at his side, gazing into his face. His eyes were still closed. I left them alone.

It took two hours to get the wounds dressed that weren't too serious and for the doctors to decide about the others. In that time the Russians had started up their pounding twice more, but the men were prepared, and not so many new casualties came in. Three or four of the worst cases had already been sent down to the hospital in Balaclava, on a wagon pulled by an ox. One was so bad they decided that moving him would be pointless. If he couldn't be operated on here, he wouldn't make even that short journey. That man was Thomas.

Once I finished helping I went in to find Emma. She sat just as before, her hand on Thomas's forehead.

"Emma, dear," I said, "shouldn't you come with me?"

"Dr. Hastings says they may be able to save one leg. They'll take off the other as soon as he . . . wakes up." Emma kept her eyes focused on Thomas. "Where is Dr. Maclean?" she asked.

I'd been so occupied assisting Dr. Hastings that I didn't have time to wonder anything, and now I realized there was no sign of him in the hospital tent or anywhere around. Then I knew. "I expect he went to Mother Seacole."

"He'd do nothing of the kind!" Dr. Hastings came in just in time to hear what I said. "She's a charlatan of the worst sort. She may be a decent enough nurse, but she sells the men medicine and whiskey and claims to have healing powers."

I fingered the sachet around my neck.

"Then where is he?" Emma asked.

"I sent him down to Balaclava. He didn't want to go, but up here we wouldn't be able to deal with his wound. Too much chance for infection."

I looked up at Dr. Hastings. "What sort of wound? I thought he had some shrapnel in his leg?" Dr. Maclean had shrugged off our help like he was only slightly hurt.

"In his leg and his side. I'm afraid there may be internal injuries."

My mind was a jumble of unconnected thoughts. I must go. I must stay. What should I do? "I must return to the hospital in Balaclava. With wounded coming in they'll need all the nurses they've got."

Dr. Hastings nodded his head toward Dr. Maclean's horse. "You might as well ride her down."

I didn't wait, but hiked my skirts up and climbed onto the beast's back. I wasn't much of a rider, but I figured I could manage. As I was about to turn the horse, Emma came running out, hair down around her shoulders, her face dirty and splotchy where tears had dried. "You tell Miss Nightingale that I won't be coming back no more! That I'm staying here with my husband, like Mrs. Duberly!"

I nodded and sighed as I rode off. She had such hope in

her face. Yet Thomas was likely to die, and soon. Only a miracle—or Emma's love—might save him.

⚬⚬⚬⚬

Balaclava seemed much closer in the daytime. I passed the huddle by the door of Mother Seacole's dispensary—as I thought, several of the wounded from the trenches had apparently decided they'd be better off here than in the hospital tent—and the stationary engine at Kadikoy. The way was easy to find: there was only one road, and a sign pointed to Balaclava at the only turn off of that.

It was altogether too quick a ride for me to decide what I would say to Miss Nightingale. With luck, I wouldn't see her at all. Sometimes she was so occupied with her meetings and inspections that she didn't come to the hospital. The others must have raised the alarm though, when Emma and I weren't there in the morning.

How did everything go so badly wrong? Our plan was to get back before anyone was awake so that nobody need know we'd left at all. Now I knew how foolish we had been. Even if we'd just got there and turned right round and come back, it would have been difficult to make it in time. I wasn't sorry I'd stayed to help the wounded. I just wasn't sure Miss Nightingale would see it like I did.

I went directly to the hospital, deciding that if I came in with the wounded from the trenches the others might have more sympathy for me. In addition to the wagon that had gone down earlier, three more arrived around the same time I did.

I didn't know what to do with the horse, so I tied the reins to a fence nearby. I went up to the orderly who was admitting the men. "Who's on the wards today?" I asked in a low voice.

"Don't you know? I thought ye was in there with the rest of them," he said.

"I had business to attend to," I said, putting on my most superior expression.

"Eh, well," he said, pointing to two stretcher bearers the way to take their cargo, a man with what looked like a serious head wound. "The usual lot, and Miss Nightingale herself. Didn't look too pleased if you ask me."

I didn't ask him, and wished he hadn't said. *Better sooner than later*, I thought. I went to check the roster. I was supposed to be in the admitting ward today, which meant I'd see the men from up above. I wondered if Dr. Maclean would be there, or if he'd been moved somewhere. I didn't know who I dreaded seeing more: Dr. Maclean or Miss Nightingale.

"Nurse Fraser."

It wasn't a question. It was a command. And I would have recognized the voice anywhere. *At least I'll get it over with*, I thought, preparing myself for the worst. I wouldn't be any worse off than before I came, at least. "Yes, Miss Nightingale?"

"I wish a word with you, after we have finished seeing to the comfort of these men."

So she was going to let me do my job a while longer. There was relief in that. I went from bed to bed, checking dressings, giving drinks of water, cleaning off faces. One bed was curtained off. That usually meant surgery, or a wound too bad to deal with easily. We weren't to go behind curtains unless asked. It reminded me of the curtain I had pulled around when Dr. Maclean and I saved that soldier with appendicitis.

I was about to skirt around the curtained bed when Miss Nightingale beckoned me closer. "Nurse Fraser, there's an unusual case I would like you to see."

Though I was surprised she asked me after what I'd done, I followed her around the screen, and my heart nearly stopped. It was Dr. Maclean. His wounds had been revealed in all their ugliness, and he was propped up on pillows, talking through clenched teeth and sudden sharp breaths, discussing the problem with the other doctor.

"I think it missed the liver. If we keep it packed, I may live." His face went white as the doctor probed inside the wound. So far he hadn't noticed me.

"There's shrapnel lodged just to the left of it. We have to get it out."

Miss Nightingale bent close to see what she could, pulling me with her. Did she know what she was doing to me? I didn't dare look at Dr. Maclean's face, which was so distorted with pain that I assumed he would hardly notice me there. His skin was torn in a jagged shape, not a neat incision like the one he'd made on the soldier that day with a razor-sharp scalpel. Blood flowed from it so fast the doctor could hardly keep a cloth from soaking through.

"Any higher and a bit farther over and it would have hit your heart," the doctor said.

"Perhaps it would have . . . done me a favor." Dr. Maclean could hardly get the words out.

"Would you hold this back for me, nurse?" The doctor glanced at me, indicating that I should take the large tweezers he was holding. I reached out my hand, but it shook so much I couldn't grasp the instrument. Miss Nightingale took it instead, her hands as steady as if she were watching someone darn a sock. I shrank back. The floor was sticky with blood. Piles of soaked bandages were lumped at the doctor's feet.

"Got it!" the doctor said, holding up a triangular metal shard covered in gore. "Best get you closed up."

Dr. Maclean didn't say anything. His face had gone beyond pale to gray. The doctor began stitching up his wound. Miss Nightingale still watched, fascinated, handing him a threaded needle. It was such a large gash, so deep, and he was still bleeding heavily, almost as if shrapnel still pierced him.

The scene was oddly unreal. I almost forgot it was a man they worked on, and which man in particular. The feeling didn't last long, though. Hardly more than a moment later recognition and fear gripped me. *He was bleeding too much.* What if, like that soldier we'd found in Scutari, there was still something vile and poisonous inside him?

I could tell something wasn't right. The swelling hadn't

gone down enough near his liver, which I could still see despite the blood. I felt as if I was back in the Barrack Hospital, watching something happen and knowing I should act. I didn't have the confidence then, and Dr. Maclean was there to do what was necessary. Only now, his life was in the balance.

They had started their stitching near the top of the wound, where they'd removed the one piece of shrapnel. The doctor's hands moved quickly because of the bleeding, and I knew I didn't have much time. Without thinking about the others, I cried out "No!" and pushed the doctor and Miss Nightingale aside. I plunged my fingers inside the gash that remained and probed gently, closing my eyes and feeling for something—I didn't know what.

I heard cries of "Molly! Don't," and was dimly aware of other angry voices. But I paid no attention, just concentrated on what I was doing.

And I found it. It was hard, and would not have been easily visible, I thought later. I grasped the object's edge and pulled gently, aware that if I moved too fast I might inflict more damage.

I felt someone grab my arm and shout, "Don't! You'll kill him!"

After that I think the doctor and Miss Nightingale must have been frozen with astonishment, because they did not interfere with what I was doing until I brought my hand out with its prize.

Silence fell. I could hear a bird singing outside the

window. I looked at what I held in my hand and saw a shard of metal, covered in blood and bits of flesh, that was twice the size of the one the surgeon had already removed from Dr. Maclean's body.

All my strength left me and darkness closed in. The last thing I remember was his voice. "Molly, it's all right."

Chapter 28

I woke up in a room I didn't recognize. There were chintz-covered chairs, a lamp with a pink glass shade, and blinds drawn down over the windows. I lay in my shift underneath soft white sheets, and a glass of clean water was on the table next to me. I pushed myself up and reached for the glass.

Someone's hands took my shoulders from behind and gently pressed me back down. I turned my head. It was Miss Nightingale.

"Oh, Miss Nightingale! I'm that sorry! I didn't mean to break the rules, only I didn't have a choice. I—"

"You mean you had no choice in sneaking off to the front lines with that Emma, a troublemaker of the first water?"

I couldn't look into her eyes. "Don't be angry at Emma. She's not coming back. She's married now, to her Thomas. What happened to me?"

"Ah . . . I expect she had her reasons. As for you—you fainted."

"I fainted? And before that?" Had my action been a

dream? Surely I'd not dared to interrupt a doctor performing surgery. I had to look up and see what was in Miss Nightingale's eyes, to see just how angry she was, what she thought. It would give me pain, but I wouldn't have done anything different. I knew I owed her so much, for taking me on when she really needn't have, and for trusting me to be one of her nurses.

She leaned forward in the chair she sat in next to the bed. She didn't look like she was mad at me, just curious. "You put your hand into Dr. Maclean's wound. Why?"

The picture of him suddenly flashed into my mind like a lightning bolt. "Where is he? Is he . . ." I couldn't say it.

"Dead? No. And the doctor thinks he'll recover. He also thinks that if you hadn't found that other piece of shrapnel, he would most certainly have died." She paused and looked off into the distance. "But, Molly, what made you do it? How did you know?"

I didn't fully understand it myself. "I saw the swelling was still there, and there was too much blood."

We were silent together for a little while. "Whatever it was that made you take such a dangerous chance, you're a clever girl, and you have learned more than many who spend a lifetime nursing. I think I knew you had a special gift when I first saw you, in Paris." She wasn't talking directly to me anymore. She stared out across the room like she was talking to herself. "I envy you. I don't see things like that. I don't see—or imagine I see—what goes on inside a living body. I see the whole mass of people and how doing things

261

differently could make more of them get well. It's laid out in front of me, like a pattern I can perceive but no one else does." She turned back to me. "Do you think that's wrong of me, Molly? Ought I to just care for people one at a time?"

She was asking me? How could doing all she'd done for the soldiers in Scutari and now here be wrong? "Miss Nightingale, I'm sure there's others who could judge better than me. But I think you've done more good than the whole army."

She smiled. Then she stood and her face closed over again. She was Miss Nightingale; efficient, strong, strict Miss Nightingale. "If you feel well enough I think you'd better go back to your quarters and pack your things. Though you're a good nurse, Molly, I'm afraid I can't overlook the way you disobeyed. It wouldn't be fair to the others. There's a boat leaving for Scutari this evening. I'll give you a letter for Mrs. Bracebridge and she'll arrange your passage back to England—and give you any wages you're owed."

"Thank you, Miss Nightingale," I said. But it was nowhere near enough to say what I felt for her.

By then it was late afternoon. I discovered I'd been taken to Miss Nightingale's own room at the commander's house when I fainted. A maid came in and helped me, gave me hot water and a towel so I could wash. It was odd having someone wait on me.

When I got back to our hut the others hardly talked to

me. I sat by myself at tea, no Emma to share stories with. I missed her, even though it'd been no more than half a day since we parted. I looked around, hoping Mrs. Drake would still speak to me, but she wasn't there. She wouldn't turn her back on me, I was sure, and I did want to say good-bye to her. She was always the one with a kind word or something cheery to say when things were difficult, and she was civil to the others who'd been sent home, too, whatever the reason. "Where is Mrs. Drake?" I asked, breaking the silence apart like a stone in a pond. "Did she return to the Barrack Hospital to nurse the new wounded?"

"Don't you know?" Mrs. Langston asked, looking truly surprised. I shook my head. "She took sick in the middle of the night. She asked for you."

I felt like someone had stabbed me in the heart. Mrs. Drake? She was ill and she wanted me? I didn't wait for any more news, but left my one valise by the door of the hut, ready to be taken to the landing, and ran as fast as I could the short way up the hill to the hospital.

"Mrs. Drake," I panted to the first orderly I met. "Where is she?"

He pointed away from the men's ward to three small rooms reserved for high-ranking officers. I ran to open the first door and found the room empty. So was the second one. I thought the orderly had deliberately told me wrong to tease me, and hearing no sounds at all coming from the third room I assumed it would be empty too.

But I opened the door to find Mrs. Drake sitting upright in her bed, her face as pale as her nearly white hair. She wore a serious expression. "I've been expecting you," she said.

"Oh, Mrs. Drake! I'm so sorry I wasn't here when you took ill. I wish I could've been in two places at the same time, but I had to go with Emma to find her Thomas. I had to—"

"It doesn't matter, Molly." She smiled at me and reached out her hand. I took it. It was very cold. "There's so much I wish I could tell you, but they won't let me."

"Who won't let you? What do you want to tell me?"

She smiled. "Poor Molly. You're confused. Don't worry. Everything will come clear in the end."

Her voice was so kind and loving, sweeter than any voice I'd ever heard, except my mum's when I was sick. Something about it made me just want to cry and cry, to weep away all the sorrows and disappointments, the pain I'd seen in the past few months, and the pain I'd caused Will and Dr. Maclean. I knelt down by her bed and buried my face in the covers. I let myself sob like I never had before, in hard, painful gasps that shook me all through.

After a while, I felt a hand on my head. I assumed it was Mrs. Drake, telling me it was time to stop crying and face my future. I looked up.

The bed was empty. It was perfectly made. Not so much as a wrinkle where Mrs. Drake had been sitting. I turned. It was Nurse Roberts, not Mrs. Drake.

"She was fond of you, Molly. She'd be glad to know you came to say good-bye."

I had shed all my tears already. Now I was just confused. "What?"

"It was her heart. Those pains she complained of in her chest. They woke her last night, so bad she couldn't breathe. She died before morning."

I stood, my knees stiff from kneeling. "I'll be going now," I said, too numb to react, and left the hospital.

Chapter 29

Emma sent me a letter that I got in Scutari, during the first week I had to wait for passage home to England, because of storms and other delays.

Dear Molly,

Thomas only lived two more days after the bombardment. Dr. Hastings said he would have been a cripple his whole life, and it would be no way to live. I was sad, of course, but at least our baby will have a surname. The chaplain told me he'd make sure I got my widow's jointure, so I'd have some money to get home on.

But I decided to stay here anyway. I'm closer to where Thomas's buried, and Mother Seacole said she could use some help. That way I'll know someone who can manage will be there when the baby comes. I wish it was you. I never had a friend before.

I know it's hard for you to write, but if you can,

send word about yourself. I expect I got you into terrible trouble. Will you ever forgive me? Maybe if you're in love like I was you'll understand.

And Molly, speaking of love, that soldier—Will, the one who looked for you in Scutari—he's been very sweet to me. Him and Thomas were friends it turns out. Take care.

Emma Mitchell

I wasn't surprised about Thomas's death. I had a sense that it would happen, as sure as I knew the sun would rise, no matter what. What I didn't expect was Emma getting friendly with Will. I don't know why it bothered me so much. I didn't treat him like more than a friend, and I knew I hurt him that day near the trenches. Truth was, I was very fond of Will, only I didn't know much about love. Was it the warm, safe feeling Will gave me or the frightening, dangerous feeling I got around Dr. Maclean? Now, I wouldn't have a chance to find out.

And it'd maybe work out for Emma, if Will could take care of her. I tried to imagine it, imagine him looking at her the way he looked at me. But I couldn't. He was my friend first. I knew it didn't make sense for me to be jealous. Still, even though I figured he'd look for comfort in someone else's arms, why did they have to be Emma's?

But I had plenty of other things to think about. Not least of which was how could Mrs. Drake talk to me when she was already dead and on her way to being buried? I decided I must have so wanted to see her, and I hadn't slept the whole night before, that I imagined it all. I had to believe that, anyway. Stranger, perhaps, was how I knew that something else was inside Dr. Maclean and had to come out before they sewed him up for good. Miss Nightingale called it intuition. But she punished me nonetheless, and it surely had nothing to do with nursing.

As soon as I got off the boat at Scutari I was treated like I had the pox. No one talked to me except to ask for the salt at meals, and the nuns even crossed themselves when they saw me. I don't know how they found out everything that had happened, but I overheard enough of their whispers to know they had.

After so many adventures in Balaclava, everything seemed different. I didn't know myself anymore. Used to be I could fall asleep as soon as my head hit my pillow. Now I lay awake every night until late, listening to the sounds of the night, trying to make sense of everything.

I thought of what I could say to my mum when I got back. Surely she'd take me in? I could maybe train for a midwife now I had more experience. It was a way to get by. I'd help her, and be a good girl, teach the little ones their letters just like I learned mine. The more I thought it through, the more I wanted to go home, until it became like an ache that wouldn't go away. But still the storms continued and the ships were full. I kept my valise packed, just in case.

Mrs. Bracebridge made sure I was busy in the wards and

was kind enough, but I couldn't talk to her—not after she'd taken such a chance on me and I ended up a disappointment. The doctors were all too occupied with the sick and wounded, and I didn't know any of them well enough to talk to, to find out more about how I might have known enough to reach into Dr. Maclean's wound like that.

Dr. Maclean. I couldn't help wondering if he was better, and whether he would stay in Balaclava or go home. If he stayed in Balaclava, there was no chance I'd have to face him again, so that was what I hoped for most—and feared.

I kept trying to imagine both Will and Dr. Maclean in my mind, but the harder I tried, the less I could picture them. I'd suddenly find Will's eyes in Dr. Maclean's face, or feel the imprint of Dr. Maclean's lips as I remembered Will's kiss. What did it mean? I couldn't be in love with anyone if I was so mixed up that way. And maybe I didn't want to be. Maybe it was never my lot to find a husband. Plenty of girls didn't.

Then I'd start back in again, picturing the moment when I'd see my mum and the little ones, my brother Ted and my dad. Would I get the strap? Or was I too old for that now? What would they know, other than what I told them? Would I lie?

While I waited and thought, the worst jobs in the Barrack Hospital fell to me. I supposed it was only fair. I had to clean the linens when men soiled them and shovel up the bodies of rats that ate the poison put out for them. I was more like an orderly than a nurse, but the work felt good. It stopped me from thinking and brooding, my mind going in circles like a dog chasing its tail.

Since no one talked to me, I didn't get much news either, about the war or what was happening outside the hospital wards. I was surprised, then, when one afternoon Miss Nightingale walked into the common room. A few of the nurses—the Sellonites mostly—got her a nosegay, picked from the spring flowers that had already started poking up in the mud of the parade ground. I sat by myself in the corner, working my way through a pile of socks to darn.

"Molly! You're still here?"

I stood and curtsied. "Yes, Miss Nightingale. There were storms and no room on the one steamer that left. Mrs. Bracebridge says I'll go next week."

She looked upset, more upset than I thought she would at finding me still there. I wasn't causing any trouble. No one could say a word against me since I'd been back at the Barrack Hospital.

I didn't find out what made her act so oddly to me until the next day, when I was on the wards cleaning up as usual, and I overheard two orderlies talking.

"Seems funny to have a doctor as a patient. They say he wanted to stay, in Balaclava, but Miss Nightingale convinced him to come here for care."

My ears burned. I continued what I was doing as best as I could, but I kept tucking in the sheets around one soldier so long he likely thought I was sweet on him.

"Aye. He wasn't no favorite with Dr. Menzies, though. Bet he's sorry he's got to care for him!" The two men laughed.

I knew right away they were talking about Dr. Maclean.

He was there. In the Barrack Hospital. Only walls and stairs separated me from him. My palms tingled. The sick men around me faded from my sight. Where was he? I wanted to go to him. That was what Miss Nightingale feared. That's why she didn't want me to be here still. What was she afraid of? He hated me, I was sure, after the business with Will. But then why did I feel this tug, like a rope was tied to my heart and he was at the other end of it?

I didn't dare just go and find him. I was only permitted to do the tasks Mrs. Bracebridge gave me, then go back to our quarters. But I'd already ruined everything, and would be going home with my head hanging soon enough. What worse could come of it?

Worse would be if somebody stopped me from finding him. So I'd make sure they wouldn't.

I finished up as quickly as I could in the wards, then went back for tea. No one talked to me, as usual. Mrs. Clarke slammed my plate down in front of me, which was also usual. Anyone who did something to upset Miss Nightingale was in her bad books for good and all.

I went to bed, just like nothing had changed. Only I planned to use the tricks Emma taught me to sneak away. I knew Miss Nightingale might be up, since she went around the wards at night checking on the men. But I had to take that chance.

As soon as I heard the other nurses snoring or just breathing slow and regular, I quickly slipped out from beneath my sheets, balled up my covers so it looked like I was still there, and stole out into the corridor.

Trouble was, I had no idea where to find Dr. Maclean. I knew at least that he wasn't in any of the wards I'd been in that day. That left the sick wards, and two or three where the newly wounded came in. I guessed it would be one of those. But the longer I was out, the more chance someone would see me and I wouldn't get to him. *There must be a way to find him faster*, I thought.

The wards were quiet. Only the occasional moan or the soft sound of a man crying held back during the day so the others wouldn't hear. The rats weren't scrambling. It seemed that Miss Nightingale's presence in the hospital was enough to put everyone—even the vermin—on their best behavior.

I found what I thought was nearest to the center of all the wards, on the ground floor. Then I closed my eyes and tried to imagine Dr. Maclean. At first, all the little night noises distracted me. The dream murmurs of the soldiers, starting out indistinct, became louder and louder, and I could hear all of them, all at once—just as I'd heard the whispers on the battlefield in Balaclava. "My poor wife." "The lads at home won't believe this." "Where is the nurse? I need water!" "I wish I could see my boy Tommy . . ." The words piled up on each other and jumbled together until I couldn't tell anything. None of them sounded like Dr. Maclean. Perhaps I was wrong. Imagining things again, just as I had imagined Mrs. Drake after she was already dead and gone. But I had to keep trying, just a little while longer. I squeezed my eyes shut so tightly a tear trickled out of the corner of one of them.

"Molly."

I heard it. Plain as day. It was the only word I could hear distinctly over the noise inside my head. I willed him to say it again. I put my hands over my heart.

"Molly."

Now the word came from a direction. From the left, up higher. I didn't want to break the spell I'd put myself under to hear it, but I had to move. I had to hurry to wherever Dr. Maclean was. I opened my eyes.

The ward was there, just as before. But now, a soft, pink-ish glow seemed to spread out in front of me, like a road of light. It was leading me, I knew it. I glanced at the men, asleep or unconscious in their beds, to see if they noticed it. There was no sign that anything disturbed them. I moved forward toward the glow. Each step I took made it retreat. It was like trying to follow a rainbow, only it gets farther and farther away the more you run toward it, and then it disappears. I didn't want this pathway to disappear, but I had to continue and try.

I walked carefully. It was torture, because I wanted to run. The light led me up the stairs to the third floor, through a ward to a room in one of the towers. It wasn't the tower that contained the medical offices. It was in the opposite corner to the tower we lived in. I thought that tower was dilapidated and not used for anything but storage. But that's where the light told me to go and every now and then I heard his voice saying "Molly."

I didn't dare call out in answer, not wanting anyone to know I was there, so I just concentrated on answering him with my heart.

At last I reached the entrance to the tower. The glow didn't stop, but instead of a narrow path in front of me, I could see it outlining the closed door. I found I was breathless, as if I'd run all the way, but I knew I hadn't.

My heart pounded. I no longer heard the call of "Molly." I reached my hand out to grasp the doorknob. What if someone else was in there? What if I had been fooling myself and I wouldn't find Dr. Maclean at all, but some other poor soul?

It was too late to change my course. I pulled the door open, prepared for nothing and everything.

The bright light I had seen around the door vanished as soon as I opened it fully. Inside, there was only a single lamp on the table next to the bed. I forced myself to look at who was in that bed.

"Molly."

This time, it was only just above a whisper, not the cry that had brought me there. I walked to Dr. Maclean's bedside. They had shaved off his long beard. He was very thin. "I had to find you," I said. This was no time to waste words.

"I'm glad. I wanted to see you one more time."

Talking apparently pained him. "What happened? I thought they said you would recover?"

He smiled weakly. His brown eyes had lost the depth I once saw in them, as if everything he ever was now sat on the surface. I reached out to touch his hand, lying on the covers like a lifeless thing. "They told me what you did. It was very brave. I would have died within hours if you hadn't."

"But . . . Why aren't you well?" My cheeks were wet, but it didn't feel as if I was crying.

"They want to try another surgery. I don't think I'm strong enough to survive it."

I squeezed his hand. He gave the smallest answering pressure. "No!" I said. "This can't be everything. What is it worth then?"

"What is what worth?" He shifted and winced. I immediately adjusted his pillow, my nursing habits too hard to shake off.

"This feeling, this love I have for you. And all you taught me to do. And in the end, I couldn't save you."

"It's worth all the world, Molly. And you did save me."

"But here you are, and you're—"

"Dying. Yes. Don't cry, Molly. There's nothing anyone can do. But I did want to tell you one thing before it's too late." He lifted his head. I helped him, since it clearly cost him great effort. "I would have asked you to marry me. We have a connection, you and I."

I couldn't speak. Tears locked my throat so I could hardly breathe. Finally I took in a raw, rasping breath that was more like a sob and cried, "No! You can't leave! What will I do without you?" Pinpoints of light danced in front of my eyes. I forced myself to take a slow breath. "Take . . . me . . . with you! Take me with you!"

If anyone saw what I did next they would have thought I'd gone mad. I reached my arms out and spread myself over Dr. Maclean like a human blanket, touching every part of him I could, as if I could transfer the life I felt coursing through me into him, as if he could draw upon my strength and live.

"Ah, Molly!" Dr. Maclean said, and gently moved me so that I lay next to him instead of on top. His arm wrapped around me, and he lightly stroked the side of my hip with his hand. "I always wanted to hold you like this. But now . . . Stay with me. I can pretend. I can imagine what might have been, with you at my side."

Now tears flowed down his cheeks. They weren't hot, like my tears, but cold. They sparkled in the lamplight. "Let me keep you warm," I said, and put my arm around his shoulders. He nestled his cheek against my hair.

"Thank you," he said. "You have beautiful hair. I've not seen much of it until now." Then he turned his head and kissed me, so lightly I might not have known, except that I wished for it so much.

"Just be quiet. Lie still. All will be well yet, you'll see,"

I said, murmuring to him as if he were my child and just wanted soothing to go to sleep.

I don't know how long we stayed like that, what time it was when I awoke, and what time it was when I finally realized that Dr. Maclean had died in my arms.

Chapter 30

I went back to the nurses' quarters. I didn't try to hide or pretend I'd been there all along. What good would that have done? I didn't try to find a doctor either. It was too late for Dr. Maclean. They'd find him soon enough.

No one would expect me to be at his burial. I had already said my good-byes, and it was time to face the future without him. But had I ever really imagined a future with him?

I felt hollow, like someone had tipped me and poured the life out of me and into the Bosporus. I went through the motions of the day in a daze. I'd done those things so often I didn't have to think about them. No one mentioned anything about me not being in my bed come morning, nor said anything to me they didn't have to.

I sat eating by myself in the common room. I'd taken to waiting for the others to finish and go to their rooms so no one would have to feel awkward. I was a little surprised when Miss Nightingale came in and sat down across from me at the table.

"There's a steamer leaving this evening for Marseille. I've managed to get you passage on it, Molly." She talked to me quiet, like somehow she knew about Dr. Maclean and me and didn't want to upset me. All I could do was nod. I was ready to travel at a moment's notice. I'd have time on the boat and the train to figure out where to go, what to do when I got back to London. I said nothing, and Miss Nightingale left me to myself.

I didn't expect anyone to see me off. Early in the evening I walked to the landing where the caiques waited to take passengers across to Istanbul to board the steamers that went to Marseille, to Arabia, to Africa. It was only then I had a single moment's regret about having to leave. My life had changed so much in Scutari and at Balaclava. Not all the memories were bad. I had Emma, after all. In spite of everything that happened, she was a true friend. I decided to write to her when I got back.

I was already half gone from there, so I nearly jumped when someone tapped me on the shoulder as I stood staring across at the minarets against the sunset. I turned and clutched my coat closed, thinking perhaps it was a beggar looking for coins.

"Molly, I wanted to give you this to take with you."

I was so shocked to see Miss Nightingale standing there that I hardly realized she was holding something out to me. A letter. As soon as I came to my senses I said, "Thank you, Miss Nightingale," and curtsied. I turned the letter this way and that, thinking it must have come from Emma, since

Will was surely done with me. But it wasn't for me. It had a name on it, someone I didn't know. Perhaps Miss Nightingale wanted me to post it in England for her, the mail being rather unreliable from here. But it didn't have a frank on it for postage, and no direction for the address. "Excuse me, but what is it?" I asked.

"It's a recommendation, from me to St. Thomas's Hospital, saying that they should employ you as a nurse, as you have proven yourself very able, but the climate of Turkey disagreed with your health."

I took the letter in its crisp, white envelope and pressed it to my heart. "But . . . why?" I had broken rules. I had been as disobedient as any of the other nurses she sent away. I didn't deserve a recommendation.

"I'm not entirely sure myself," she said, looking off into the distance. "You were rash and gullible. But you're also one of the best nurses I have ever known. You understand healing. You understand the need for cleanliness, air, and good food. I have watched you around the patients and see that you know the essential truths of nursing care. You take your job seriously. I can only hope that when you are a little older and wiser, your faults will be smoothed away."

She didn't smile when she said any of this. I was sorry I'd not been more perfect—and yet I wasn't at the same time. I wouldn't have helped Dr. Maclean save a life. I wouldn't have given him a second chance to survive. But now that I knew my life ahead would include caring for the sick, I was happier than I had ever been. I didn't have to worry what I would do when I got back to London. I would go straight to St. Thomas's. I owed that—and so much more—to Miss Nightingale. I knew I would miss her when I was home as much as I missed my mum while I was here.

We didn't shake hands, although my heart was so full I could have kissed her. I just thanked her and waved. She watched my caique go until I was nearly across to the other side, then turned away. That's the last time I ever saw Miss Nightingale.

<hr>

The journey home was easier than the way there. The season for storms was over, so the Mediterranean crossing was smooth, and I didn't stop in Paris, so although the train ride was long it seemed faster. How different it felt to hand an actual ticket to the purser on the Boulogne Packet and take my place in a deck chair for the short channel crossing.

I had tea in the tavern where I'd waited outside for Mrs. Bracebridge and the nurses five months before. I paid for my hot scone knowing I had plenty left to take home to my mum, then boarded the London train—third class, to save money, in spite of the fact Miss Nightingale had given me plenty of money for the journey.

But I'd already decided I wouldn't go home first when I arrived in London. And St. Thomas's would have to wait a bit too. I owed it to Will at least to visit Lucy and bring her news of her brother. I'd give her the rest of the money I didn't have for Will when he came to visit me in Scutari. It was supposed to have been hers anyway.

I don't know how I remembered the way to her house but as soon as I saw the door, I knew I'd found the right place. I hoped Jim was at work so I could talk to Lucy without holding anything back. I knocked.

I heard a baby's cry somewhere inside coming closer to the door, and in a moment Lucy cracked it open to look out. "May I help you?"

"It's me, Molly," I said. "I'm home from Turkey."

She opened the door a little wider. "Molly! I didn't expect... Come in." She pulled the door all the way open and motioned me in with her free hand. Her other arm was occupied with her baby, whose red cheeks and teary face made it obvious she was cutting teeth. The little thing stopped crying in a trice when she saw me, no doubt stunned by my unfamiliar face.

I put down my valise and reached out for her. "I was with your mum when you came into the world!" I said. She squirmed and stuffed her fist in her mouth.

"Let me make some tea," Lucy said, handing her little girl over to me. Something about her had changed. She was reserved toward me. Although she didn't turn me away, she seemed hesitant about me being there.

I waited in the parlor, bouncing the baby on my knee, who didn't once take her round blue eyes off mine. Soon Arthur came in carrying a wooden top. He looked taller than I remembered, but then in five months he must've grown some. "My daddy made this for me," he said.

"How clever! Can you show me how it works?" I asked.

There was something so normal, so quiet, so sweet about the modest house that it made me want to cry. When I thought back over the past several months of my life and how much I'd seen that was the opposite, how men blew each other to bits and suffered terrible disease and hunger on the other side of the world—for what?—I couldn't make sense of it all. But I'd have to think about a life here, living in a hospital and caring for people, with half days off to visit my family and bring them money. I wondered what my mum would say. Now, with Miss Nightingale's recommendation, she would have a good reason to be proud of me. I would not shame her again.

Lucy came back with the tea. She looked as though she'd recovered herself a little and had something all ready to say to me. "I didn't expect you to come here. Will told us you were going to marry a doctor in the east. I'm glad you came, though, so I can wish you joy in person."

"He died," I said, too shocked to think of a better way to say it, reeling with the knowledge that Will had thought enough about me to write of me to Lucy.

Lucy stopped with her mouth open, closed it, and poured us both tea. "I'm sorry."

"It's all right. We were never anything but friends. Will was mistaken. We didn't get married." What point would there be in saying anything else?

"I don't . . ." Her voice faded off and her cheeks went red.

I didn't want her to be embarrassed or uncomfortable, so I thought I'd better make conversation. "I hear that Will has been very helpful to my friend Emma, a widow. Please wish them joy for me the next time you write to him." I looked down. Much as I'd thought about it, I'd never said the words aloud before. It hurt me more than I expected to let them go like that, as if putting them out there gave them power, made them real.

"Emma? He's never mentioned any Emma." A dawning look came across Lucy's face, like a cloud cleared away and light spread all over.

At that moment the little girl started crying again, perhaps because I was so caught up in what Lucy was saying that I'd stopped bouncing her on my knee. Lucy reached her arms out and I gave the warm, cuddly body back to her, sorry I couldn't hold on to her longer. "I'll just put her down for her nap. Wait here . . . Come, Arthur!" She reached out her hand and little Arthur took it, with a sad backward glance at me as they went through to the kitchen.

I sat in the quiet for a few moments, the muffled sounds of children playing outside making me feel wistful for my home. *I'll have to leave soon,* I thought, and reached in my valise for the money I meant to give to Lucy.

"Molly?"

I stood up so fast that I dropped the purse with the coins and they scattered over the wood floor.

"Will!"

There he was, in front of me, plain as day. He leaned on a cane. "Will, I thought—"

He walked right up to me, matching each step of his right foot with the cane. "You thought wrong, from what Lucy tells me. The question is, did I?"

At first I couldn't look into his eyes. I didn't expect to see him, and yet it seemed so natural that I would. I wondered if I was talking to a ghost, like that time with Mrs. Drake. "I didn't . . . I mean, it's not . . ."

Will reached out and touched my chin with his fingertips, tilting it up so I'd have to look right at him. His hand was warm. This was no ghost.

And his eyes. They were clear and blue, as I always remembered. But didn't I also remember that look in them that reached out to me without any tricks, with no hiding or deceit, nothing complicated or shadowy, only something honest and true?

I let my eyes answer his. I felt my heart overflow, like it was reaching out for his, across the space that separated us. How could I not have seen this before? How could I ever have thought that Will wasn't the one, the only one, who cared enough about me to follow me to Turkey, and who I cared enough about to come to the one place in London where I would find him, if he was home?

"The answer, Will Parker, is yes."

He smiled. His lips touched mine, like he was afraid I'd change my mind all of a sudden. But I put my arms around his neck and held him to me. I heard his cane drop to the floor as he leaned into me and wrapped his arms around behind my back, pulling me close. We kissed so long I nearly lost my breath.

"You're not going to go off to Turkey again, are you?" he asked, gently pushing a curl of my hair out of my eyes when we'd separated enough to look at each other again.

"No. I don't think Miss Nightingale would have me, for one thing!"

"Don't worry. I'll take care of you." He nestled his nose into my hair, tipping my hat off and onto the ground.

"But she gave me a recommendation. I can work at St. Thomas's."

Will pulled away from me enough to see me. "Very impressive. We'll have to talk about it, decide what to do."

"I thought this called for a celebration," Lucy said, walking back in with a tray, three glasses, and a bottle of beer. She was smiling so wide her eyes crinkled up.

———

Will courted me properly for a few months while I worked at St. Thomas's. It took some convincing, but he agreed eventually I could work after we got married. I promised I'd stop if a baby came, though. They'd not let me work if I was in the family way anyhow.

I took him home to see my mum and dad. They were so proud of me they invited all the neighbors in just to wish us good luck.

I never told Will about Dr. Maclean, what really

happened. I think about him now and again, though. I imagine him looking down, happy for my happiness. That would have been like him.

I didn't see Miss Nightingale in London, but I knew she was there after the war ended. They said she was sick. I would have gone to visit her, only she was a fine lady and I was just a parlormaid turned nurse. But every night in my prayers I thanked her, more than even the rest of England thanked her for all she'd done for the soldiers. I thanked her because she understood me more than anyone else ever had, and she still let me be what I was.

Will did too, in his way. I'm as happy as a body has a right to be. We expect our first little one soon, sometime around my nineteenth birthday—my real nineteenth birthday.

But happy as I am, I'll never forget Dr. Maclean and how he made me understand what love was. I know now it could never have been. There was so much more separating us than keeping us together. But it was Dr. Maclean who taught me there were different ways to be and to do things, that taking a chance could have good results if it's done for the right reasons. Most of all, he taught me how love could bind two people across oceans and through walls, living or dead, forever.

Author's Note

In the Shadow of the Lamp was as much a discovery for me as I hope it will be for the reader. Finding out about the life of the famous Florence Nightingale, who established modern nursing practices as we know them, was a revelation. She had a powerful effect on everyone around her, was unflaggingly energetic, but was also abrasive, single-minded to the point of obsession, and self-sacrificing in the extreme. Her ideas about nursing were no-nonsense and entirely based in practicality at a time when the idea of contagion and germs was hardly understood. Pain was thought to be an important part of surgery—evidence that the bad was being purged—and the idea of cleaning surgical instruments unheard of.

Nightingale's common-sense precepts of cleanliness, nourishment, and fresh air revolutionized nursing. She strongly advocated for the use of chloroform in surgery and for shielding patients from other patients' views while being treated. Most remarkable of all, she was a well-bred, upper-class lady whose family initially resisted her call to nursing as a profession. In Nightingale's day, nursing was practiced by low-class women with no skill and little inclination for the work.

One of the things that made writing this book a challenge was that when the British government asked Nightingale to go to the Crimea and improve the care systems for injured and ill British soldiers, she did so only on the condition that she could choose her own nurses. The ones she selected had to be older than twenty-four, have nursing experience, and preferably not be too attractive or marriageable. This does not describe a heroine I'd necessarily like to read about! And Nightingale herself was in her thirties by this time and had turned down a very good marriage proposal to dedicate her life to nursing, making her unsuitable as a teen protagonist.

Enter Molly Fraser, a character entirely of my own invention. There was no question that everyone's imagination was fired up by reports of the conflict in the Crimea and especially of Nightingale and her nurses going to save the day. So why not a young parlormaid who finds herself in a difficult situation? There's no evidence that anyone stowed away to go with Nightingale, but stranger things have happened in history.

As to which characters are historical and which are not: the names of all the nurses, except for Molly and Emma, appear on the lists of nurses who were at one time or another with Nightingale in the Crimea. Volumes of Nightingale's writings and letters exist, and she has been the subject of many biographies and studies. Yet very little information about the nurses who accompanied her remains, apart from the journal of Sarah Anne Terrot, one of the Sellonite Sisters of Mercy. She did not remain long in Turkey, having been sent home as an invalid after a few months.

While Nightingale wrote numerous letters to the authorities and to her family, they rarely mention the nurses unless it is to complain of their incompetence and bad behavior. She was primarily occupied with the big picture: managing the ambitious enterprise of getting supplies to the hospital, caring for the men, laying down rules, establishing schedules and systems, and recording data about illness.

As to the doctors featured in this book: a real Dr. Menzies was in charge of the Barrack Hospital at Scutari, but my Dr. Menzies is an amalgamation of several doctors Nightingale dealt with there. Dr. Maclean is an invention, as are the doctors at the front in Balaclava.

Another important historical figure whom I touch briefly upon is Mary Seacole. She was a Jamaican nurse who went to London in hopes of traveling to the Crimea with Nightingale, but after finding that the services of a black woman were not wanted, raised enough money to get there on her own. She established an outpost near Balaclava that was part infirmary, part general store, part tavern. Nightingale probably met her, and is reported to have said that Mother Seacole did some good for the soldiers—although she also said her establishment was little better than a brothel. Seacole arrived in March 1855, and so would have been very new to the soldiers at the time of my story. I have taken the small liberty of establishing her there a little earlier so that Molly and Emma could meet her.

In the annals of Nightingale's time at Scutari there is almost no mention of the individual soldiers she came into contact with, and so Thomas and Will are also fictional. The conditions they faced, however, are not.

Particularly fascinating is the mystique that attached itself to Nightingale despite her pragmatic, businesslike approach. "The lady with the lamp" became a common figure in the newspapers and magazines of the times and showed a caring Nightingale with a lamp that looked a bit like the kind a genie might pop out of. In 1858, *The Ladies Repository* wrote:

"She is a 'ministering angel' without any exaggeration in these hospitals, and as her slender form glides quietly along each corridor, every poor fellow's face softens with gratitude at the sight of her. When all the medical officers have retired for the night and silence and darkness have settled down upon those miles of prostrate sick, she may be observed alone, with a little lamp in her hand, making her solitary rounds." (p. 361)

Nightingale did indeed patrol the wards at night with a lamp, but the true irony is in her reason for those nightly vigils: she didn't trust any of her nurses to check on the wards at night because they might make mischief with the men. Her solution was to take that duty upon herself.

One historical fact about Nightingale that I took license

with was the trip to Balaclava. Nightingale did go there, but not with the first group of nurses who established the Field Hospital. Mrs. Langston led that party with a few nurses on her own, with Nightingale's sanction. Nightingale went out some months later to inspect the facilities, and it was there that she first became very ill.

Despite her iron will and unflagging efforts, the illness Nightingale contracted in the Crimea was debilitating and stayed with her for the remainder of her life. Not long after returning to London when the conflict was over, she became bedridden and remained a virtual prisoner in her room for the rest of her days. Astonishingly, although she was an invalid, she lived to the ripe old age of ninety, dying peacefully in her sleep in 1910. The British government offered to have her buried in Westminster Abbey, but her relatives declined.

Her legacy lives on. The rolling screens used in hospitals to give patients and doctors privacy during examinations are called Nightingales. Many schools of nursing owe their beginnings to her, and the original Florence Nightingale School of Nursing, established in 1860, remains today as the Florence Nightingale School of Nursing and Midwifery at King's College London.

The Crimean War—the scene of the infamous Charge of the Light Brigade—is perhaps most remembered for the reforms brought about by Florence Nightingale and her nurses. It remains a rarity among bloody conflicts for having had such a lasting and positive effect on humankind.

Acknowledgments

I would especially like to thank my wonderful editor, Melanie Cecka, who was not only instrumental in making *In the Shadow of the Lamp* the best it could be, but whose fascination with Florence Nightingale was the true inspiration for this book.

Thanks are also due to the staff of the Florence Nightingale Museum, who were forthcoming with information that would have been difficult for me to find.

Finally, a huge thank you to my agent, Adam Chromy, with his army of astute readers who always manage to see the big picture; to Stephanie Cowell, a superb writer, who despite her own busy schedule of writing and promoting her books is ever ready to read and give thoughtful advice; and to all my cohorts of writers, fans, friends, and supporters on Facebook and Twitter, who shared the gestation of this novel with me.

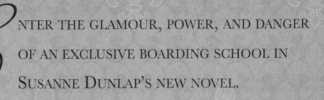

ᴇɴᴛᴇʀ ᴛʜᴇ ɢʟᴀᴍᴏᴜʀ, ᴘᴏᴡᴇʀ, ᴀɴᴅ ᴅᴀɴɢᴇʀ
ᴏꜰ ᴀɴ ᴇxᴄʟᴜsɪᴠᴇ ʙᴏᴀʀᴅɪɴɢ sᴄʜᴏᴏʟ ɪɴ
sᴜsᴀɴɴᴇ ᴅᴜɴʟᴀᴘ's ɴᴇᴡ ɴᴏᴠᴇʟ.

When Eliza Monroe, daughter of the future president of the
United States, is sent to boarding school in France, she discovers
that her classmates, Hortense, daughter of Josephine Bonaparte,
and Caroline, sister to Napoleon, are mortal enemies—and she
is about to be caught in the middle.

Eliza

I spent my entire first day at school observing Hortense and Caroline. I hardly had to observe! The bad blood between them is so obvious it could be embarrassing in any other setting. Here there is no one to pretend for. Even the young ones watch and wait for an opportunity to play one girl against the other. I thought the young students were all Caroline's creatures in the morning. But by the end of the day, I wasn't certain. Hortense has a quiet command that draws some of them to her with their needlework, as if copying her motions will make them more like her. And it is clear that Madame believes Hortense to be the ideal student. There is something about Hortense. Not just her beauty. She is fragile, as if some secret weighs on her, or some sorrow is always in her mind. I find myself wanting to protect her, despite the fact that she is older than me.

As to where I am to be in this intriguing game—I have not yet decided. I promised my mother I would write to her each day, and so now I must try to remember every detail, every nuance of expression and meaning so that I can get my mother's advice on how to play along without exposing my own hand. What is that hand exactly? What do I want to accomplish for myself in this place?

I can see that the school itself is a grand enough setting now that I have resigned myself to being here. In addition to the large, airy parlor, there is a dining hall big enough for all forty students to sit down to dinner. And this leads to a ballroom. It must have been a lovely place once, although the chandeliers are swathed in netting and the gilding on the trim is worn off in most places. Still, I could imagine dancing here, my gown trailing behind me and my jewels glittering in the candlelight....

That is not likely to occur here, however. A school is hardly the setting for an elegant ball. So what then? What do I want?

And suddenly, I know. I want to fall in love. Paris is so full of dashing young officers, and between Caroline and Hortense, I must be able to meet some of them. Oh, I know I shall likely return to Virginia and marry someone from a good family. But there is always the possibility of a lieutenant or a colonel, or perhaps even a marquis....

And there is a school full of boys just across the street. One of the younger girls told me they sometimes watch them from the windows on the second floor as the boys take their exercise in the garden of the old convent building that houses them. I imagine they must be much more interesting than the rough lads in Virginia, who are good only at plowing the fields or killing birds with their guns. I have heard that there will be a tea party here in a day or two, and that some of the students from the boys' school will come. Madame Campan thinks it's important for us to learn how to behave among young men so that we are not flustered when we first go out in society.

It will be difficult to accomplish even a flirtation, though, that is not fully in view of everyone. I promised my mother that I would behave and follow all the rules. One false step, she said, and she would send me back to Virginia while she remains in Paris to enjoy the society. She is thinking of the time at school last year, I know, when I found out that our teacher had a lover and threatened to expose her for it if she did not make me first in the class. I did not know the man was my teacher's fiancé. She went to my mother. I had to be very obedient after that, and was never first, no matter how hard I tried. My spirits were so low. That is when Mama decided to bring me back to Paris.

It is very quiet in the school. I expect everyone is asleep except for me. As my pen scratches on the page, I imagine it being as loud as a banging gong. This is the hour when Mama and I normally go over the day, whether we are in Virginia or in Paris. She sends the servants away, brushes my hair herself, and we talk. Whenever I feel uncertain about something that has happened, she helps me sort out the meanings and threads. So what if the daughter of a minor Virginia landowner pulled my hair and called me a snob? She is not worth bothering about, my mother would say. Her family rose to prominence only because her grandfather was a thief and swindled his partner out of his half of the business. And if the teacher pays more attention to a boy who wants to go to Harvard, I must simply accept that I am only a girl and there are other ways to make a name for myself.

A small blob of ink drops onto the page. I have been sitting with my hand poised above the paper. Yet I still hear scratching. At first it is quiet, but it becomes louder.

"Eliza!" The whisper is just audible. I lay down my pen and go to the door of my room. Those of us with maids have private rooms. The other girls sleep in dormitories on the top floor, one for each class. Except for Hortense, who as one who has been at the school for a long time—Caroline told me it has been four years—has her own room down the corridor.

I open my door and am surprised to see Caroline standing there, not in her nightdress but in an evening gown and a velvet cloak.

"Come! We have no time to lose."

She brushes past me into my room and heads straight for my wardrobe, opening the doors and rifling quickly through my gowns. She pulls out my best evening dress and tosses it on the bed.

"Quickly!"

Not a word of explanation. She simply expects me to dress and go with her! Where? I can't help wondering. But if I am to dress for evening, it must be a party! Perhaps I will meet someone handsome and dance.

"I'll tell you all about it on the way. There's nothing to worry about. I simply need your help. Do you have any jewels?"

While I slip out of my nightdress and into the silk gown with lace at the neck, she plunges her hands into my jewel case, tossing aside a few pieces until she reaches my pearl ear bobs and sapphire necklace.

"These will have to do. Now get your cloak. It's cold."

As we run quietly as ghosts through the dark corridors of the school, I realize that Caroline never gave me the opportunity to deny her, that she simply assumed she could command and I would obey. From all I've heard of her famous brother, this presumptuousness is a family trait.

An unmarked but very comfortable coach awaits us outside the gates of the school. As soon as we close the door behind us, the driver cracks his whip and we lurch forward over the cobbles.

"I only hope we are not too late!" Caroline says with a cross glance at me, as though the lightning speed with which I prepared myself had somehow delayed us.

I reach up my hand to pat my hair. I hadn't yet taken it down for the day, but if I'd known I was going anywhere, I would have repinned it to catch up the strands that had fallen loose.

"You're fine; don't worry. No one will look at you." Caroline chews the side of her thumb and stares absently out the window. Her words hurt, just a little.

"Where are we going?" I ask since she hasn't volunteered any information.

"To Paris. To a party at a lady's *hôtel particulier.*"

I want to ask which lady, thinking it possible my mother will be there, but the abrupt way Caroline answers discourages me from saying anything more.

And besides, isn't this what I want? To go out to parties? I just didn't expect to be doing so in secret in the middle of the night, without my mother's knowledge or approval. Why does Caroline need me by her side? What purpose will I serve?

The carriage is racing through the streets toward the gates of Paris. How will we get through at that hour? Must we pay a toll? I didn't bring any money with me.

Caroline remains silent most of the way. I think about trying to make small talk, but it feels out of place in these circumstances.

After what seems too short a time, I hear the coachman telling the horses to pull up. I see a gate and a watchman ahead and the lights of Paris beyond. Caroline sits forward in her seat, fumbling for something tucked into her cloak. To my surprise, she draws out two silk masks.

"Here! Put this on!"

I quickly tie mine over my eyes, positioning the slits so that I can see out. Caroline has fastened hers remarkably quickly. Though she thinks I don't notice, I see her take a small note from the folds of her cloak. The watchman comes to the window. She smiles and leans on the top of the door.

"*Merci, monsieur,*" she says, putting out her gloved hand with the folded note tucked into her palm. I catch the fellow's eyes. They are that lively dark brown I have noticed in the faces of some attractive Parisian gentlemen. He casts them rapidly over the note, and almost before I can register his reaction, he yells "*Allez!*" up to the coachman and we are off again.

"Are you planning to tell me why we're going out at this hour?" I ask by now so mystified and curious I can stand it no longer.

Caroline turns to me, now smiling and calm, the way she was at school earlier. "We are going to meet a particular friend of mine, at a masked ball."

"Why have you brought me with you?"

"Because, my dear Eliza, I wish to make you my particular friend as well. And in order to do that, we must have a secret together, *non?*"

We arrive at the gates of a very grand house. I see many coaches ahead of us, letting out their passengers at the door.

All the ladies are masked, but not costumed. They are the kind of masks that make the wearers feel protected but do not fool anyone acquainted with them. If my mother is here, she will surely recognize me. I pray she has either not been invited or is at home with one of her headaches—ungracious as that sounds.

After we descend from the coach Caroline takes my arm as if we are sisters, or at least the closest of friends. She is rather short, and so anyone might think we were quite close in age, not separated by four years.

We enter the ballroom after letting a maid take our cloaks. I have never seen anything so dazzling. It's as if all the jewels women hid away during the revolution and the *Terreur* are on display at the same time, glittering in the flicker of thousands of candle flames.

"Don't gawk!" Caroline hisses in my ear, squeezing my arm a little too hard. Her eyes scan the guests. She is affecting ennui, but I can tell she is searching for someone. I don't have to be a genius to guess it is a gentleman.

"*Merde!*" she whispers. An elderly lady standing nearby turns quickly and glares at her, but Caroline doesn't notice.

"What?" I ask.

"See, over there?"

She lifts her chin toward a corner of the room, where a knot of men in uniforms with sashes is standing, their backs to the dancing couples in the center. They are clearly in deep conversation with each other. I shrug. "What is it?"

"My brother is with them. I did not think he would be here."

I still don't know who Caroline is looking for, but if Bonaparte is here then surely Joséphine cannot be far. As I look around, I see the most extraordinary lady, her skin so dark I could almost imagine she is one of the slaves who work our land, but she is dressed in a column of silver silk, with jewels draped over her. Perhaps she has darkened her skin because of the party? "Who is that?" I ask Caroline, turning her so she can see.

She tosses her head. "An actress. She is all the rage at the *Comédie Française*, I'm told. She is supposed to be the estranged wife of a *vicomte*, but that is only by her word."

I continue to stare at the woman, fascinated. She has sharp, high cheekbones and large eyes. Her lips are full, but that is the only feature aside from her dark skin that makes her appear to be a Negro.

"Don't act like a child!" Caroline says, forcing my attention away from her. "Look! There he is!" She points toward the group of men again, but not in the direction of the one I recognize as Bonaparte. "He's looking this way!"

Before I can get a good look at who she means, she yanks me around so that I almost lose my slipper and drags me after her as she walks rapidly away. I am practically limping, until I manage to slip my foot more securely into my shoe. Caroline pulls me into an anteroom that is empty except for a maid who stands ready to fetch something for whoever asks her.

"You see, that is my secret. It is Murat. I am in love with him." She whispers fast and low, her eyes glittering.

"Why is it a secret?" I ask.

"Because my brother will not consider it. And right now, I don't know if Murat even notices me. He is so handsome. All the ladies love him. I must see him, alone. And I will need the help of my friends."

Now I'm beginning to understand. She wants me to do something for her, perhaps carry messages. I hear my mother's warning voice in my mind. *One false step, and it's back to Virginia.* "Oh, Caroline! I can't help you. I'm only young, after all."

She takes hold of my upper arm and squeezes so her fingers are digging into me and I have to grit my teeth not to cry out. "Oh, but you must—you *will*! Because now I have your secret, too."

My secret? So that's why she woke me and brought me here. She can hold this over me forever. My first instinct is to be angry. But then, I have to admire her. It was cunningly done.

"Well, then, Caroline, what next?" I say.

She smiles.

SUSANNE DUNLAP graduated from Smith College and later earned a PhD in music history from Yale University. She has taught music history at the college level and is the author of two historical novels for adults, as well as three other novels for teens: *The Musician's Daughter*, *Anastasia's Secret*, and *The Académie*. She divides her time between Brooklyn, New York, and Northampton, Massachusetts.

www.susannedunlap.com

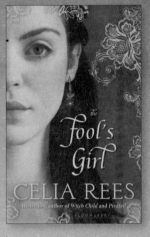